I0760527

Secrets That Remain

The Emil Fricker Story

Secrets That Remain

The Emil Fricker Story

Julie Rose Bawden-Davis

Lynn Rose Ann Kelley

ISBN 13: 978-1-955265-52-2

Library of Congress Control Number: 2025914804

Published and Distributed by Roses Are Red Publishing

rosesareredpublishing.com

Printed in the United States of America, Orange, California

First Edition: October 2025

To our lineage—those women and men who came before us.
May your trials and tribulations mean
something for future generations.

Acknowledgments

As they say, it takes a village. Here's my village. I'm supremely grateful to the following people.

ARC Readers:

Julie Schlueter, Susa Fraccaroli, Trish Darrenkamp, Beth Helm, Chelle Young, Jacquelyn Gray, Penny McCulloch, Amber Mancebo, Heather Wamboldt, Pamela Bloink, Tara Bradley, my father, Monte Bawden, my sisters, Mandy Stanley and Katie Weissberg, Jan Huston, and my Aunt Vicki Britt.

Pros:

Judy Bullard, cover design

Kyle Kane, Roses Are Red logo design

Sabrina Wildermuth, design consultation

Jeremy Davis, technical support

Contents

Author's Note

In many ways, this is more the story of my Great Grandma Rose than it is of my Great Grandfather Emil. Though he and his actions lie at the epicenter of this book, it is my great grandmother, affectionately referred to by my family as "Little Granny," who is the true heroine. Though Rose may have been small in stature, my great grandmother was a giant spiritually and emotionally.

As you will see in these pages, Rose Wilhelmina Jenny Fricker overcame great odds that would have broken most people. She retained her spirit, strength, and faith until the day she took her last breath at the age of ninety-six.

I will be honest with you. This was not an easy book for me to write, especially after my mother and co-author passed in 2020. In many ways, this is a heartbreaking tale, and I teared up often as I chronicled our family history. At the same time, I greatly enjoyed getting to know my Great Grandma Rose on a deeper level. Though I knew her when I was a teenager, and I lived with her daughter, my Grandma Blanche, as a young adult, it wasn't until my mother, Lynn, and I wrote this story that I saw the indomitableness of both of their spirits. Through sheer willpower and a willingness to look to the "bright" side, even when the bright consisted of fleeting rays of sunshine in between savage storms, both women and others involved soldiered on. While their stories are tragic, at the same time their ability to overcome tragedy and ultimately live fulfilling lives brings great hope and faith.

I am extremely proud to say these two women, as well as my Great Aunt Arline, are my lineage. You will see as you read that my Great Grandma Rose was a woman of great accord and backbone. In fact, her backbone was made of steel that could not be broken. She fiercely and deeply loved my Great Aunt Arline, Grandma Blanche and Great Uncle Richard, and in turn my mother, Lynn, and that shows in all she did for them. During extremely dark times that would have crushed the average person, Rose kept putting one foot in front of the other, while offering love and encouragement to those she held dear.

The components of this story were gathered and written over a period of twenty-six years by my mother and myself. Mom started the journey with her cousin Jan back in 1999 after my Grandma Blanche passed. After Jan and my mom's initial trip to Highland, Illinois where this story takes place, my mother asked me to help her write a book about what occurred. When we returned to Highland on several occasions to do more research, it became clear to me that telling the insider perspective was important, as much that had been publicized was overdramatized and one-sided.

Our quest to find out how my great grandfather ended up on the gallows included talking to descendants of those involved and gathering newspaper articles written at the time, the latter of which you will see reprinted in this book. As my mother and I dug through court records, birth records, and the like, the quest found us walking through labyrinths and sliding down rabbit holes, often finding answers after many hours of searching. This book also includes information gleaned from conversations we had with those in our family involved when they were living.

Though my mother didn't live to see the publication of this book, she and I spent many hours working closely on this, and for that time together I am immensely grateful.

My hope is that as you read my Great Grandma Rose's story, you find inspiration and solace in knowing that with faith, hope, and love, all things—even the most tragic—can be overcome. And that a person can truly conquer and soar to great heights amidst great sorrow. There are no bounds to the human spirit when the human spirit alights on angel wings.

Julie Bawden-Davis

Orange, California, May 2025

Lynn Kelley, Granddaughter of Emil Fricker

Growing up in my house was like growing up with a secret that shows itself in intermittent rays of sunlight when you're deep in the forest. The sunlight peeks in, and then quickly disappears. When slivers of illumination crept in, my grandmother or mother would spot the breach, and the forest would once again fill with darkness—often for years at a time.

I'd prefer it was a real secret. A mystery that I hadn't ever heard anything about. That I just stumbled upon one day, rather than wondering and worrying throughout my childhood and even adulthood. When the rays appeared for short periods of time and then shot back into the shadows, darkness enshrouded the house, muffling and stifling the voices that seemed to want to communicate the whole, real, true story.

The few times I opened my mouth to ask what those voices seemed to wish for me to hear, I was shut down. Even my father, who would talk about everything and anyone, never discussed the secret.

It wasn't exactly that lies were told. It was the omission of enormous, life-changing events. For years I felt like large chunks of my mother's and grandmother's lives were missing. Those chunks were like blank spaces in a puzzle not quite completed.

It wasn't until my mother and father died that I had the courage to cut through the vegetation to reveal the secret. To see what was so dreaded and dark we couldn't talk about the subject for most of my life until my parents passed.

When Mom died in late 1999, slightly more than a year after Pop passed, I went to Illinois out of curiosity. At least that's what I told myself. But the truth is, deep down, I somehow knew the journey to my mother's and grandmother's past would change me somehow. Change who I'd become and who I once was. Family secrets have a way of doing that—rewriting your history.

At the time, I went to my birthplace in South Bend, Indiana seeking a sense of family. Losing my parents made me yearn for years past, and the children of my mother's brother, Dick, my cousins, Jan and Jon, were a part of that past. I wanted to visit and recall the many happy years we spent as children.

Seeing Jan when I got off the plane in Indiana was comforting. It was reassuring to know there was still someone out there who knew me way back when. When we got to talking about our parents, we had a conversation that ended up turning both of our lives askew and making us question everything we'd ever known about our backgrounds and even ourselves.

It all started when Jan asked me if I knew the story of our Grandfather Emil. I shared what I had been told by my mother, Blanche, but it wasn't much. Jan suggested we visit the place where (I was soon to find out) my infamous grandfather had lived. I thought, why not? The trip should be interesting. Let's unveil the secret once and for all. Little did I know what I would be stepping back into and where the secret would lead me.

When Jan and I traveled to Highland, Illinois to explore the secret, I had no idea I'd be walking into a tunnel of sorts—one that would lead me to myself in many ways, and to my mother, Blanche, and Grandmother Rose, who both raised me. I soon discovered I didn't really know who I was, after all.

It was one of those experiences where the light shines in front of you and the dark lies at your back. You can't help but keep moving forward to see what you'll see next along the path. Turning back into the darkness isn't an option once you've entered the tunnel. It's too dark back there in the not knowing; in the wondering; in the confusion. The way in front of you, while it brings shock, dismay, and even deep sadness, is lit and brings clarity in its own way and in its own divine time.

I never planned on writing this book or accessing my ancestors and their secrets. But the further I walked into the tunnel, the more I knew this story should and could be told by me and my daughter, Julie, with the help of my passed on loved ones, whose presence, just as the lingering secrets, remain to this day.

Would it have been better if I'd never known? I think about that sometimes. It might be cliché, but ignorance can truly be bliss. Walking around with this truth, I must tell you, has created a peculiar sort of awe and horror. What have I come from? Where has it led me, and where will it still lead me? Could I ever? Have I ever gotten close...?

Spring 2000 remains etched into my very being. That was the day Jan and I traveled to the Highland, Illinois Courthouse. We wanted answers, and we figured we'd find them in the transcripts from the trial our parents had skirted around talking about for decades.

When the clerk told us they didn't keep court transcripts, but she could give us a list of jurors, we said we'd like the list and waited while she left her desk to get them. A clock ticked in the quiet room as we stood there, its sound seeming to become more ominous as we waited. Finally, she returned and asked a question that ping-ponged around in my brain for a time, rattling me, until it finally settled like a bowling ball in my stomach.

"Which trial would you like the list from?" she asked.

To say that Jan and I were stunned at the question is a monumental understatement.

Finally, I found my voice. "How many trials were there?"

"Two murder trials. I can make a copy of both lists, if you like."

We requested documents from both trials, and a few minutes later when we checked out the lists, we noted the jurors were all men. That made sense, since women couldn't even vote in 1924.

Of course, the lists only brought more questions, so we made our way to the largest library in the county. We were quiet in the car as Jan drove. Our journey to the truth had begun. There was no telling what we would soon discover about Jan's father, my Uncle Dick, my mother, Blanche, and the woman at the center of the maelstrom, who helped raise me. She was home every day after school to give me a glass of milk and a plate of homemade cookies—my Grandmother Rose.

Chapter One

Fricker Dairy Farm, Highland, Illinois

September 15, 1924

Rose heard the knock even before it was a knock. She'd known they'd be coming for Emil. He didn't know—never suspected, but she knew. Not exactly what was happening, just that something was doing, and it wasn't good.

When the doorbell dinged, Rose ran to the top of the staircase and watched as Emil yanked the door open, his hand remaining on the doorknob.

"Why boys, what brings you here on this fine, fine evening?" he said to the two uniformed police officers.

"We're here on official business, Emil."

Rose knew without seeing his face that her husband's smiling demeanor changed to steel and his eyes narrowed.

"Official business? What kind of official business?" He made the O in official a long O—making himself sound more like a farmer; something he did when the occasion called for it. As he spoke, Rose saw his giant hand squeeze the door handle.

"We been hearing something about a homemade still on your premises. Don't have to tell you homemade brew—any brew—is against the law."

Rose saw Emil's hand loosen on the door and his shoulders relax as he laughed. "That so? You need to tell that to some of your boys downtown."

The two young police officers exchanged glances, and the smaller of the two cleared his throat and continued. "We got to take you down to the station and ask you some questions."

"You can't be serious."

"We are, sir. Got the arrest warrant right here." The taller of the two officers held up a piece of paper. Emil, who'd been interrupted from his post-supper time in the parlor, smacked at the paper.

"You think I got nothing better to do than play your silly, little games?"

"We can take you in peaceable, or we can do otherwise. But I suspect that would rile up your wife and kids."

Emil's back straightened like a pocketknife opening and he lashed out in a hard, low voice. "You leave my wife and kids out of this. They have nothing to do with it. You hear?"

The officer with the warrant stepped back and lost his composure for a second. Emil had a way of doing that, Rose thought, taking quick and steady control of almost any situation.

"Look, no offense Fricker, we're just doing our jobs. Let's just get this over with." He almost pleaded now.

"All right," Emil said, reaching for his black hat and adjusting his suspenders before he pulled on his coat. "Don't imagine I'll be gone long. Should be back in an hour to inspect the evening milk—providing you boys don't drag your feet."

The officers said nothing as they escorted Emil down the front walkway of the big farmhouse.

Rose heard a thudding even after the front door banged shut. She realized it was her heart when a small hand took hers.

"What is it, Mama? Why are they taking Papa away?" Ten-year-old Blanche looked up from her halo of black curls into her mother's face.

"It will be all right, child. Your Papa should be back soon."

"Back in an hour, right Mama, that's what Papa said. He's supposed to watch me ride my pony tomorrow morning."

"That's what Papa said," Rose murmured, stroking her daughter's springy curls. But Rose knew somehow that Emil wouldn't be coming back by nightfall.

Chapter Two

Sheriff Edward Deimling

Sheriff Edward Deimling sat outside the Fricker farmhouse in the driver's seat of the police car waiting for the boys to pick up Fricker. He shook his head as he looked out at the property with its barns—three of them—and the Holsteins pasturing beyond in the waning light of early evening.

All of this—every single inch—was Fricker's. And did he appreciate any of it? Deimling snorted. Probably not. Too busy messing around with another man's wife to see what was right in front of his face. Deimling would like even a corner of this. He hadn't grown up with the world in his lap like Fricker. Hell, he was lucky to get a meal sometimes when he was young. But no matter. He had pulled himself up and out.

Here he was, Sheriff in the next city—much bigger city than Highland. Being Sheriff, he didn't have to explain to anyone why he was taking a personal interest in this case. Fact was, he wouldn't have it any other way. He planned to see this through himself. Since Highland wasn't officially his town, he had to have the Highland Police Department pick Fricker up and get him into the police car.

He knew Fricker to be the riley sort—so he insisted he go along. The Highland police chief didn't seem to mind any. Looked relieved even. Fricker would be ornery as a bull when the ranchers separated them in the summer from the heifers. Deimling knew the dairy baron wouldn't create a scene in front of any of his farmhands, though, who might be out and about this evening. He could be a spiteful devil, but he had his pride. They would be able to get him into the car peaceably.

Sure enough, when the boys escorted Fricker to the car and motioned for him to get in, his eyes met Deimling's in his rearview mirror, and it looked to him like steam erupted from his eye sockets.

"What the hell you doing here, Deimling?" huffed Fricker as he folded himself into the back seat.

"Just in the neighborhood and thought I'd take a nice evening drive."

"Bull shit," Fricker muttered as he settled in his seat and the door closed. "Let's get this charade over with, Deimling, so's you can get home to your little life."

Deimling gritted his teeth as he turned the car over, and the other officers got in. Once the rage at Fricker's comment subsided and they were on the open dirt road back to town, he spied Fricker in the rearview mirror. Sitting there all high and mighty. Humph.

Well, just wait until a few minutes from now. When they were booking him for murder. Deimling knew he shouldn't be feeling like this. He knew he was gloating, but this had been a long time coming. Fricker had always looked down his nose at him. Always viewed Deimling as a gnat flying around he could squash just like that. Well, he'd show him. They'd all show him now.

Deimling had been to the scene of the "accident"—if that's what you could call it. Poor boy was riddled with bullets. Just for being in the wrong place at the wrong time and with the wrong woman. He didn't stand a chance against Fricker, who'd been king of the hill for far too long.

He'd heard about Fricker's father. His own papa had told him about all the good Rudolph had done. He had started the Fricker school and had helped many people. He was a 'right fine man, that one,' his papa had told him. 'Respectable, upstanding.' Now as for this one. A whole different story. The apple fell a long ways from that tree.

"What you looking at?" Fricker snarled when Deimling took another peek at him in the back seat of his police car. "This is all a joke, you know. When the boys at City Hall, who are probably drinking my alleged moonshine right now, hear about this, you'll be the laughingstock of the town."

Deimling's blood pressure rose, and he felt the anger clouding his head. Breathe, he told himself. Breathe deep.

"Just doing my job, Fricker. Taking orders, that's all."

"Taking orders? Since when the sheriff take orders?" Fricker laughed.

Deimling ignored Fricker as he turned into the Highland Police Station. He heard the cracking and popping as the police car drove over the gravel, and then he stopped in front of the small station. After sliding out of the driver's seat, he walked around to the back and opened the door.

Fricker looked up at him with those dark eyes of his and snorted. "Let's get this charade over with so I can go home to my wife and family."

Your wife and family? Deimling thought. Fricker sure wasn't thinking of his wife and family when he had that poor boy killed on account of Minnie. He felt his hands shake a bit as he motioned for Fricker to get out of the car.

As they walked toward the front door of the station, Deimling felt glad he had called in backup. This wasn't going to be easy—getting Fricker booked and into a cell. He was a big man at 6'2". Not that Deimling couldn't hold his own, but Fricker also had a way with sarcasm. That tongue could stop you up. And in these kinds of situations, a moment's hesitation could be the death of you.

They walked into the small station house and Fricker laughed when he saw the deputy and a couple of boys from another precinct.

"What's this? Some kind of joke? Everyone knows I got a still on the property. So what?"

"This here ain't no joke, Fricker. You're under arrest," said Deimling.

"For what?"

"Murder."

"Murder? What in the hell are you talking about!" Deimling could see the veins in Fricker's throat bulging now.

"For the murder of John Nungesser."

Fricker spied for the first time the boys in the back jail cell.

"I have no idea what you're talking about. That Minnie's husband? He's dead? What're Wernle and Landert doing here?"

"Never you mind that. We need to get you booked."

"Like hell you're going to book me!" Fricker bellowed, stepping back toward the doorway.

The boys who came to help Deimling started forward. He'd warned them they might have to take Fricker forcibly. The dairy baron's demeanor shifted as they all approached—a snake, that one.

"Fine. Go ahead and arrest me. This'll all be worked out in the morning once I talk to the boys at City Hall, including the mayor."

Chapter Three

Rudolph Kamuf

Rudolph Kamuf had seen them take away Fricker in the police car. He'd been coming out of the barn when they walked him out of the main house.

In some ways, Kamuf, a farmhand and homesteader for decades, always expected something like this to happen. But on the other hand, he was right shocked, if he was going to be honest with himself. Because Emil Fricker always seemed to land on his feet. On those big boots he often wore. Kamuf always wondered about those boots. Why he wore them. It wasn't as if he did all that much work. Most days he just went around and told the farmhands what to do. And then got himself into mischief tinkering in that still of his.

Kamuf didn't reckon this was about Fricker's still—seeing how the whole town, including the mayor, guzzled his moonshine first chance they got. Kamuf wasn't partial to the stuff. He'd seen the evil it could cause, and he didn't want no part of it. His mama—God rest her soul—warned him against the evils of drink. 'Sides, it was currently against the law. Not a good thing in his book at any time.

Once the police car was out of sight, Kamuf headed back toward his one-bedroom shack in the back-forty of Fricker's property. He had to do some trimming of 2 x 4s before the sun set. Better get to it. Fricker would likely be home soon, and he'd be right ornery if he didn't finish the work 'for sunset. Though truth be told, Kamuf wasn't feeling so good. Not for a long while now. His missus died a decade ago, and there was no one to tend to him. Not that he wasn't always able to tend to himself. Doctors called it asthma. Said his lungs didn't work right no more. That likely was the problem, because he could barely breathe most of the time. The sawdust from cutting wood for the fences didn't help neither.

Maybe since Fricker was being hauled in he'd be too busy tomorrow to notice, and Kamuf could just hold off on the cutting until then. Get himself a good night's sleep and get up with the sun. That's what he'd do.

Chapter Four

Home of Minnie Nungesser

Deimling dreaded this. Deep down in his bones, dreaded it. How to tell the girl—the poor waif—that her second husband was dead. How did you tell such a thing to a girl whose whole life had been one tragedy after another?

He pulled up in front of her house and sat there for a moment—thinking about his own daughter and how she had a right fine life. She'd met a good man. Deimling thanked the Lord every day for that. She had settled down and now he could look forward to being a granddaddy.

But what did this poor child have? Minnie had been literally kicked to the curb when she was a baby by her parents—those ne'er-do-wells. He knew the father and mother from childhood. The folks who ended up taking care of the little girl loved her up right as best they could, but Deimling could see in her eyes and feel in her heart the pain that early abandonment wrought on her soul.

He sighed deeply and got out of the car, lumbering to her front door, then rapped on it gently.

"Who's there?" Minnie called out. Her voice sounded to him like the squeak of a mouse.

"It's Sheriff Deimling, Mrs. Nungesser. Sorry to be calling so late, but I've got some important news that can't wait until morning."

Minnie pulled open the door, her eyes wide and beckoning. "News Sheriff?" she asked.

Deimling cleared his throat and looked at the threshold. She had a threadbare rug there. Seemed like it was once a black color, but now it appeared gray.

"Perhaps I could come in?" he implored.

"A' course, sorry, Sheriff, forgive my bad manners." Minnie stood back and opened the door wide for Deimling to make his way through. "Please sit down. Can I get you something to drink? I don't have much, but I think I've got some apple juice pressed from last year's harvest."

"No, Minnie, Mrs. Nungesser," he corrected himself. "No need." He had taken off his hat and clutched it in his hands.

Minnie looked at his hands grasping the hat and her eyes flew open wider. "What's the matter, Sheriff? Something's wrong. I can tell."

He cleared his throat and began. "Afraid so. Seems your husband, John, they found his body along the dirt road leading up to Saint Rose."

Minnie stumbled back, her hand grasping for the chair behind her. "Found his body? Do you mean he's not alive?"

Deimling helped her sit in the cane backed chair, finding himself saying, "There, there. I'm afraid he didn't make it, Min—Mrs. Nungesser."

Minnie slumped forward, grabbing her head and crying out something that sounded like a cow being slaughtered. Deimling didn't know what to do, so he patted her shoulder and repeated, "There, there, Mrs. Nungesser, it'll be okay."

Minnie's head shot up and she cried, "Sheriff, please stop calling me Mrs. Nungesser! I'm not Mrs. Nungesser anymore, now am I? Oh, my, God, I'm a widow! I'm not even thirty-years-old, and I'm a widow again! All alone in the world!"

Tears streamed down Minnie's face as she pounded her lap. "I don't want to be alone! I'm not supposed to be alone!"

Deimling felt terrible watching the girl realize she was all alone. What were the odds?

After a while, when her crying subsided and she was left gulping air, Minnie raised her face covered in angry red splotches and managed to ask, "What happened to John?"

Chapter Five

Rose Jenny Fricker

Rose sat in her rocking chair holding her Bible, unopened. The sun had set hours ago. Usually, she loved this quiet time all to herself just before bedtime when she read her Bible. She rarely missed a night. It was the words she read in this book that supported her and sustained her through each and every day of her life, no matter what the situation.

Darkness enveloped the room, and that usually soothed her. But tonight, she was so tired. A deep down tired. Every bone, every fiber, exhausted. She couldn't remember ever in her entire life feeling such profound fatigue, not even the days after giving birth to her babies. As she rocked, she felt certain the level of her tiredness would be far greater soon.

It had been five hours since her husband of seventeen years had gone to town with the Sherriff. When Emil first left, she was concerned but then reassured herself he'd be back soon. That wasn't the case, though. She knew now her husband was in a lot of trouble after asking George, one of the farmhands, to go into town and report back to her what was doing. When he returned with an ashen face and couldn't meet her gaze, she knew something terrible had transpired.

"It's okay, George, you can tell me," Rose said softly, waiting for him to find the words.

"They're saying something mighty peculiar, Ma'am," he said, finally raising his eyes to hers. "Looks like the mister is being accused of murder."

Rose kept her eyes locked on his; she couldn't look away. Instinctively, she knew this was a test she had to pass. She stood up straighter, the vertebrae in her back filling up with liquid steel that hardened immediately. "And who do they say he murdered?"

"They're saying Minnie's husband." George blushed and looked at the floor. "And there's something else just as peculiar."

"Go on." Rose encouraged him.

"Arline's husband, Eldo, and Jake Landert, they were arrested, too."

Rose stifled a gasp. "They have something to do with what happened?"

George raised his gaze to meet Rose's. "Not sure Ma'am. I know them to be right fine men. I wouldn't worry about this. The Mister is very important in the town and county. Likely this'll be sorted out soon."

"Thank you, kindly, George, for gathering that information for me. That'll be all for now. Please check on the cows. I'm going to need you to oversee the milking until further notice."

"A 'course, Ma'am." George bowed his head and ducked out of the room.

Now, sitting here in the dark, Rose realized she rocked faster than when Blanche cried with colic. Willing herself to slow the chair's movement, she looked down at her new blue dress. She had worn it for the first time last week. Emil had smiled at her, his face softening and becoming handsome. He said she looked beautiful in the color. Now that was the man she married. Not the one George talked about. Murder. Was Emil capable? And Minnie's husband? She recalled the ferocious flash in her husband's eyes when he glanced at their milkmaid, and her heart rattled around uncomfortably in her chest. After setting down her Bible, she made her way up the farmhouse's sweeping staircase to her son, Richard's, bedroom door.

As she stopped in the doorway and peered in, Rose's heart filled with love and concern for her child, who lay deep in slumber. Although no artificial light shone in his room, moonlight poured through both windows.

She spied Richard's schoolbooks neatly stacked on a small table next to his papers and lessons. He was such a good student, putting much time and effort into his studies. Since he started school as a little boy, he always expected the very best of himself, and the result was a report card with all As. Now manhood had started to leave small, subtle changes in her boy. He was becoming tall, like his father, and his feet and hands appeared slightly too large for his body, which was lean and sinewy from working hard on the farm whenever and wherever he was needed. Richard also had a full head of brown, smooth, wavy hair. So different from his sister, Blanche's, with her unruly, tight, kinky curls that announced their own mind.

Both were wonderful children, but totally different. Richard had a soothing manner about him. He'd listen to whatever someone said, quietly and completely. Before replying, he took time to seriously think about what he would say. He seemed to evaluate all elements of a situation in a calm and rational manner.

Baby Blanche, really no longer a baby, reacted in essentially an opposite manner. She was four years younger than her brother and truly idolized him. When she was a toddler, she followed him around and mimicked his actions. From a very young age, she managed to do the most aggravating things around her big brother. He always seemed unfazed, though. In fact, when her shenanigans reached an unbearable point, he'd laugh in a kindly manner, reach out for her and say, "Stop, stop, stop." She seemed to understand even before she could speak well and would retreat to another room. The two had always had a strong bond. Rose silently asked God to maintain and increase the depth of their relationship.

Next, she moved to Blanche's room and tiptoed in to watch her daughter. Her often-animated young face was surrounded by a torrent of long curls sprinkled with small tendrils and little corkscrews of dark, almost black, hair. Blanche wasn't enamored with her wild tresses. She tried many times to decrease or eliminate the curls, but all attempts failed. Arline, her big stepsister, was the only one she allowed to take a brush to her mane. The older girl was gentle but firm with her younger sister when brushing her hair, and in general.

All three of her children had a strong, loving relationship with each other, and for that Rose was grateful. Shuddering, she thought that before too much longer they may desperately need each other.

Chapter Six
Arline Fricker Wernle

Eldo should have been home by now. Night had fallen, and the moon shone bright outside. Arline got up gingerly, little Eldo asleep in her arms. She padded softly into the next room and laid him down in his cradle on her side of the bed. Then she went out to the living room and pulled the curtain back and checked outside. Nobody.

She hoped Jake hadn't talked Eldo into going into town and playing in one of those back-of-the-building penny ante games. She'd warned him about gambling. Besides being against the law, they couldn't afford him spending his earnings on nonsense like that. She had little Eldo to think of now. He was five months and growing an inch a day, it seemed.

Arline sat down and picked up the recent issue of *Vogue* she'd splurged on in the local drugstore a couple of weeks ago. She had read it cover to cover already, but she would read it again while she waited for her husband to get home. Certainly, he'd be home soon. His dinner, a tuna sandwich, sat on the table. No doubt the bread was dry by now. Served him right for being late to supper.

Just as she was settling down to read the article on skirt length again, someone rapped on the door. She got up from the couch and yanked open the door, ready to ask Eldo where his keys got to. But his friend Abe stood on the front steps.

"Abe, what's wrong?"

"I thought I should come and tell you, Arline," he said, his eyes earnest and confused.

"Tell me what?"

"All's I know is they took him. They took Eldo right there from the corner store and said he was arrested!"

"What for? Did they say what for?" Arline felt the tension that had been building all day fill her head, making it hard to see and hear.

"I think it might have something to do with your pa. It was all so confusing. But I think I heard them say something about Emil and maybe murder and John Nungesser. I'm sorry, Arline, that's all I know," said her husband's friend, who she noticed had been twisting his hat in his hands as he spoke.

"Thanks, Abe, that's a lot. I really appreciate you coming to tell me. I would have been up all night wondering what was happening."

"If you need anything. Anything at all...."

She nodded and shut the door.

After she heard his truck pull away, Arline sat down on the couch in their little living room and struggled to catch her breath. Her father? Eldo? Arrested? Murder? John Nungesser, Minnie's husband?

Irritated rage made Arline want to say some filthy words she'd never uttered before. There she was again, that Minnie, in the thick of things. Arline felt the familiar helplessness slither throughout her body when she thought of the woman who came flouncing into their lives years ago and had been upsetting the apple cart ever since.

Chapter Seven
Highland Jail

Sheriff Deimling should go home. It was nearly midnight and his wife had probably put his dinner in the icebox hours ago. But something kept him here. He worried if he left for the night, when he returned in the morning, Fricker's jail cell would be empty. He'd be home sitting in the lap of luxury once again with a big grin on his face, while those boys, Jake and Eldo, sat shut behind bars.

From his vantage point, Deimling could see Fricker in the jail cell, sitting without a care in the world, boredom on his face, while that poor girl cried her eyes out over the loss of her second husband. Fricker obviously thought this wasn't going to touch him. Deimling would see about that. He looked at the arrest papers, snorting when he remembered how Fricker demanded to know why he had to sign them when all they contained was "lies."

"You have to sign these arrest papers just like everyone who is arrested, Fricker. There's no exceptions for you."

Deimling could admit it. He'd never liked the man. Fricker had always looked at him through those hooded eyes—as if he could make him do what he wanted, like he did with the other puppets in town—the council members and the mayor. Well, he wasn't them.

And worse, he'd seen the devastation done to the girl. Seen how this was tearing her up and had been tearing her up for some time now. Like Deimling, she wasn't born with a silver spoon in her mouth. The opposite, actually. Minnie's parents abandoned her, so she ended up with foster parents from the get-go. And now she'd been abandoned by two husbands.

Deimling hoped Fricker didn't get out of this one. The Old Boys Club liked their moonshine, and they liked Fricker's the best. But this was murder, for crying out loud. They wouldn't sweep this under the rug, would they? He sure hoped not. If they did, well, he didn't know if he could continue to be Sheriff anywhere near here. He'd have to pick up and move west, like some of his family had.

With any other prisoner, he wouldn't be worried. But Fricker had that way about him. He could do the damnedest things, and they would just slide right off him and disappear. Or, if it was something that just couldn't disappear, then it'd grasp ahold of someone else and not let go.

And Fricker could intimidate. Boy could he. All he had to do is give someone that dark, cold stare that made men cower inwardly and even outwardly. He'd seen it many times. He could only imagine how it made that poor girl feel.

He'd never forget that first time Minnie came to him. She'd been weeping for hours, looked like. Had a kerchief in her hand she'd wrung so many times it looked like a rag.

"I'm sorry to bother you, Sheriff," she had apologized. "But I—I—just didn't know what else to do!"

"Come and sit down, child," he'd instructed when she came to him in his office. "Close the door and shut out the chill. What's happened?" He perched on his desk as she sat in the chair in front of him.

"It's," her lower lip trembled and new tears sprang to her eyes, "my employer, Sheriff."

"Who, Fricker?"

She nodded, tears making their way down her pink cheeks.

"What has Fricker done now?" Deimling had heard some strange, disturbing rumors about things doing at the dairy farm. "He hurt you, Minnie?"

"Not exactly."

"It's okay, child, you can tell me anything."

She nodded. "I know. That's why I come to you. I know you're a right fair man." The tears came out faster now while Deimling waited. "He's keeping some of the money he owes me, Sheriff. Me and John, we need the money. I'm fixing to hopefully be a mama soon. Without that money..." She looked up at him through teary eyes. He noticed how her long, black lashes glistened with tears.

"Let me see what I can do. I'll call on him and ask about your back pay."

"No need, Sheriff! I wouldn't want to bother you."

"No bother, Mrs. Nungesser. Keeping someone's rightful wages is against the law. That's my job. Anything else you want to tell me?" He gave her an intense look, hoping to pull the whole truth out of her.

Finally, she wiped her eyes with the kerchief. "That's mighty nice of you, Sheriff. If you could just inquire about my back wages, that'd be fine. Just fine."

Chapter Eight

All night long, Rose had tried to plan how she would handle the children. She'd been holding off telling them anything since Emil left last night, hoping it'd all be over by now. They would definitely stay home from school today. Richard would be unhappy about missing his classes and would balk when she told him his father would be absent for a while. How could she broach this subject? Tell the whole truth? Part of the truth? Either way, it would wound both children. How could it not?

Rose thought about Richard and his friends and what would be said to him and how he would handle going to school. Because the news was certain to be everywhere, and she knew the school children would not be merciful. Richard liked school and he was an excellent student. His father had an appreciation for that, but Rose knew Emil always secretly wished for a tougher son.

When she heard Richard up and around, she tapped lightly on his door and went in. He had his britches on and was pulling on a shirt, his feet bare. Rose continued into the room and sat on the edge of his bed. That alone caused her son concern, as sitting on a bed was never allowed. Rose had Richard's full attention immediately.

He sat down next to her, and sensing the gravity of the occasion, took both of her hands in his. As she relayed how his father had been arrested, her son maintained a perfect look of stoicism on his face. However, Rose noted his lower lip quivering when he asked if his father would ever be home with them again.

Rose was a quiet woman, but when she said something, it was one-hundred percent truth. She never meant for anything she said to hurt anyone, much less a child she carried beneath her heart. However, pain flooded Richard's face when she honestly told her young man/boy that from all she had learned, she wasn't sure when or if his father would return.

Richard did ask what difference going to school would make. She reminded him of the cruelty of some of his classmates. He looked surprised to hear that, but suddenly grasped what she was saying and agreed they might prove to be an aggravation. He rose when she stood, and they reassured each other with a hug.

***

After his mother left the room, Richard pulled out his desk chair and sat. He didn't move for at least fifteen minutes as he stared ahead, seeing nothing. Finally, he got up quietly, closed his door and laid down on his bed as tears formed in his eyes. He brushed them away and vowed he would never, no matter what happened, cry about his father ever again. Oh, Richard loved his papa, and Emil had always been good to him. He'd overheard his papa telling other folks what a good son he was, an excellent worker. And he bragged about his son's school reports. However, the boy knew his little sister was Papa's favorite. That was truly okay with Richard, because she could be such a cute little thing. Blanche seemed to cast a spell on her father, and Emil couldn't resist her magic. Richard knew only too well, because he himself succumbed to her wily ways almost daily. She was basically a good girl, and he loved her a lot and enjoyed most everything about her.

No, Blanche had nothing to do with the disdain he felt toward his father. The truth was, many times he'd seen his papa leave a barn only minutes after Minnie left from the same barn. Papa had no idea his son was watching him carefully, nor did he realize Richard had observed him leaving Minnie's bedroom in the small hours of the night. The soon-to-be young man felt bile rise in his throat as he imagined Papa and Minnie having relations. He just couldn't understand why he'd do that to his mother. Papa knew if she found out it'd hurt her something terrible.

What did Papa see in that horrid woman? She was built sturdy, with big bones and rough skin, and she sounded crude when she spoke, whereas mom was small with delicate hands and bones. And mom never spoke loudly. Her voice was soothing, caring, and she was so very loving, kind and understanding. What was wrong with Papa? Richard wasn't a little boy anymore. He knew what Papa and Minnie were doing. Of course, that woman pranced around Papa, showing him her petticoats, and when she was dusting in his office room, she leaned far forward, causing the top of her big breasts to be seen.

Shaking the thought from his head, he sat and picked up a book and began reading.

***

Rose leaned against the wall just outside of Blanche's room. She knew talking with Richard was simple compared to what she feared would soon transpire when Blanche learned of her papa's predicament. Delicate Blanche, Rose sighed. What would news of her father's situation do to her? She adored him, and Rose herself knew how important the love of a father was. Her own father supported her and all she did, including caring for her younger siblings and making sure they kept up with their studies and had clean clothing after her mother died. What would Blanche do with this news? She was feisty, but at the same time delicate.

Rose digested the totality of what might lie ahead. Arrested for murder kept repeating in her head. Murder, how can that word even be associated with her family? Could Emil have actually killed another human being? She just could not allow her mind to attach the word murderer to her husband, who was rather clumsy, but always soft and gentle with their children. How horrid it all seemed, because no matter what the future held, right now, today, Blanche's papa could be described as a possible murderer.

Rose moved into the room and stood next to the bed watching her baby, her little firecracker, sleep. There was no listening patiently or evaluating for Blanche. As soon as she heard something disagreeable, she let everyone within earshot know how she felt. Her slender, little body was lying in a tangle of sheets and blankets, her hair spread out over her pillow. Many tight, little corkscrew curls framed her face. Rose thought her child had beautiful hair, exactly the opposite of the way Blanche regarded her tresses. The girl fussed and carried on when Rose attempted to brush her hair, which was unruly and almost impossible to run a brush through. For several years, Arline, Blanche's half-sister, allowed her to do her hair. Now that was no longer an option, as Arline lived in town with her husband and infant son. So, Blanche was doing her own hair, and some days it was obvious. But Rose felt that as long as she wanted, Blanche should care for her own hair. She was no longer a baby, and she would improve with time.

Just then, her child's eyelids fluttered, and she opened her eyes wide, looking at her mother and asking, "Why are you a standing there, Mama?"

Rose had stood perfectly still with what she felt must have been a soft, warm look of love on her face as she watched her sleeping child. Once Blanche's eyes opened, she promptly replaced the expression with a bland, noncommittal one. Many years ago, Rose learned to never reveal her feelings with her face, as doing so could expose information she might not want divulged at that time.

She brought herself completely into the present and sat on the side of the small bed that Emil had built with his own hands for his little princess. Rose noticed as she did so that Blanche's perfect-sized bed would probably become too small in another year or so. Feeling emotion well in her chest, Rose gathered her baby into her arms and rocked back and forth.

Soon Blanche pulled away and looked deep into her mother's eyes while asking in an insistent tone, "What's wrong, Mama?" Her face suddenly lit up then. "Where's Papa? I want to remind him he's going to watch me on my pony after school."

As she began to hop out of bed, Rose took hold of her arm. "Please sit, child," she said.

Hearing the seriousness in her mother's voice, Blanche stopped and sat immediately.

"Papa might not be home today, and he didn't return last night." Rose sighed and thought how only the truth could be spoken now. She explained that suspicion of murder was why Emil was in jail and not allowed to come home. As Rose talked, her little girl's dark eyes filled with tears and spilled over and down her face. Pulling her baby close, she held her as she sobbed.

When the crying ceased, Rose informed her she wouldn't be attending school today. The expression on Blanche's face changed then from pain to anger. Her daughter sprang from her bed and began to put her school clothes on.

"What are you doing?" Rose asked.

"I'm going to the jailhouse to bring Papa home," she fumed.

Rose convinced her child to come downstairs with her and talk about her plan while they ate breakfast. As they made their way down the sweeping staircase, Rose's heart raced at the realization she was the only lifeline these two young children had.

And then there was Arline, her stepdaughter, Emil's daughter from his first wife, who passed when Arline was quite young. It was true that Arline met all situations head on and managed them. Truth was, she didn't allow anything to manage her. She will get through this and survive better than any of us, Rose thought. But it wouldn't be a good feeling for her to walk through town with all the whispers about her father. Arline had always taken such pride in her family and physical self. Like her legendary mother, she had metamorphosed into a stunning woman.

Chapter Nine

Arline would stare at the picture of her mama, Annie, often. Stare right into her eyes, and it felt like she was talking to her. After Mama died of blood poisoning, no one mentioned her, except strangers. They would tell Arline she looked like her mama—but she could tell they meant not quite as pretty. Papa never talked about her mother, though, ever.

Arline didn't have a lot of recollections about the day her mama died, but she did remember the look on Papa's face. She saw deep lines of sadness etched there. Funny how she remembered that now. Those lines. How many young children would remember the lines etched on their parents' face? Arline remembered how her mama would call Arline an "old soul" sometimes. She also remembered that.

More than anything, Arline remembered the deep sense of despair she felt when Papa told her that Mama wouldn't be coming back. That she'd gone to a really nice place called Heaven and she'd be staying there until Papa and Arline would one day go see her again. Now with what had happened, it looked like maybe Papa would be seeing Mama a lot sooner than he'd thought that day he told Arline about Mama not coming back.

Gazing at the picture made Arline feel better, and worse. If Arline's mother had lived, all this probably wouldn't have happened. That Minnie wouldn't have come and taken her father's attention. They said that her mother was the prettiest woman in the southern part of the state, and they were right. Arline remembered brushing her Mama's hair—so soft and full. Like the mane of a lioness, or at least what she thought a lioness's mane might feel like.

Everyone stopped to look when her mama entered the room. She was almost too beautiful to look at, at least for Arline. After her mother got so sick and passed on, Arline couldn't hardly think of her. It was too hard to know she would never come back and tell Arline how pretty she was or touch her cheek. Papa was sad then. Really sad. He didn't say anything—he never did, but Arline knew. Who wouldn't be sad to lose such a beautiful wife? It made Arline sad for a long, long time. And then she got angry. At Mama for leaving and at Papa for getting a new wife.

Why did Papa get a new wife, anyway? She could never replace Mama, ever. Of course, he couldn't have picked a better new wife, and Arline realized that. Rose was kind and gentle and never, ever raised her voice to Arline. Of course, Rose was totally different than her mama. Where her mama was pretty and elegant, Rose was plain and humble, where her mama was loud and outspoken, Rose was soft-spoken and gentle. Arline's mother never went anywhere near the animals and would never talk to the farmhands, but Rose would talk to them all the time, as if they were just like her, and she loved to milk the cows and feed the hens. The kitchen was her favorite place to be. Did Papa plan it that way?

Sometimes Arline wondered about her mama and papa. She knew Papa loved her mama—but sometimes it looked like he loved her too much. It was as if he wanted to gobble her up and eat her alive. They both had forked tongues, and their arguments could get ugly. Like the time Mama threw a vase at Papa when she was angry about something. Could Papa have gotten tired, no matter how beautiful Mama was, and poisoned her blood? They said it was blood poisoning—and the cause was unknown. Was Papa the cause? Arline shuddered to think about it.

But she didn't worry about Rose. Papa never raised his voice to her, because Rose rarely spoke. She always just listened and then stepped into the background. She never cowered, though. Rose wasn't a weak woman. Arline saw her stepmother watch everything with all-knowing eyes. Arline guessed in some ways Rose was a lot smarter than her own mama, but she felt guilty whenever she thought that.

Was that why Papa had become interested in Minnie? Because she had that same kind of fire her mama had? That Rose just didn't have, even if she tried.

Arline had watched Minnie flounce around the house and giggle nearly from the moment she moved onto the farm. It had made Arline want to spit nails at the woman. Who did she think she was batting her eyes like that at Papa? The last few years before she moved out and married Eldo, any attempts Arline made to talk to Papa—well, just forget about it. She could leave the room, and he wouldn't even notice, he was so fixated on that vixen. And now here they were, Papa in jail for the supposed murder of her husband.

Chapter Ten

Fricker was a loner, thought Kamuf. Like he was cursed to walk the earth by himself—arm's distance from everyone. He'd seen Fricker in his youth in the woods all alone, his head down, like he was checking the ground for rattlers. But Kamuf knew he wasn't, cuz even the rattlers stayed away from him.

He'd get a gleam in his eye sometimes, and it got a lot worse when he drank. And boy, did he drink. Fricker could drink any man under the table. As a matter of fact, he could be three-four sheets to the wind and most people wouldn't even know it. Kamuf knew, though. Probably on account of his own papa. He liked the drink, too, and Kamuf could smell the telltale signs. Fricker's wife, Rose—what a fine woman she was—could tell, too. They both knew when he was a-drinkin'.

So, when Fricker asked Kamuf to take the gun that one time and go take care of the poor fella, he wasn't at all surprised. No, truth be told, he was kind of surprised something didn't happen sooner—seeing how Fricker was so enamored with that Minnie. Damn, the day she walked onto the farm. Damn that day to hell. Kamuf thought about that sometimes. What if she never came? All the people now caught in the crosshairs of Fricker's decisions when it came to that girl would be living out a different life right now.

Kamuf remembered the girl when she was a youngin.' Got everybody to play her way, do the stuff she wanted and wasn't supposed to do. It was just a certain group of them following her around like puppy dogs. Poor mutts. Whenever trouble was doing in town, she would be in the middle of it, but disappeared right before the ruckus hit. She never took ownership of any of the things she set in motion that got topsy turvy. No, she'd be sitting there batting them eyelashes like she didn't know what was doing. But Kamuf had this gut feeling she was play acting all of it. So, when she came flouncing into the Fricker house that first day, maybe no one else noticed, but Kamuf saw it. That same gleam in her eyes as Emil's. They were like torpedoes hitting one another, and the destruction began. What a mess. Damn sure it would have been better if they'd never met or laid eyes on each other.

Kamuf wasn't surprised when the scuttlebutt said the poor girl was "beside herself" about her husband's death. Funny thing, if they only knew that she knew. She knew he'd be killed. She was planning on it. Fact was, she had big plans for herself on the Fricker farm. He couldn't prove none of it, though. So, Kamuf just sat back and watched. What else could he do?

Chapter Eleven

It was quite late when Rose finally settled into her rocking chair, Bible in hand. She was exhausted. For days now since Emil had been gone and was still being held by the Sheriff, she had tried her best to carry out his daily duties.

She oversaw the milking of the cows, and all entailed with getting the milk to market. Additionally, the workers who tended to the other animals and the crops required instruction. Rose took care of all her own ever-present duties as rapidly as possible, sadly cutting corners. This was most evident with the three meals a day she planned and worked beside Cook to produce for the farmhands and household help. Preparing such large amounts of food was more than one person could accomplish without help. Rose also truly enjoyed cooking, and she particularly loved baking. She found it soothing in many ways. In fact, she sought refuge in the kitchen ever since she could remember. The compliments she received about her cakes, pies, and desserts from the hired help were important to Rose. They reinforced her self-worth.

Sitting in the dark now, only a small lamp illuminating the area in which she sat, Rose began reading her Bible. When she turned the page, she stopped, realizing her mind hadn't comprehended one single word of what she'd just read.

She sighed and stared into the darkness, looking down at the floor-length nightdress she wore, which was quite comfortable. Rose had sewn it herself out of muslin. To add some beauty to the coarse, unbleached fabric, she had crocheted several inches of ecru-colored lace on the sleeves and cuffs and around the high neck of the gown. Before putting the garment on, she had brushed her long, dark hair with its occasional silver threads and braided it. Now, sitting here in the quiet, she felt her hair against her back in its soft, loose braid.

Rose was so very tired, but also anxious and tense. She felt cloaked in uneasiness and dread all the time and knew she wouldn't be able to fall asleep for quite a while. For goodness sakes, she couldn't even read her Bible right now. Instead, she allowed her thoughts to go places she had forbidden herself to visit. The most forbidden of all those places was the what ifs. What if Emil didn't come home? What if there was some truth to why they held her husband? What if he truly was involved in murder?

Rose chastised herself. What good would such treacherous thinking do? She needed to snap herself out of this. It was crucial she remained strong for her children like she'd done for her siblings when her mama died. She had skipped college to raise them, and now they had their own full lives.

Shaking the disturbing thoughts from her head, Rose decided it was far better to think of the beginning. When she first met Emil. When times were better.

Her thoughts traveled back to 1907, seventeen years before when she learned of Emil's interest in her. One of her mother's closest friends, Mary Margaret, had started coming to her parents' home to help when her mother became bedbound. From Mary Margaret, Rose learned how to move and position Mama in bed for comfort, as well as what foods to prepare that she would be able to eat. Everything Mary Margaret did for her longtime friend was done with kindness and love. For that Rose felt beholden.

Even after Mama's passing, Mary Margaret continued to visit periodically and would share the latest gossip. Rose always listened politely as the woman became animated while she embellished the activities occurring in town. On one occasion, she shared Emil Fricker's plans to remarry and his intentions to court herself, Rose Jenny.

When Mary Margaret revealed Emil's plans, Rose was taken aback and thought about being courted—an absolutely foreign concept when thinking of herself. She had never been the object of a man's or even boy's affection. As Rose served her guest rhubarb pie and tea, she listened to the details Mary Margaret had gleaned from an overheard conversation in the store.

"Thank you," gushed Mary Margaret, who took a bite of the pie before continuing. "Land sakes, it's no wonder your pies are known throughout the county. This is delicious, and I'm sure I'll want a second slice."

As Rose listened intently to the gossip about Emil's intentions for her—spilled between mouthfuls of pie—her heart picked up speed and excitement grew within her. Externally, however, she remained calm and unaffected.

When their visit ended and Rose walked her guest out to her waiting buggy and Mary Margaret climbed in and bid her goodbye, there wasn't even a moment when Rose's inner turmoil was visible on the outside. Externally, her demeanor projected the epitome of cool calmness.

Once back in the house alone, though, Rose released her thoughts and emotions. Every now and then she'd make a statement out loud, including verbalizing the fact that her siblings were finally all able to care for themselves. Even the youngest planned to go away to college in the fall. Rose's work for the family was done.

With that realization, she dared to imagine the gossip about Emil Fricker was true. As her thoughts raced, she became certain he would want more children, as he only had a daughter, about five years old. Her name was Arline, if Rose's memory served her. Surely, he'd want a son to care for the small empire Emil's father had built.

Could it be she was going to be a bride? A wife? And maybe even a mother? Rose realized she was indeed ecstatic. Then she remembered her mother's teachings and immediately quelled her excitement. She and her father had emigrated from Switzerland and spoke Swiss German between themselves. Displaying emotion was not something they encouraged. Her mother would likely chastise her and insist what Mary Margaret had told Rose was simply gossip. With that in mind, Rose told herself not to expect anything. However, a spark of hope materialized. This spark of hope was something she had previously tucked away deep in her heart and had planned to never resurrect.

Mary Margaret's words also took some of the sting out of Papa's decision that Rose would not go to college but instead care for the children after her mother's passing. It had been the only logical solution for the family, as Rose was quite capable of loving and nurturing the little ones. She eventually accepted her role and ended up reaping much joy and many blessings from seeing the children to adulthood. Despite this, the one sting she could not accept and release was the dream of having her own family and home.

As time has a way of slipping away without notice, she observed her youth being carried with it. She recalled the fear and sadness that filled her entire body in those days whenever she imagined holding her own child—one birthed from her body. Often in that time, long ago, she would stare into her looking glass and wonder if any man could ever love her, or was she just too old?

It was nearly two days after speaking with Mary Margaret that Emil appeared at the door of the Jenny home. Rose had been in the chicken coop gathering eggs when she glanced toward the house. Seeing a tall man on their front porch caused her to freeze and unknowingly release the grip she had on the egg basket. She looked on the ground at her feet, as if viewing it from another dimension, watching the yellow yolks and clear albumen roll down and over the white and brown eggshells. As she stole a look at the man on the porch—most certainly Emil Fricker—her father opened the door and moved to stand next to the visitor. They exchanged an energetic, possibly forceful, handshake. Then they moved to the table and chairs set up on the porch and sat down. From her vantage point, Rose observed that Emil never seemed to quite become comfortable in the too small chair.

She believed her appearance to formally meet Emil was mandatory. She'd simply walk to the porch, smile and introduce herself to him. Oh, Lord, what was truly happening? Every nerve ending in her body was on full alert. She was so nervous, but it was a tingly, good sort of nervous. Then she realized she was neither dressed nor groomed properly to meet someone, especially a possible suitor.

Momentarily, she ducked back into the shadows. Putting her hand to her hair, she felt that a lot of tendrils had escaped the bun she had secured near the nape of her neck. She pulled the pins holding her hair out, quickly smoothed it back and secured them once again. Then she lifted her skirts and released them, checking they weren't twisted and did not show her legs. She pinched her cheeks and picked up her egg basket but then set it back down. Best to leave the jumbled mess of eggshell pieces with yellow and white still oozing and spilling over onto the coop floor.

Holding her head high, Rose walked toward the house and the two men on the porch. The closer she got to Emil, the faster her heart seemed to beat. She could feel the rhythm throughout her entire body. As she approached, her face felt flushed with excitement, and she thought how pointless it had been to pinch her cheeks. Taking the few steps to the porch, she found herself looking up at one of the tallest men she had ever seen.

Towering over her, he took her petite and delicate hand in his gigantic one, and said, "Mighty pleased to meet you, Ma'am."

Rose nodded her head in response and then sat on the edge of a chair; her ankles crossed daintily.

Her father began speaking, telling of Emil's desire to marry her. Nevertheless, he planned to come courting until Rose freely gave her hand in marriage. And he did. As a matter of fact, a few days later she went on her first outing with him.

Emil arrived in a large, ornately extravagant carriage. After wishing her father a good day, he offered Rose his arm as they left the front porch. She held it lightly while they made their way to his buggy, where he assisted her up and into the carriage. As she sank into the buttery leather of the buggy seats, surrounded by shiny metal and more brown leather, Rose thought the carriage was outrageous and that she could never handle such a showy buggy. Or would she have to?

She moved her attention away from his carriage and looked forward to his horses. A matched pair, and what beauties they were. Tall, black and dark, with excellent conformation. Both acted anxious to move. When Emil signaled his team to go, they started forward in a surprisingly gentle and steady manner. After a few minutes, Emil inquired about her comfort. When she replied she was very comfortable, his attention went back to driving the buggy.

After they had traveled for some time, Rose thought, he didn't seem like a man of many words. Where on earth was he taking her? And alone! Just the two of them. Was that even proper? Rose briefly closed her eyes and prayed, dear God, please help him keep his hands to himself and don't let us go anyplace where something's doing.

As they continued on their mystery journey, Rose felt her anxiety level rise. Where is he taking me played over and over in her mind as uneasiness moved into full bloom. She realized her breathing was far too rapid, and she began to experience some lightheadedness. No stranger to nervous spells, in response Rose closed her eyes and focused on taking deep, slow inhalations and exhaling all the air within.

Soon, she felt better, and noticed Emil was talking to her. Oh, goodness how could she reply to him? He continued to talk about the effects of the weather on his various crops, speaking of the yields and saving specific crops. He mentioned the methods used to save those crops were all his making. He spoke in a conversational, not boasting way.

As the carriage went up and over a rise in the road, Emil continued to talk while Rose silently thanked God for orchestrating the last few minutes. Sitting close within the carriage, she was able to glance at her intended frequently, noting his strong profile and the way he sat extremely straight. He was such a large man—big bones and tall—but upon closer inspection, she noted he appeared merely skin and bones. Right away Rose thought of her love of cooking and hoped to fatten him up.

As she watched him, she noticed the expression on his face remained unchanged, whether he was relaying a tragic death or telling of a humorous situation. His reputation around town indicated he was always stoic, cold, and ruthless. Sitting so close to him, she felt uplifted and safe, as well as excited. She certainly felt nothing negative about Emil.

After a spell, Rose became concerned again. Where on earth was he taking her? Out of Illinois? Finally, she couldn't help herself and asked, "My dear Emil, where are we headed? I mean, this is a lovely outing."

Emil demonstrated briefly the start of a smile followed by concern as his hand closed over hers, so large and safe, and he asked, "Is there anything you need?"

Rose shook her head. "Everything is lovely. It's just that I expected something shorter."

Emil turned to Rose with that almost smile and replied, "Our destination is up around the next bend in the road."

The two dark animals were suddenly no longer being instructed by Emil, and Rose knew exactly where the buggy was going. She looked up at her suitor with a full smile and said, "This is wonderful."

The buggy came to a halt directly across from the large entrance of the massive home belonging to Emil. The front door opened then, and a bundle of skirts, petticoats, and curls came charging toward them.

"Papa, Papa!" the child called.

Emil quickly said, "I thought you should get to know Arline and look through the home that will be yours soon. I've been a-praying on you and my baby girl getting on. 'Course, once I met you, I knew there'd be no problems, as long as you're able to manage my little fireball."

For a moment, Rose was taken aback as she thought about all the men she knew. Which one would go out of his way, as Emil had, to make certain mutual respect was established between his child and a possible caretaker/mama? Rose knew no man who would extend that courtesy. Honestly, it seemed many men saw their children as future farmhands. Sadly, Rose knew of quite a few children living in such a situation.

So touched was Rose by his gesture that tears formed in her eyes. She blinked rapidly, unwilling to have tears be associated with the events of the day. She thought this man certainly couldn't be ruthless. If he was cold to someone, possibly there was a reason. Stoic, now that was likely. However, she couldn't think of any way his stoicism could harm another, except maybe his loved ones. She gulped, as she soon would be one of them.

Despite her size, which was around the same as most five-year-olds, Arline climbed up and into the buggy in a heart-beat. She threw herself onto her father's lap, gave him a peck on his cheek and said, "I love you, Papa." Then she began talking to Emil rapidly, moving from subject to subject, barely taking time to breathe. While she did so, Rose and Emil made strong eye contact.

Finally, he said, "Let's go in and show Rose the house. Most likely she'll move in with us soon."

The smile on Rose's face was immediately squashed when Arline looked directly into her eyes and said, "You're not my mama. You'll never be."

Rose watched the little girl's face soften, however, as she continued almost shyly, "It would be nice to have you move into the house. Do you know how to make French braids and brush hair without hurting someone?"

Rose smiled and replied, "I can be gentle when I brush a little one's hair. And I truly enjoy all types of braiding."

At that, the three of them left the carriage and went into the home. Right after they entered, Emil announced, "We're not staying here long. Just enough time for Rose to see every room. We're taking the carriage and going on an outing."

In response, Arline squealed in delight as she jumped up and down, clapping her hands.

"Now let's get this show on the road," said Emil as he led Rose through the parlor, where she admired the tapestries and rich fabrics used to decorate the room, along with the thick, soft rug covering most of the shiny, hardwood floor.

When she entered the dining room, Rose was speechless. China, porcelain, silver and cut glass glistened throughout the room.

Fresh cut flowers adorned the center of the massive dining table. Taking in the totality simply took her breath away.

After a few moments of silence as Rose continued to gape, Emil kindly told her, "This will all be yours, but not until you're ready to be my wife."

They moved on through several more rooms and ended the tour in the kitchen, where Emil said, "My dear Rose, I doubt you have any interest in here, as we have a cook for all meals. You'll meet her soon."

"On the contrary, my dear Emil, the kitchen is my favorite room. It's where I create delicious recipes." She went on to describe some of her creations to him, and again he smiled.

Then they went upstairs and peered into each beautiful room. Rose had never even allowed herself to dream of such elegance.

As they toured the lavish home, Arline stayed close to her father and seemed to be a very well-behaved child. The three went downstairs and back to the kitchen where a large picnic basket awaited them. Again, Arline clapped and exclaimed, "I love, just love, picnics."

It was a brief carriage ride to a green pasture filled with wildflowers blooming under trees. Emil took a tablecloth from the basket and spread it out over the grass. Being careful to choose a place with some shade, he asked his daughter to remove the food and place it on the tablecloth. Arline jumped to the task while smiling constantly. They sat around the cloth laden with food and ate. A bit of conversation occurred; however, eating was their priority. The food the cook prepared Rose had to admit was delicious.

When they finished and all was cleaned up, Arline surprised Rose by asking, "Will you go walk with me in the woods? Not real far, just a short walk."

Rose agreed.

As they moved through the forest, Arline posed many questions to Rose, such as, "Do you have your own children?" She followed this with, "If you have no children, how can you know how to take care of me?"

Rose explained about raising her brothers and sisters and helping her mother from the day they were born. Arline listened carefully, then skipped ahead, but soon made a sudden stop. She turned around to face Rose with a twinkle in her eyes surrounded by an aura of excitement. In her hand, she held a beautiful black and yellow butterfly.

Rose took the opportunity to share what she knew about butterflies and their symbolism of new beginnings. Again, the child listened intently and then asked, "Can we take this one home?"

"We could, but wouldn't it be kinder to allow that beautiful creature to fly about freely during its short time on earth?" Rose answered.

Arline was very quiet and continued to watch the butterfly perched on her hand. Suddenly, she released it and waved her arms upward, crying out, "Go see everything, pretty butterfly."

They held hands as they made their way back to the pasture and Emil. When they arrived at her father, sprawled out on the grass, Arline ran to him and leaned down to put her mouth to his ear, whispering loudly, "Let's keep her. Can she come home with us today?"

Chapter Twelve

September 17, 1924

Deimling sat in his study after dinner, waiting for his evening meal to digest. Reaching for his current book, he opened it but soon found himself staring at the words on the page without truly seeing them. He sighed and looked up at his giant bookcase—built by himself from roughhewn lumber he'd found in the nearby forest. He had collected it all over the course of a month, then sanded it by hand for hours until it was just right.

A twitch of irritation hit his belly then, and he snorted. Had Fricker ever done anything like this, besides his God forsaken still? Deimling had been offered the evil brew, as he often thought of it, but he had always turned it down. Least of which he was the law, and it was currently not legal to possess or drink spirits. Even more importantly, his own father had a problem with liquor back when it was legal, and he wasn't about to turn out like that.

Deimling could tell Fricker had a deep-seated problem like his pa. He'd seen him pacing his cell with the same hunted look in his eyes Deimling had seen in his pa's when his ma threw out the liquor. Not that it did any good, because after a round of pacing and yelling, his pa would go buy more. But Fricker couldn't get out of the 10 x 10 cell they had him in to go make himself some more.

When they first took him into custody, he was ornery as hell. But now, he looked defeated. Like he didn't want to think, but he couldn't stop himself from doing so anymore. Although, he kept insisting he was innocent.

What came first? He wondered. Was it the moonshine, or was it Fricker himself? Not that it mattered all that much, because as far as Deimling was concerned, Fricker had to pay for what he'd done. It was a curiosity, though, not knowing the process. It wasn't the first time he'd seen men with a lot of promise throw away everything for the brew, and women, of course.

The attorney for the district said Fricker's case was airtight. Deimling had to admit to himself he wasn't going to take a deep breath until the man paid. Of course, if they did manage to catch Fricker in the net, many other people would unfortunately pay, including his family. Not much was known about Fricker's wife, because she tended to keep to herself. As far as Deimling knew, Fricker had been married to her for a good amount of time.

Chapter Thirteen

April 1910

Rose (Jenny) Fricker

Rose was in her garden once again. Spring had finally arrived. She gazed upward and smiled at the tiny wisps of white clouds hanging in the otherwise perfectly clear, bright blue Illinois sky. The sun was full and shiny. Colorful little bits of green were evident on every plant, tree and grass.

She adjusted her sun hat. Her mother had taught her as a young girl to never go out in the sun without protecting her head, arms and hands. It was a fairly common belief that the rays of the sun turned a woman's skin dark, and porcelain skin was revered. In fact, the lighter a woman's skin, the more beautiful she was considered to be. Rose had a medium complexion tone. She believed this medium skin shade put her behind other fair-skinned women. Consequently, she kept every inch of herself generously covered when she was out in the sunshine.

Now with the sun shining so brightly, she wore a pale gray, long-sleeved blouse, and her hands were totally covered with gloves. She thought how they were possibly an old pair of go to meeting gloves, as they were long enough to tuck the tops under her shirtsleeves. A dark gray heavy cotton made up her skirt and reached the ground. Every day she spent on the farm, she wore a pinafore apron that covered the front and sides of what she wore. Whatever the chore, her skirt apron was always pressed smoothly and without wrinkles. She believed in bringing dignity to every activity in which she participated. She also preferred a nice warm undershirt as opposed to the fancy underpinnings many women were drawn to.

A slight breeze suddenly came through, and she felt her clothing define her silhouette, clinging to her slender frame. It was then that her body shape was discernible, she thought. Proud she remained slim, even after giving birth to Richard, her first child, just a month before, she assessed her body. True, she had small breasts when she wasn't nursing, but they fit her perfectly above her tiny waist, which curved smoothly into her hips, leaving her legs a mystery. Her long, dark brown hair was twisted and pinned securely at the nape of her neck, and she knew her dark eyes held numerous emotions. Rose was clear she wasn't a beauty in the classic sense, however, with her slim, well-proportioned shape and body language, many thought her immediately to be quite handsome and an extremely strong woman. A woman to be reckoned with.

She stood in the center of the lawn appraising all areas of the garden out to the very edges. It was quite a large area, possibly the biggest in the county. This was saying something, considering it was likely the only one planted and harvested by a wife. Sure, some of the farmhands and occasionally one of the house girls helped her in the garden, but she chose every vegetable and fruit planted. She felt it was a passion, because nothing could compete with the feel of fresh earth in her hands and the thrill of watching plants break through the barrier of the earth, producing beautiful fruits and delicious vegetables. She also enjoyed her flowers, particularly her namesake roses. Lily of the valley, too. The garden was her favorite place—even more so than the house, though she loved the kitchen, and the garden gave her a lot of opportunities for cooking.

Rose thought about the harvests to come in the summer and fall and looked forward to them, like the grapes. She gazed out toward the raspberries and considered. Maybe she should change their location, if possible, to the northeast corner. That would be a lot of work, though, considering their roots had dug deep into the earth. And she'd likely lose some plants along the way. Better to leave them be.

She relished the thought of all the harvests and the boiling and canning that would ensue. Then she would store all the jars in the cellar for the long, cold days of Illinois' fall and winter.

Emil liked her pickled beets the best, so she tried to always make sure to include as many as possible in her early spring planting. She felt so proud when he grinned at the pile she placed on his plate.

Perhaps the best part of gardening was the hope new plant life brought. Hope for something new, something fresh, something untainted by life's darker side. Rose's heart fluttered then when she thought of her husband, and anxiety threaded its way through her belly.

They had hired a new milkmaid by the name of Minnie with the idea of having her help oversee the milking since Rose had baby Richard to now care for. The girl had started the other day, bringing her meager belongings into the bedroom Rose had prepared for her. Though Rose usually liked the farmhands and housemaids and welcomed them, there was something off-putting about the girl. She had a sly way about her that reminded Rose of a fox. Truth be told, Rose didn't like the way Emil looked at Minnie, either.

Chapter Fourteen

September 1914

Rose sighed. It was time to dress the children. Putting four-year-old Richard's clothing on him was a struggle every single day. He was so willful and disagreeable when it came to what he wanted to wear. She reached for him as he bounced by, acting such the four-year-old boy he was. Rose pulled her son close and gave his wiggling little body a long hug.

As he wriggled from her grip, she looked at his sparkling eyes and impish expression and her heart instantly melted. He squirmed and pulled on his nightshirt as he told her he was a big boy and could put on his own stuff. She quickly slipped an undershirt over his head, and he thrust his arms through the holes. With little difficulty, she removed his nightshirt and helped him into bloomers. Then she popped his carefully ironed shirt right over his head. Rose managed to fasten only three buttons before he swiftly bounced away from her, stating he'd be in the bathroom, sounding as much like his father as he could.

Rose was grateful for this little reprieve before the commotion regarding the length of his pants.

Within moments, however, he was in front of her, saying, "No short pants. Short pants are baby pants. Richard's a big boy. He wears long, big boy pants like his father."

A bit of a struggle then followed, but once he was all buttoned up, pants, shoes and socks on and his hair brushed, he was a handsome boy. As she watched him scamper off, Rose's heart burst with love. Richard and his little sister were her entire life. She could not express how much love she felt for them. For her babies.

Rose paused then, thinking herself selfish in the way she thought about Arline, her stepdaughter, who wasn't the same to her as Blanche and Richard. She was now eleven years old, and physically quite lovely. This was expected, as her birth mother had been referred to as the most beautiful woman in the county. Arline was a kind, loving girl. She spent much time holding, talking to, and playing with baby Blanche. Rose knew she truly loved Arline. But there was a difference between her and the two babies that grew beneath Rose's heart. She said a quick prayer, asking for forgiveness for her selfishness and for help to be the best mother possible to all three children.

Just then, Sally, one of several women who helped Rose run the large farmhouse, entered the room. Rose asked her to take Richard downstairs. After Richard and Sally left the room, Rose immediately turned her attention to her beautiful, perfect baby girl now beginning to stir in her crib. Scooping up little Blanche, she cooed and cuddled her daughter. Whenever Rose simply watched her babies, she became overwhelmed that such perfectness was a part of her. After a long night of sleep, she knew her tiny bundle would be ravenous. Rose quickly changed her diaper as her daughter worked toward a large and hungry cry.

Holding Blanche close, Rose settled into her rocking chair, her breast feeling so full and stretched, gradually relaxing as the baby emptied one, then the other. After expelling a few little air bubbles, Blanche was a happy, content child. Rose began to dress her for the day, talking to her little beauty constantly. Blanche responded by waving her arms and kicking furiously as babies do. Time and again, she broke into a big smile for her mother. After another diaper, she put a tiny shirt on her baby, securing each of the three ties carefully into small bows to keep it snug around her. Rose then put on her tiny feet a pair of beautifully crocheted booties and pulled a long white gown over her small body. She tied the pale pink ribbon that kept the gown closed under her chin.

Taking a moment to notice the handiwork on the gown, Rose admired the small, pink embroidered flowers with light green leaves and the booties, also embroidered. She decided that both turned out quite lovely, most likely because of all the love with which she had created them.

After picking up discarded clothing and putting the room in order, she pulled her daughter into her arms and headed downstairs for another day. No matter what that day might bring.

Chapter Fifteen

January 1915

It was morning and Rose polished the silver. She had just put baby Blanche down for her morning nap and checked on Richard, who happily played outside. Usually, settling her children and doing simple household chores gave Rose a brief sense of peace and order. At least for a few minutes. Not so lately. She continued to feel a sense of impending doom. She shook her head and instructed herself to ignore her feelings. After setting down the silver polish, she went to check on the kids again. They were just fine.

There was no reason on earth Rose should feel anxious. She willed herself to focus on her polishing, noticing the smoothness of each piece as she ran her fingers back and forth over them. She admired the beauty of the silver in her hands and even felt overwhelmed by the bold patterns, most of the pieces engraved with the letter F for Fricker.

It never ceased to amaze Rose that one man could have such a large and beautiful home filled with exquisite belongings, all so personal. She still felt surprised that she, Wilhelmina Jenny, actually lived amongst such loveliness. Not that the home she grew up in wasn't nice and had its own beauty. Especially the intricate doilies and tablecloths made with love by her mother's hands.

Now Rose spent her spare time creating needlework handworks for her own home—though it hardly needed any enhancement.

Still, despite the gorgeous, billowing window coverings made from fabrics from overseas and the rich, velvet-covered furnishings, a harsh coldness permeated each room. It was a stark contrast to the cheery, love-filled rooms of her childhood.

Her thoughts turned to herself then, and she wondered what happened to that cheerful, lighthearted woman she was when she married Emil nearly eight years before. Where did that girl go? She knew she should be happier than ever. Her dream of motherhood was now fulfilled, and her hopes of a home far exceeded her expectations.

Could it possibly be the storm clouds that seemed to follow Emil into each room and the gloom that settled in the house every time he came home? Rose willed herself to push away such thoughts of her husband and instead admired the rich, sparkling silver pieces, caressing each bowl, knife, fork and spoon as she placed them in their designated spaces in the beautifully walled and decorated dining room.

Just as she closed the cupboard, the main entrance door flew open, and moments later, Minnie entered the living room in a flourish. Her face was flushed and her breathing hard. Rose paused for a moment, thinking that tending to the dairy cows never left her in that condition. Rose remained perfectly still as she continued to observe Minnie while the woman prattled on and on needlessly. Rose realized suddenly she was staring at the girl. Her mother had taught her at a very young age that good, polite girls never stared at anyone. She had cautioned that it was impolite and actually rude, and it could possibly be hurtful to another. But Rose couldn't take her eyes off the young girl. As Minnie's mouth moved, Rose was unable to hear the specifics of what she gushed about. This reminded Rose of the way her eyes flashed, and how her smile often appeared to invite the men she spoke with to her bed. It seemed that Minnie wasn't particular as to who the man was—young or old, fat or thin. They all seemed mesmerized by her suggestive manner and the exaggerated sway of her hips. She wasn't all that attractive, but she flirted and made men feel ten feet tall.

Rose continued to stare at the very plain face of the girl. She definitely wasn't pretty. However, her overtly sensuous and seductive mannerisms held most men captive within her gaze. She often watched her own Emil look at Minnie with longing and something totally foreign. When this occurred, he was impervious to anything happening around him or anyone, including the apple of his eye, little Blanche. She believed Emil looked—what man could resist—but that was the extent of his wandering.

Rose continued to evaluate the young woman, noting the firmness of her face. Even her slightly plump body had a glow of youth. She was, after all, sixteen years younger than Rose. Minnie wore her golden-brown hair in two braids pulled up and across the top of her head. Despite the probable care spent on her hair, multiple wisps escaped the braids and fluffed around her face and the back of her neck. She dressed okay for her job, although always looked a bit disheveled.

Minnie's dress seemed similar to the other housemaids—once new but now faded green chintz with little yellow and pink flowers on it. But the difference was it seemed all of Minnie's dresses were quite fitted in the hips and then flared out unlike those of the other women workers—her contemporaries. The dress also spanned tightly across her breasts. She indeed had a large bosom. Rose, on the other hand, was quite small, even though she nursed both of her babies for at least a year. She had always been pleased she wasn't larger, as once her breasts served their purpose feeding babies, they seemed to be a nuisance. However, she noticed most men enjoyed looking at Minnie's large bosom, and Minnie seemed to like the attention.

Rose again thought about Emil's wandering eye and assured herself he was truly a good man. Her mother had told her men eventually become their fathers, and Emil's father was known throughout the county as a solid, generous citizen. She prayed that was the case for her husband. But when he drank that poison from his still, he got mean and even cruel. Hopefully he would soon come to his senses and quit.

Chapter Sixteen

May 3, 1920

Rose moved to a deeper corner of her dining room so as not to be conspicuous and continued to evaluate Minnie. She wore her hair braided and affixed closely to her head. A dull brown in color, the braids so small, Rose thought when they were unloosed, her hair would surely be limp. Rose compared her thick, wavy mane to Minnie's and felt a bit smug as she recalled the looks of admiration from Emil on the nights she brushed her curls and waves before joining him in their bed.

Reaching for a few stray hairs to twist into the bun at the nape of her neck, Rose noticed the wiry stiffness of some strands. They were silver in color and multiplying rapidly in her dark hair. Minnie certainly had no silver or gray interwoven in her coiffure.

Rose gazed at the girl's round face, noting how line free it was. Not surprising for a young, barely woman. Rose didn't know exactly how old Minnie was but had been told she was fifteen when she began working at the Fricker farm. As Rose continued to watch Minnie, she pictured Emil's face when he looked at the girl. Not every time he saw her, but when he probably thought no one was watching him. As he took in Minnie, his eyes filled with desire and his entire demeanor changed.

Emil had never looked at her, his wife, that way. Rose felt his looks to her were most often filled with kindness and even appreciation. Sometimes she wondered why he was so grateful toward her. Most likely mainly for the fact that she cared for him, and more importantly, gave him a son and his little princess, Blanche.

Rose hoped she was wrong about what his eyes held regarding Minnie, but deep in her heart Rose knew what she saw. Lust. Pure and simple. The kind of lust she just read about in the Bible. The lust King David had for Bathsheba.

The body that went with the round, laughing face of Minnie was strong and sturdy. Her coarse, rugged hands had thick, almost masculine looking fingers. Rose stared at her own hands. Essentially the opposite of Minnie's, the fingers on her hands were long and slender and tapered into manicured fingernails. Rose worked hard but took the time to keep her delicate hands soft and supple.

She also noted that hers and Minnie's bodies were also almost opposite in appearance. Much of Minnie reminded Rose of a bullet. She was without smooth curves. Instead, she stood stocky and sturdy, with the exception of her breasts. They protruded from her body in hulking mounds. Rose unconsciously put her hands on her hips and continued along the same vein of thought. Her waist nipped in quite small, and she was particularly proud of it, along with her flat stomach. Especially considering she had birthed and carried two healthy sized babies. Her hips were full and just right, and they ended with long, shapely legs. Not that anyone had or would ever see them, except for herself, Emil, and a glimpse by the town doctor. Rose admitted she liked the secret of having her body hidden beneath her long skirts. Of knowing she had an attractive body underneath.

Still evaluating Minnie, Rose focused on the girl's large, full breasts. Rose had oftentimes heard others refer to the girl as buxom. That word definitely would not describe Rose. Her breasts were small and invisible in her clothing. Practical in all areas of her life, Rose didn't wear a brassiere; her tiny breasts had no need. The sleeveless shirt she wore daily provided extra warmth and was a perfect substitute.

Rose really didn't understand the fuss many men made of breast size. Women had breasts for only one reason—to feed their offspring. Her breasts had performed wonderfully well with that important work. During the first months of their lives, Rose produced more milk than either Richard or Blanche could consume, and both babies grew and thrived because of her bosom.

Rose shook herself back to the present work in the dining room. She had to check her thinking. These thoughts of Minnie's breasts were ridiculous and not at all like her! After all, Rose's mama had taught her right, so what was her problem? Rose truly believed with every fiber of her being that being a devout Christian woman, reading her Bible every night before bed, and being good and kind inside and out was most important in life. She'd done her best to teach both Richard and Blanche the same, probably before they could even understand words. She wanted to set an example for her children that living a righteous life was the best way to live. That meant being kind, giving, loving, and forgiving. All of this was certainly not in keeping with her current thoughts about Minnie. And besides, why did she even have these thoughts in the first place? Minnie was a married woman now. She and her young man had been married for a couple of weeks—they were newlyweds.

Rose willed herself to think of something else, managing for a short while to make a mental list of the seeding she planned to do for the late spring garden. But before long, her thoughts wandered back to Minnie. Rose hated to admit it, but she felt Minnie was deceitful, cunning, and dishonest at times. To be sure, she had witnessed many examples of the girl's dishonorable actions.

Most recently, Rose was near the top of the stairs when she heard a definite breaking of glass or china in the dining room. She wondered what had broken but remained perfectly still on the steps. It was only an object—most likely a replaceable one, not terribly important. But for some reason, she wished to know exactly what happened. So, Rose quietly descended a few more steps until she could see downstairs, remaining hidden in the shadows. She observed Minnie quickly brush china pieces and chips into the table crumber and then scurry out of the room with it. Before doing so, she glanced around as if to see if anyone was watching. When the dairy maid returned to the dining room, she was empty-handed. She placed a small rose-covered saucer minus the cup in the very back of Rose's china cupboard and left the room.

Rose was certain the breakage was an accident. However, what ensued soon after left her almost speechless. When she went into the kitchen to help Cook get the next meal going for the farmhands, Minnie came rushing up to her, wringing her hands.

"There's something I need to tell you, Mrs. Rose," Minnie said. "Can we go in the next room?"

Rose nodded and followed Minnie into the dining room, noting how she didn't sashay for Rose like she did for the men.

"Mrs. Rose, I don't want to be causing anything to be a-doing, and I don't abide by telling on other folks, but I seen Cook break one of your very best china pieces. A cup decorated with roses, it was. She cleaned up the broken pieces and hid the matching saucer in the china cupboard over there." Minnie pointed to the cabinet.

Shocked at the blatant lie, Rose mumbled, "Thank you" as Minnie looked at the floor and rushed out of the room.

Chapter Seventeen

"Shot Himself in Head"

Highland News Leader, May 11, 1920

Robert Kehrli, a young man of Highland, in the employ of Emil Fricker, a prominent dairy baron living east of town, committed suicide by shooting himself in the head with a 33-caliber revolver some time Friday evening.

His dead body was found by Emil Fricker, for whom he had been working on his farm where Fred Koehler lives about 9:30 a.m. Saturday. The county coroner was notified and with his permission the body was removed to the Spengel Undertaking parlors in this city where Deputy Coroner Kueker, of Troy, held an inquest Saturday afternoon.

The coroner's jury was composed of F. M. Mueller, Henry Graimmer, Wm. Schuepbach, Geo. Steinegger, Nick Hoffmann, and S.M. Drum.

The testimony at the inquest showed that the deceased had been working of late much the same as usual, that he had seemed in low spirits and threatened recently to end it all. Friday evening, he told Mr. Fricker that he was coming to town and would be back in time for work the next morning. When he failed to appear, Mr. Fricker searched for him and found his body. He was last seen alive by Fred Koehler about seven o'clock Friday evening.

He was found on the flowery side of a green hill with the revolver which he had ended his life lying close by. He had shot himself in the side of the head above the level of the eye and ear. The verdict of the jury was that he came to his death from a pistol wound, self-inflicted.

Funeral services were held at the home of his mother, Mrs. Carolina Kehrli, yesterday afternoon. Rev. C. E. Miche officiating and interment made in the City cemetery.

The deceased was born in Pierron on Oct. 15, 1889, making his age 30 years, 6 months and 22 days. When he was a child, his parents moved to Highland where he grew to manhood. After reaching maturity, he worked for a time at the Milk Factory and later for many years on a farm and for Mr. Fricker. He was overseas during the World War and returned last summer. On April 13th he was united in marriage to Miss Minnie Schlicht and is survived by his young bride, by his aged mother, by three brothers, Andreae, John and Louis Kehrli and by four sisters, Mrs. Sophie Weisenberger, Mrs. Louisa Schuepbach, Mrs. Emma Rutz and Mrs. Rosa Daniels.

Robert was a good, hardworking boy and we deplore the rash act that ended his life.

Note: This article has been reprinted verbatim from the original article, including any grammatical errors.

Chapter Eighteen

April 1921

It seemed she wasn't in the house. Good. Arline needed some time to search the harlot's room. Figure out what kind of spell Minnie had cast on her papa. Arline had heard about those kinds of things before when she was in town, from Lucy Ruthers. There were women who cast spells on men. They'd mix up potions and stick in some of the person's hair and clothing. Arline was going to find whatever Minnie had in her room and burn it.

She started with under the bed. Nothing except dust bunnies. Humph, no surprise there. The girl couldn't clean to save herself. In the closet, Arline hit pay dirt. There on the top shelf was a wooden box. Yes, she was sure she'd found her secret stash. Reaching up on tiptoe, she tried to reach the box but couldn't. She looked around the room for a stool or chair or something to get up on, but there wasn't anything. Just the bed, and she'd make too much noise pulling it over to the closet.

Suddenly, Arline heard a door open and close downstairs, and her alarm bells sounded. She always knew when Minnie entered the house. The energy shifted—in a bad way. Arline closed the door to Minnie's closet, looked around to make sure she didn't drop anything and slipped out of her room and down the passageway, away from the stairway.

Sure enough, the floozy yanked her bedroom door open and went inside. Arline took the chance to glide by her doorway. Just as she started to slip down the stairs, she thought she heard a door open. Arline stopped and held her breath, one foot in the air over the stairs. Was Minnie about to come rushing around the corner and catch Arline?

The door shut again, and Arline heard movement in Minnie's room. She stole down the stairs as quickly and quietly as she possibly could.

***

Arline just couldn't help herself. The thoughts of what could be in that wooden box on top of Minnie's shelf ate away at her—kept her up at night, even. It was a few days before Minnie left to the barn and there wasn't any help hovering about that Arline could slip into her room again and take a look at the box. Bringing a stepping stool with her, she turned the doorknob in silence, then slipped inside and stole across the room, sucking in her breath when she hit a floorboard that creaked.

Opening the closet with a satisfied smile on her face, she looked up to the top shelf and scowled. It was empty! Where had she hidden the box? Arline checked through the closet, finding nothing but Minnie's dairymaid uniforms and a worn-out pair of shoes.

Maybe under the bed? Arline knelt and peered underneath, vexation growing at what she saw. Nothing! Then she had an inspired idea and felt underneath the mattress. Still nothing. Maybe on top of the mattress? Nothing still. Aggravated, Arline strained to imagine where Minnie would have hidden the box, when she spied her out the window coming back from the barn. Damn that tramp! Every time Arline stepped into her room, it was as if she knew.

Reluctantly, Arline left Minnie's room and made her way back downstairs. When the milkmaid entered the house, she found Arline studying a book in the parlor. No words were exchanged; they rarely spoke to one another. Minnie knew Arline wanted nothing to do with her—and she seemed to share the same sentiment. Good, thought Arline. Best we don't talk. I might slap your face off.

Chapter Nineteen

Fall 1922

Rose looked up from her crocheting and paused to watch Emil pacing the parlor. He was such a big man—more than six feet tall, every bone in his body oversized. She knew she never saw any man bigger than her Emil. Right now, she could see a flicker of the younger Emil she married. The man who took such long strides, one to her two. He'd take her hand ever so gently, and they used to laugh together. He'd always been clumsy, but so much kinder than the man he was today.

It was when he created his still and began making moonshine that he changed. Rose could tell he drank a good amount of his own product. She was grateful that for today it seemed he had abstained. When he didn't and came home full of the drink, he was horrid. Everyone stayed their distance, not wanting to be on the receiving end of his cruelty. He had never raised a hand to Rose or the children. Sometimes it seemed he placed the three of them on a pedestal. But moonshine was evil, and so was Emil when he drank it.

The frown on his face and his pacing revealed he was totally absorbed by some difficulty. There were times it appeared to Rose that a demon within tortured him. He was a strong man but definitely had his weaknesses. One possibly being that girl. Rose stopped herself then and shook her head. She refused to go there or think that. She couldn't shake off the feeling of impending doom and disaster, though. It was stronger now than ever before. Forcing herself to tune out Emil and his anxious energy, she put her attention to her hook and yarn.

Chapter Twenty

Winter 1923

Dang nab it! That woman showed up everywhere Arline went. They would run into each other on the staircase, in the hall, out in the garden, even. When they did, Minnie would give Arline that smug look that said, "I got your Papa's attention a lot more than you do!"

Humph, thought Arline. Well, she had to go to great lengths to get that attention, now didn't she?

Oh, what a tangled web this was. It just made Arline mad as a hornet and sick, really. Sick to her stomach. That's what it did to watch this farce. This disgusting dance between the two of them. Her own father and that she-devil.

Arline sighed and threw some more feed at the chickens. How she wished she was a hen right about now. Just pecking away at the feed without a care in the world.

A chicken in the coop began laying then, its loud clucking soon turning to squawking. Arline wasn't fooled. She knew exactly what Minnie was gunnin' for—to be the "lady" of the manor. Just that thought made Arline snigger. As if that could ever happen. Arline would see about that. She'd expose the harlot and have her thrown out on her behind is what she would do.

She and her stepmother Rose might have the same birthday, but they were miles apart in the "niceness" department. If Minnie ever tried to take over as mistress of the dairy farm and hurt Rose in the process, Arline would rip the girl's hair out, strand by strand.

Chapter Twenty-One

Spring 1923

Though the boy didn't need the money, he sold the moonshine. That was the way Fricker was. He didn't give nothing out for free. At least to the folks who worked for him and homesteaded. Funny how Kamuf called him a boy. He thought of him like that. Most likely, because he'd known him since he was a young-in. And then there was the fact that Kamuf knew his pa. A right fine man was Rudolph Fricker. He would never have made no moonshine and certainly wouldn't have sold it.

The moonshine. Lord almighty. That was like poison to Emil. Turned him into someone that Kamuf had never seen before. There was a stark difference between when Fricker nipped at the bottle and when he was stone, cold sober. Kamuf hardly couldn't stand being around him when he drank. He was right mean. That was for sure. And definitely not like himself.

Kamuf never was a big fan of the moonshine, even when it was legal. He never did like how it made him feel squirrely and jumpy—especially afterward. He wondered now, how did Emil feel when he woke up after tying a hard one on? Did he ever wonder where'd he'd been and what he'd done? Did he remember any of it? Kamuf suspected he didn't.

But Fricker sold moonshine and made it, often late into the night. And then drank it. There were plenty of times when Kamuf saw him stumble out of the barn where he kept the still in the early morning lookin' like he'd fallen asleep in there. Kamuf didn't go near the barn or try to look inside. He'd seen one of the farmhands take a peek once, and the boy got his head near chewed right off. No, Kamuf had no desire to go and take a look at the still or into Fricker's lair. He knew well enough what a still looked like, and he hated the smell of alcohol. It was the same stench his own pa brought back home after drinking with the boys. Made Kamuf sick to his stomach, that was sure.

What made him sicker, though, was knowing what was going on with Fricker and that Minnie. He wasn't no fool. But there was nothin' he could do about it if he wanted to continue homesteading on the Fricker land. Truth be told, there weren't all that many places like this with such fine and fertile land to farm and raise steer. That's why he put up with Fricker's shenanigans. Kamuf did his best to pay no mind to all that was a-doin' on the dairy farm. Though that was mighty difficult to do at times.

Chapter Twenty-Two

Late Spring 1923

Rose got out of bed and peered out the window at the early morning sky. It looked like it would be a nice day. Maybe she'd take the buggy into town today. Anything to get this gnawing sensation out of her belly.

Emil didn't come to bed again last night—and she always woke up not quite right on these mornings. He never said anything about his absence. Instead, he'd scowl at her as if he dared her to ask, so she just kept quiet. Better not to get him angry. That only made things worse.

On the ride to town, she could forget—for a little while—all her cares. It felt so good to have the wind whipping back her long braid and the sun on her face. Sometimes jack rabbits hopped in front of her across the road. Other times she spotted a deer in the distance.

As she was splashing some water on her face, Emil entered, bringing with him the telltale smell of alcohol. The odor always made her feel nauseated—like when she was pregnant with Blanche. She grabbed hold of the edge of the washbasin and sucked in a sharp breath, trying to regain her composure, but he noticed.

"What's wrong with you, woman?" He demanded, pulling open the closet and taking out his black and gray suit.

"Just a sore tooth," Rose lied, feeling the floor moving slightly underneath her.

"I want an extra egg with my breakfast."

"I'll see to it," Rose said, bowing her head and leaving the room.

As she descended the stairs, she ran her hand along the wooden banister. Polished regularly by the servants and sometimes herself, it was smooth and cool to the touch. Good thing, too, because Rose's insides were hot and uneasy. And her stomach felt upside down.

Chapter Twenty-Three

For several years of my life when I was young, I attended church every Sunday with my Grandma Rose. During these outings, she engrained in me that it was improper to turn around and look at people seated behind me.

Her rule of never turning and looking backward extended to all situations, such as graduations, or presentations of some sort. To this day, I find it difficult to look behind me in church or similar settings. It would be impolite. Additionally, I believe I passed this foible onto my children.

It is such seemingly little things like this you experience when young that one day suddenly don't seem so insignificant. At some point, these realizations echo loudly—a deafening sound that shows you how actions, beliefs, and even feelings of shame and humiliation, transcend generations.

I came to see during the writing of this book that my grandmother's insistence on not looking behind her in church because it was impolite meant a lot more than it looked like on the surface. I realized for my grandmother and even for me, there was protection in not looking back.

My Grandma Rose's inclination to not turn and see who was looking at her back had more to do with survival than politeness.

By not seeing who might be watching and maybe judging, she could keep putting one foot in front of the other all those years ago.

Chapter Twenty-Four

Early Spring 1924

Rose took a deep breath of fresh air. It was a beautiful day, and she looked forward to her ride into town and a long visit with her closest friend, Suzy Saunders. She took a seat in the buggy and smoothed her skirt. Unlike her plain, around-the-house attire, she wore a going to meeting church type skirt and blouse. She fastened her bonnet on her head, her usual chignon touching the nape of her neck as she did so. Then she took the reins and signaled the horses to head out, soon enjoying the ride, with its peaceful bump, bump of the buggy's wheels on the dusty road.

It was a thirty-minute trip, if she took it nice and easy and didn't push the horses. Familiar with the route and the woman driving them, the two strong and steady animals required very little guidance, so she held the reins loosely in her hands.

The only time she'd ever really needed to hold the reins tightly was about a year before when a large snake appeared in the middle of the road. Both horses reared and started to run wildly, forcing her to grip the reins and slow the horses in a very gradual manner as she led them off the path and away from the snake. At the time, her heart beat like the horse's hooves on cobblestones, and it took her a bit of time to get her breathing under control before heading out again. Hopefully, that was the last time she would experience a ride with nearly runaway horses.

Her mind returning to the day in front of her, Rose realized her euphoria about getting away from the farm ran deeper than spending time with Suzy. Emil had been out of sorts lately, coming home every day or night full of drink. That made everyone tiptoe around and try to stay out of his path. Steering clear was almost impossible for Rose. She didn't try to communicate with him at all, though. She had learned long ago to never say a word about the moonshine she knew he consumed in the daylight hours. That would throw him into a rage. He would claim he only had a drink or two to relax and then would go into a tirade about how he had so much land, cows and farming to be responsible for, so she and the children could live in a beautiful home.

Today, just getting away from the farm and into a different setting was Rose's goal. Enjoying her friend's company and catching up on the news in town was a sorely welcome escape.

As the buggy progressed along the road, Rose allowed her mind to quiet as she observed all the beautiful nature the Lord had placed around her. The trees with their deep, rich green leaves against a piercingly beautiful blue sky were almost breathtaking. She looked down at the edge of the road where little bits of white wildflowers peeked through the tall, green weeds lining the path. Looking to her left, she spied an enormous field of corn not yet ready for harvest growing strong, tall, and healthy. The cornfield went as far as she could see, meeting with the lavender hue of the horizon. To her right were the woods with green moss growing like a blanket covering the floor of the woodlands. She looked up for a moment as a flock of crows soared overhead. For some reason, she felt they were enjoying their freedom tremendously. She realized now that freedom was something Rose hadn't felt since the day she had exchanged wedding vows with Emil.

Breathing deeply again, she saw two small, fluffy white clouds in the distance high above. They contrasted with the dark, stormy clouds that had filled the sky a few days before, bringing torrents of rain that reminded Rose of her life in general. She much preferred this freedom she felt now on the road—light and unfettered.

Rose thought for a moment. Had she feared the worst since the beginning whenever her beloved husband came through the door, or had this dread begun recently? She really couldn't recall when things had changed. It seemed so subtle, like a wolf sneaking up on a lamb. She once again pulled her mind back to the present and the bump, bump, bump of the carriage as the horses made their way to town unguided.

Riding in her buggy was her indulgence and made her feel so happy and so free. As her heart lifted at the day ahead, she felt as if she could sing, though she didn't have a good voice.

Why didn't she feel like this at other times, Rose wondered? She couldn't even reach this level of lightheartedness on Sundays when she went to church. Possibly it was the trepidation as to what she might find Emil a-doing when she returned from her place of worship. Sundays really filled her with mixed emotions. At times she would breathe a sigh of relief when she and the children returned from church to find Emil taking Blanche's little pony out of the stables all saddled up and ready for his princess to ride. Some days he even rode with her on his big, strong, dark brown steed.

Emil loved his little girl so very much, although that didn't diminish his love for his son, of whom he had much pride. Emil knew, as Rose did, that Richard would really be someone when he returned from college. Sometimes Emil took Richard out to split wood with an axe and do other manly activities. He made certain he knew how to milk a cow and move bales of hay and get grain into the trough feeders for the various animals. Emil knew Rose could also show her son these things, but he had happily and willingly assumed the chore of teaching their son some of the basics of life on the farm.

Rose wondered suddenly if Emil had been as thorough with the "facts of life" with their son. Well, she'd simply ask him when he was in the right frame of mind.

Coming up over the ridge, Rose could see downtown Highland, a community that made her feel so at home, so comfortable, so safe. Before long, she found herself heading down Main Street. As she passed the general store and other small businesses, she thought how the town was essentially unchanged from when she was a little girl. She remembered the delight of being allowed to choose a penny candy when she was the one who came to town with her mama. Looking at all the beautiful fabrics sold in the general store nowadays reminded Rose of when she and her mother would choose material to make a frock for her, Rose, or Rose's sister, Elise. Those were carefree times when Rose's heart floated freely, and there were really no true cares. She had been so happy as a child.

Sure, Rose worked hard on Papa's farm, but so did everyone. Her brothers toiled more than she and her sisters. As the eldest, Rose tended to the young ins, and Mama had taught her to cook. Actually, Rose felt she was an excellent cook because of her mother's teachings. Having only those chores and duties as a child, as opposed to the worries that weighed so heavily on her now, was such a blessing in comparison.

But then suddenly, Rose realized she was jealous of her brothers and sisters. She understood that Mama had been too sick to care for the little ones, and Rose was the best substitute for her. She had been old enough to teach and nurture them. Rose had held each and every baby minutes after they were born into the Jenny family and energetically helped her mother care for all of them. She knew practically as much about each little person as her mother. Most importantly, her love for each was deep and unconditional.

Rose tried to remember her life without a baby brother or sister, but there was always a small one for her to help with. Like Mama said, babies were a blessing from God. That thought reminded her of an incident when she was in grade school. She was taken aback when one of her friends had blurted out on the play yard about her younger brothers, "I just hate them. I wish they were never born."

To this Rose replied, shocked, "You're not serious. You're just saying that to be dramatic."

The friend didn't smile or laugh, as if joking. Instead, with a solemn expression on her face, she said, "I swear to God. I'd like it if my mum gave um away. They're just a lot of trouble."

Rose knew her face must have expressed the horror she felt at what her friend had just divulged. To avoid eye contact, she bent down and brushed at the dust on her shoes. When she stood up, her friend grabbed her hand and urged her to join the other girls jumping rope. Rose followed along, but her mind churned. She thought how tiny and helpless each new brother and sister was when they entered the world, and as they grew and smiled and laughed, she thought them truly precious. When they began talking, the funny little things they said were just darling. Rose believed that each sibling, while so very different from the other, captured her heart. She couldn't have resisted caring for them. She loved them totally. She was glad she loved them, for it would be horrid to want them gone as her friend did.

When Mama passed, every relative, as well as numerous friends, offered to help and take the children. Rose declined them all. She simply had to care for them. It was her responsibility. It was in her heart.

As she continued slowly down Main Street heading for Suzy's house, she knew the Lord would not want her feeling sorry for herself. She had a beautiful home, wonderful children, and she should be grateful—not complain and feel vexed about her lot. Again, she pulled her mind to the present as she directed the horse and buggy off onto a long street filled with arching elms. Sunlight filtered through the canopy of the trees, forming irregular patterns on the path below.

About halfway down the street, Rose pulled the horse and buggy to the right and came to a complete stop. There was Suzy's small house, so perfect and neat outside with the grass so green and the bushes pruned tidily. In the abundance of early spring, Rose could see green shoots with tiny buds on the hedges and the tips of bulbs—most likely daffodils and tulips—emerging from the path lining the entry to the front door. The house and small front porch were painted white with a crisp green trim surrounding each window. Window boxes hung under the front two windows. The porch featured green trim that made the small house seem larger.

There was no farmhand to take the horses and buggy as was always the case at Rose's home, so she held the reins and walked the horses around the back of Suzy's house. Emil always insisted she unhook them from the buggy, but this was Rose's business, so she just kept the horses hooked up and ready to go home later.

Before heading to the house, Rose gathered the items she brought with her. One was a jar of last summer's strawberry jam. Suzy always made a big fuss over it and seemed to like it, as it disappeared quickly. She also brought some of her embroidery and knitting. As both women talked, they did their handiwork. Talking with Suzy comforted Rose, who didn't mention Emil's drinking or that anything was awry. Instead, she talked about the children and her vegetable and flower crops. In turn, Suzy shared with Rose all the tidbits she'd heard since they'd last met that had made their way over back fences.

Today, she found Suzy in the backyard removing sheets and towels off the clothesline as they billowed in the slight breeze. Why, Rose wondered, did she always come on Mondays—wash day? Maybe it was the need for companionship after spending a weekend on the farm with Emil while he holed himself up in his still. She shook off the heavy feeling and smiled when Suzy turned to greet her.

***

Even though the days were getting much longer, it was dusk when Rose put her things back in the buggy and prepared to ride home. She would have to hurry the horses along if she was going to get to the farm before sundown. Rose tarried until the very last moment before gathering her things, though. She'd had a wonderful time talking about pleasant subjects. As she and her dear friend conversed, Rose's mind sprang to life and became active and light as the day progressed. How she wished this feeling could remain—suspended in time.

As she said her goodbyes and then guided the horses and buggy away from Suzy's house toward Main Street, an unwelcome, yet familiar feeling of dread and pessimism blanketed Rose. The closer she got to home, the more the heavy feeling suffocated her. Although her heart lifted briefly at the thought of little Blanche and Richard and the hugs they would exchange when she reached home, darkness had settled in Rose's heart once again.

Chapter Twenty-Five

Early Summer 1924

Kamuf could hardly believe his eyes the day he visited Fricker to discuss the steer on the back lot. He had gone around to the kitchen, but Cook informed him "the Lord of the manor" was in the front of the house.

Who should answer the front door but Minnie, her eyes full of almighty mischief.

"Why, Mr. Kamuf, Emil is expecting you. He's in the study," she said, trying to make her voice sound high-falutin'.

Kamuf headed for Fricker while Minnie turned to Sarah, who was on her knees polishing the stairway, and barked at her to do a better job.

He wondered how Minnie could be so brazen but then remembered seeing the buggy leave earlier that day with the missus in it. The real Mrs. Fricker on her way to town. She tended to stay awhile when she left. Kamuf couldn't say he blamed her.

The real Mrs. Fricker was such a nice lady—so kind and mild-mannered. She reminded him of his Becky, God rest her soul. Minnie was nothing like his Becky or Mrs. Rose, though. No, that she-cat had an air about her that said she was up to no good. Kamuf kept his mouth shut when she sashayed about but sometimes found himself grinding his teeth.

Kamuf had watched Minnie grow up and become a woman. If he remembered correctly, she started working on the farm at about fifteen. She had always been a wily one. Had a way about her that darn sure turned men's heads. While Kamuf understood it, he didn't fall for it. It was that little girl lost thing, he thought. Brought out the "man" in some men. They wanted to help her somehow. Anyhow they could. When the right darn truth was, she didn't need any help, and she knew it deep down.

But on the surface, well, she was just a young girl, really, looking for approval from the mama and papa that done abandoned her all those years ago. Looked to Kamuf like her father not wanting her was what drove her. Approval from the male species was her obsession. Wanting, needing that approval at every turn.

So, when she got that approval from Emil, the "man of the land," that fed her something mighty. Filled her up and overflowed her, and it showed. She got full of herself in many ways from that. But on the other hand, he saw the little girl come out sometimes. The real little girl—scared and sorry, she was. She was a right fine mess that one, really. Not sure which end was up half the time. He felt sorry for her. Sorry that she wove that web of hers and that she caught Emil in it. Because Emil wasn't a docile honeybee that would just struggle for a minute and then give in and die and get eaten. No, he was a hornet. And hornets keep stinging, again and again and again, while the honeybee only had one sting in him before he died.

Chapter Twenty-Six

August 1924

Here they were again, she and Minnie working side-by-side in the parlor. Truth be told, Rose didn't like being this close to the woman. Something about the way she carried herself made Rose's skin prickle with irritation and something else—unease.

As Rose picked up a finely-cut-glass tray to dust it, she became awestruck once again by the treasures such as this that adorned the parlor tables, especially the pieces of silver and exquisitely cut glass.

She continued dusting as her mind refocused upon the other woman in the room, who was wiping the wooden steps and polishing them to a bright shine. Minnie was a substantially built young woman, much younger than Rose. She had a presence about her, but she wasn't truly pretty. Especially if you placed her next to Emil's first wife.

The thought of the odd comparison Rose just made—of a farmhand with Emil's first wife—shocked her a bit and made her pause with the dust rag in hand. Why had she made that association?

Rose had seen Emil's first wife, Annie, at church years ago. She truly was the most beautiful woman Rose had ever seen. That made Rose wonder now as she had many times, why had Emil chosen Rose to raise his children and share his bed?

Now looking at Minnie, she wondered about the girl's relationship with her husband as she had many times. Was it more than employer/employee? Then she shook her head and reminded herself. Minnie was remarried now after losing her first husband to suicide. Of course, she was simply an employee.

Every now and then, Rose would give Minnie instructions. The girl would keep her eyes averted but answered in a polite and courteous manner. Rose had concluded a few years ago that she wasn't much of a talker. At least not with Rose.

Chapter Twenty-Seven

"John Nungesser Foully Murdered Yesterday"

Highland News Leader, September 16, 1924

John Nungesser, a young farmer who resided on the Jos. Wagner place northeast of here was foully murdered at a late hour yesterday afternoon. Full details of the horrible crime cannot be given at this time, as the coroner's inquest has not yet been held but will be sometime today.

From the best information we can get early this morning, Mr. Nungesser was at work yesterday on some land which he has rented on the Mudge place where he intended to move next Spring. His wife stated that he left home in the morning and took his lunch with him. On his way back home in the evening, he was murdered.

The first anyone knew of any mishap to him was when his team was caught while running away. Neighbors thought he had been thrown from the wagon and started a search for him. Meantime, Robt. Bellm had chanced along the road and found his dead body at the side of the road and gave the alarm. It was at first thought that he had been thrown from the wagon and killed in a runaway, but when Deputy Coroner B. D. Tibbetts arrived, he quickly discovered there had been foul play.

Mr. Tibbetts found no less than a dozen bullet wounds in his body and head. Several bullets were extricated by the coroner and indicated that more than one person had had a hand in his murder, or at least that two different weapons had been used.

From circumstances surrounding the murder, it looks as though Mr. Nungesser had been driving home from his work in the wagon when the murderer or murderers attacked him. Apparently, he had jumped from the wagon when first wounded and attempted to flee but had fallen in the ravine at the side of the road. The gunmen had evidently then followed him and shot him several times through the head. He had evidently thrown up his left hand to protect his head, as it was also pierced by several bullets.

When word of the murder reached Highland, Deputy Sheriff Taylor of Troy was here and went out there immediately. Knowing there had been foul play; he made what inquiry he could and came back to town and arrested Eldo Wernle and Jacob Landert Jr. Later in the night, we understand that he got into communication with the sheriff's office of Clinton County and caused the arrest of Emil Fricker, a farmer who resides east of here in Clinton County. Our information this morning is that all three of these men are now in jail at Edwardsville.

The information that caused the arrest of these three has not been made public yet. Many rumors are being circulated. We have no definite information as yet, but it is likely that the murder will be cleared up and the guilt definitely fixed sometime today.

The murdered man is survived by his wife, one child, and his parents, Mr. and Mrs. Ferd Nungesser. He was aged 24 years, 1 month and 17 days.

Funeral services will be held at the Evangelical church at 9:00 A.M. Wednesday, Rev. C. E. Miche officiating, and internment will be made in the City cemetery.

Note: This article has been reprinted verbatim from the original article, including any grammatical errors.

Chapter Twenty-Eight

Evening, September 16, 1924

Oh, how could he! How could Papa do this? Send Eldo Sr. to kill an innocent man? Eldo had told her. Told her to her face that Papa had "ordered him to 'shoot him up good.' Just like that," Eldo stated.

"Just like that? What do you mean, Eldo? Just like that? Just like what?" She'd asked her husband when she went to visit him in jail the day after his arrest.

Eldo sat on a bench in the cell just a couple feet from Arline. The deputy had put a chair near the cage, so she could sit and talk with him.

Her husband's eyes had filled with tears, and he put his head in his hands. "I don't know what happened, Arline. It's all such a darn mess! We was just taking orders. That's all."

"Taking orders?" Arline hissed, looking around the station to see if anyone was listening. "You're telling me that my papa told you to get rid of Nungesser?"

Eldo kept his head in his hands while he nodded, and a sob escaped his throat. Then he looked up at Arline. "This all got out of hand so quickly. I—I don't right know what happened."

Arline pulled at the hem of her skirt and wondered about little Eldo, who was with Rose. Was he taking his bottle? And how tired would he be when she went out to the farm to pick him up?

She looked at Eldo—the man she thought she was going to spend the rest of her life with after turning down so many suitors who obviously would have been better choices. Then she replied, her voice low, "Well, you're going to have to figure it out real quick, Eldo, because a man is dead. And you might want to stop crying. Anyone sees that, and they'll finish you off, too."

Eldo gulped back another sob and sat up straighter. "You're right, Arline, as always."

"Was he drinking?"

"Who? Your Pa?"

Arline nodded.

"Yeah, he had been in his still nearly all day and was right liquored up when he told us to kill that S-O-B. Or should I say when he demanded we kill him or else he was figuring on firing us."

"If he was all liquored up, do you think he was going to even remember to fire you?" demanded Arline. "Why didn't you come to me?"

"I didn't want to get you in the middle, or little Eldo," he said. "I guess I wasn't thinking."

Arline shook her head and snorted. "You don't ever think, Eldo. That's your problem." She closed her eyes and ran a finger over her hem again. Now she had to think. Hard. About what could be done about this mess. If anything.

***

That night after putting a now sleeping little Eldo in his basinet and sliding in between the sheets, Arline thought about Minnie and was overcome with hate. She knew her stepmother Rose wouldn't condone her feeling like this, but she couldn't help herself.

Why, oh, why did that tramp walk into their lives? So high and mighty, she thought she was. With that little girl way she had about her. Arline knew about that. Knew about women who showed that little girl to get attention and sympathy, and she hated it. Hated to see men fall all over themselves when women used that vice. That's what it was, a vice. Not any different than drinking or gambling or gossiping. It was a vice.

That thought gave Arline pause. Maybe that was the girl's problem—something she just couldn't help herself from doing—all that flouncing around to get men's attention. Arline had heard how Minnie's parents abandoned her. Her mother gave birth to her, and then just threw her away, nearly literally. They tried to make it sound good. That the parents who ended up taking her when she was an infant and raising her, that they wanted her, and most likely they did. But the bottom line was, Minnie's mother and father, her flesh and blood, didn't want her. Arline had a feeling that fact ate away at Minnie. That it drove her to do the things she did when it came to men. Especially men she could talk baby to. Like Papa.

Oh, what a tangled web this all was, Arline thought as she turned over and looked at the wall, willing herself to fall asleep. Hopefully into a deep, dreamless slumber that only little Eldo could penetrate, if he needed her.

Chapter Twenty-Nine

"Held for Murder: Grand Jury Indicts Fricker, Landert and Wernle/New Evidence Implicates Fricker in Robert Kehrli's Death"

Highland Journal, September 25, 1924

Charged with the murder of Robert Kehrli and John Nungesser, successive husbands of the woman with whom he was infatuated, Emil Fricker, a Clinton county farmer, is in jail at Edwardsville awaiting his fate at the hands of a jury of his peers.

With Fricker, Eldo Wernle, his son in-law, and Jacob Landert, were indicted by the grand jury of the circuit court Monday for the slaying of Nungesser, whose bullet-riddled body was found on a roadside five miles northeast of Highland on Monday evening of last week. Landert and Wernle have confessed the crime, but both charge that Fricker instigated them to commit it. Wernle through threats of personal harm and Landert on a promise of $250.

The story of Nungesser's tragic end was told in last week's Journal. The crime recalled the sudden death four years ago of Robert Kehrli, whose lifeless body was found on May 8, 1920, in a patch of timber belonging to Fricker. Less than a month previous to his death, Kehrli was married to Minnie Schlicht, who for years had been a victim of Fricker's lust. Prior to and following the marriage, Kehrli and the woman had been employed on the Fricker farm.

In as much as Kehrli had previously made an ineffectual attempt to take his own life, his death looked upon as suicide and such was the verdict of the coroner's jury. Kehrli's relatives, however, were never satisfied with the verdict, persistently contending that the young man had been murdered. Their claim is substantiated by a sworn statement issued at the City Hall Sunday night by Rudolph Kamuf, aged 65, who for more than thirty years had lived at the Fricker home with Emil Fricker and his father, Rudolph Fricker.

Kamuf has a serious heart ailment and has been treated by Dr. Hediger of Jamestown, who informed him recently that death might suddenly overcome him at any time. Kamuf thereupon informed the doctor there was something of which he wished to relieve his mind and related at length what he knew concerning Kehrli's death. With his consent, Dr. Hediger reported to Madison county officials and in the presence of Sheriff E. R. Deimling and others Sunday night. Kamuf told of the affair as follows:

My name is Rudolph Kamuf. I am appearing before Sheriff E. R. Deimling on September 21, 1924, of my free will.

I have lived at the Fricker home in Clinton county the past 30 years or more, first with Emil Fricker's father until the time of his death, 12 or 14 years ago, and since that time with Emil Fricker and family.

I am not well: have been doctoring a long time, and fearing an early death. I voluntarily make this statement.

Several times, before the death of Robert Kehrli, which occurred on May 7th, 1920, Fricker urged me to kill Robert Kehrli. I had a rifle, and he suggested that that would be just the thing to use. I flatly refused. After I had refused, Emil Fricker said he wished he had a gun. I replied that he could get one. I asked him what he wanted with a gun, and he answered that he wanted to kill Robert Kehrli. Fricker said he could kill Kehrli just like he could a rabbit. On the day of the shooting of Robert Kehrli, I went down to the Hehling building where Fritz Kohler lived. Kohler at that time was employed by Fricker. My job for that day was to mend a door sill. Fricker and Robert Kehrli went to the timber about nine o'clock on the morning that Kehrli was shot. About an hour later, I went to the Hehling building with the finished door sill. Finished putting in the door sill about 4 o'clock the same afternoon. About the time I had finished, Fricker came to the Hehling building to get water. Kohler and I were talking together at the time. Fricker approached and said: "Well, I've got him about where I want him: he is pretty near asleep." Fricker said he had filled Robert Kehrli with drinks. Fricker had wine, cider and whisky with him when he went to the timber on the morning of the shooting.

Kohler and I argued with Fricker to let the matter drop, but Fricker said: "No," he said. "It will be now or sometime later. I am going to kill him." Fricker left Kohler and me and went back to the timber with the water. A half hour after Fricker left, Kohler and I heard a shot. Before he left us for the timber, I told Emil Fricker that if he intended killing Robert Kehrli I was going home. Fricker said: "No you won't; you are going to stay right here." I was afraid he might kill me if I disobeyed, so I remained at the Hehling house. About ten or fifteen minutes later after the shot, Fricker returned to the Hehling house, where I then was alone, Kohler having gone to the field. Fricker said to me: "Well, he is done for." Fricker and I returned to Fricker's home a little before sundown.

The next morning, May 8th, 1920, Fricker took me to the timber; he left me stand and pointed out where Robert Kehrli lay. Kehrli was dead. While I stood there, Fricker walked to three or four wood piles in the same patch of timber. He said he did that to mislead blood hounds in case they were put on the trail.

I saw a .38 caliber revolver about a foot from Kehrli's right hand.

After Fricker had made the trip to the wood piles, he came back to me and took me past Kehrli's body. Then we started back to the Hehling house. Before reaching the Hehling house, Fricker sent me back to the body of Robert Kehrli, saying that somebody might disturb the corpse. Fricker went on home to get Robert Kehrli's wife, who was working at the Fricker home, and sent Fritz Kohler to notify Supervisor F.M. Mueller of Kehrli's death. Fritz Kohler, Louis Spengel, Supervisor F.M. Mueller and Emil Fricker reached the corpse about the same time. I was nearby when they arrived.

When Fricker took me to the timber on the morning that Robert Kehrli's body was found, Fricker pointed to the wound and said he had shot Robert Kehrli. His further remark: "I told you I could shoot him down like a rabbit." The wound was on the right side in or near the temple.

Emil Fricker instructed me what to say at the coroner's inquest. I was instructed to testify that I was first to see Robert Kehrli's dead body. I so testified at the coroner's inquest.

About a month before Robert Kehrli's death, Emil Fricker promised me a home for life if I would kill Robert Kehrli.

Four or five days after Kehrli's death, I said to Emil Fricker, "What good does Robert Kehrli's death do you?" and he replied: I have the satisfaction anyhow that he (Robert Kehrli) did not get ahead of me.

When Fricker first asked me to kill Kehrli, he said the reason he wanted Robert Kehrli out of the way was because Robert Kehrli had sneaked Mrs. Kehrli (Kehrli's wife) away from him (Fricker). Mrs. Kehrli, before her marriage with Robert Kehrli, was employed at the Fricker home.

When arraigned before Judge J.F. Gillham Monday, Fricker entered a plea of not guilty and announced that he would employ an attorney to defend him. "Guilty by force" was the plea offered by Landert and Wernle. They were advised by Judge Gillham that he would accept no plea with conditions and a plea of not guilty was entered on the docket and Attorney John F. Eeck appointed to defend them.

Note: This article has been reprinted verbatim from the original article, including any grammatical errors.

Chapter Thirty

Oh, the torment deep in his soul. What could he do but testify against the man who had been good to him all those years? Or as good as he could be.

Kamuf had lived with this burden for so long now, he knew it had settled in his lungs. That's why the asthma and why he became less than a man. A mere shell really, lying here, so out of touch with the world, yet wrestling with his own thoughts as he tried to tie them down and shut them off. But the thoughts, the memories, kept coming at him now, and he knew his time was near. Marching back and forth, they were, the thoughts. About the day he had talked to Emil about Kehrli.

Why hadn't Kamuf done something to stop things? Why had he just stood there with the hammer he was fixing to use on the door sill when Fricker announced his intentions? The memory tormented him. Kept eating at him and tearing up his insides. He could have done something. Maybe saved the boy's life. Hell, he could have agreed to go and do the dirty deed and told the boy to run as fast as he could—to get out of town; to go far, far away with Minnie. But he didn't. He kept hammering each of those nails into the doorsill, one by one. While Emil, all liquored up, went to end the life of an innocent. Why, oh, why did he just stand there?

He thought about this over and over again—especially now he was lying here, waiting for his maker to come for him. So, when they asked him to testify, he just had to. Maybe he could right things even a little bit before he passed on.

Kamuf wiped his brow when they put him back down on his cot in his cottage. Little ramshackle place he had lived in for forty years now. Irony was, in recent years, Fricker tried to get it fixed for him. Offered maybe a dozen times, but Kamuf always refused. Lying here, taking his dying breaths, he realized suddenly why he'd refused Fricker's assistance with the cottage. He felt guilty—that was it—guilty he was complicit. He coulda stopped it. Coulda redirected Fricker that day. Even though he was ornery, Kamuf coulda offered to have a drink with the fella. To divert his attention. But he did nothing. Nothing!

So, when Fricker wanted to fix up his place, Kamuf knew that while he didn't like to see no one living in squalor, he also wanted to make sure Kamuf didn't do what he just did, which was tell the truth.

Fact was, though, Fricker weren't in his right mind that day. Other fact was, there was a good chance Fricker truly didn't remember it. Might think to himself, even, that he couldn't possibly do anything so vile. But he had to have woken up in the morning after many a night's moonshining and known he did things he couldn't and probably wouldn't ever imagine, didn't he? Fact was, a man's soul, his heart, his very being, didn't change, with the moonshine or without.

In retrospect, Kamuf could see it all clearly now. Funny how that happened. Now that he got that load off his chest about the murder, so much was so clear. Fact was, Fricker had succumbed to something as old as time. What pushed him off the precipice into the arms of that unfortunate woman, though many would have liked to have thought it was pure lust, in reality, it wasn't.

No, what pushed him off into the abyss of madness, because that's what it became, was grief over the death of his first wife. Oh, how he had loved her. Kamuf could see it in his eyes. A fierce love, it was, but a firm one. He didn't see anyone or anything but her.

So, when she died, in a way, Emil died right alongside her. He'd always been the moody, glum sort, but not when Annie was around. During his years married to her, he was a different man. So, the day she died; the day she left this earth, well, a part of Emil did, too. Kamuf wondered now—was that his best part that left? Maybe, just maybe, it was.

So, when Minnie came into the picture and couldn't keep herself from him, that's when it all started to unravel for Fricker. Seems like it was his way of striking back at the universe. It was a fiery situation. Way too fiery and ornery for most. That was the problem. Like fire and water, they were.

For Fricker, it became obsession. That's what it was. Pushed and got him to do things he wouldn't ever have done. Kamuf knew a thing or two about obsession. Saw his papa obsessed with the farm, with making it work, even when the soil wanted to give out and the drought hit for those long ten years. Back in Oklahoma, it was. Back where the earth wasn't as forgiving as it was here in Illinois.

That obsession. It could eat at you. Put you out of your right mind and into a mind you never, ever thought you'd be in. A mind you never could have imagined. Nothing like you woulda thought of, even if you coulda. That's the way the obsession was. Took you over; ate at your soul and good sense until there was nothing left but cold, mean want and need. He'd seen the obsession, and he'd seen it right good in Emil. That's what was gonna get him hung or in a jail cell for the rest of his life.

Obsession. What a damned thing it was. Like it had a life of its own. Like it was a beast without a soul, that obsession. Kamuf thanked the Lord right then and there that he never had the obsession overtake his heart and soul.

And then there was Minnie. Was it obsession for the girl, too? No, Kamuf thought. That wasn't it. What did Minnie truly want? Lying here struggling to breathe, he knew what she wanted. To be lady of the manor. That's why, he hated to say this even to himself, she "sacrificed" her husbands. The realization made him start coughing something awful. After he finished and slowed down his breathing, he reassured himself he'd be okay. But the truth was, he wasn't alright—none of them stuck in this tangled web was.

Chapter Thirty-One

September 26, 1924

Deimling got a start when his wife asked him a question he never considered. What if Emil isn't guilty? Truth be told, that thought never entered his mind, not even for a second.

"He's guilty as a fox with a chicken in his mouth, woman, what makes you say such a thing?"

"You got all the proof you need then?"

"Sure, I got proof. We've got the boys who say Fricker told them to kill that boy. That's proof enough."

"So, it's a case of he said/they said?"

Deimling snorted. He didn't want to have this conversation. "You should have seen him there, all high and mighty."

"How do you know he was high and mighty? Maybe he was scared. And what does him being all high and mighty have to do with him being guilty?" asked his wife.

That last statement made Deimling stop for a second. Fricker scared? He was about to discount the notion, when his wife continued.

"Didn't you say he could get the death penalty? The way I see it, that could scare any man. You are right stoic, too, Ed. Maybe stop casting stones and do your job."

"And what job is that?"

"How about you make sure he's guilty before you convict him. Isn't it supposed to be innocent until proven guilty?"

"We'll find out soon enough about that," he said. "Likely he'll be going to trial, since he keeps insisting he's innocent."

Chapter Thirty-Two

"Fricker Trial in November"

Highland News Leader, September 30, 1924

Emil Fricker, who is charged with instigating the murder of John Nungesser of Highland on September 13 last, and with the murder of Robert Kehrli on May 7, 1920, will be tried by the Madison County Circuit Court on the first charge on November 12. The two slain men were successively the husbands of Mrs. J.M. Nungesser, and jealousy, the state charges, prompted the killings.

In the recent murder of Nungesser, Jacob Landert and Eldo Wernle, Fricker's son-in-law, both of Highland, are to be tried jointly with Fricker. They plead that Fricker forced them to take Nungesser's life.

Note: This article has been reprinted verbatim from the original article, including any grammatical errors.

Chapter Thirty-Three

October 1924

School was not easy for her children now that Emil had been indicted and would soon be going to trial. Though Richard's grades remained all As, she knew he endured verbal cruelty from some of the students because of his father. He had shared with her before his father's arrest he looked forward to the time he spent in school. Often, the hour or two after the school day ended Richard could be found with a teacher learning even more than the class presented. Other times, he simply visited with a teacher.

While keeping up with his studies, Richard always found time to help his mother with anything she needed. She was so proud, but her heart broke when she thought about the torture and occasional horrid practical jokes he endured. She desperately wanted to intervene, but he was adamant about tending to his own problems.

And then there was Blanche. Her once sweet-natured daughter had become a real handful. Rose mulled over some of the incidents her baby had been embroiled in since her father was arrested.

There was the older boy who had made some snide remarks about Emil and the entire family. Blanche had flown into a rage and ran at the boy with her fists swinging and legs kicking as she screamed, "liar, liar."

Of course, the boy wasn't injured. Several other boys and two of Blanche's girlfriends watched the scene unfold. All seemed so shocked that no one moved for a brief while. The boy simply protected himself from her blows. Finally, the other boys and her girlfriends separated Blanche from the boy and moved her a good distance from him. Both girls clucked and soothed their friend's ruffled feathers.

Another particularly painful event for Blanche was when some older girls made up a jingle they sang while jumping rope in the schoolyard. The words were hideous—referring to Emil not as a cold-blooded murderer, but as hot for sex with Minnie. That time Blanche just yelled obscenities at the girls and went into the schoolhouse out of hearing range. If Rose hadn't understood her child's pain, Blanche's mouth would have been washed out with soap many times over.

Chapter Thirty-Four

"Fricker May Ask for Change of Venue"

Highland News Leader, November 4, 1924

Court arrangements were made last Tuesday whereby Emil Fricker, Highland farmer and under two indictments for murder, will have a few more days to prepare his case before going to trial for the death of Robert Kehrli who was mysteriously shot in a timber tract northeast of Highland two years ago. An arrangement was made that day in which the attorneys agreed to a resetting of the case for November 17.

The trial had been set for November 5, the day after the election, but with a crowded docket and the election coming in the early part of the week, the resetting was easily arranged. The possibility of a congestion will be escaped on the new date.

Fricker is also under indictment in connection with the death of John Nungesser on September 13 and that case had been set for November 7. It has been stricken from the present setting and will come up at a later date.

In resetting the case, Fricker's attorneys indicated that they would be ready to enter the hearing on the reset date.

It was rumored about the courthouse that Fricker will ask for a change of venue from the county in at least one of the trials. One of his attorneys was questioned and said he had not definitely decided. If a change is asked, it will be in the Nungesser death.

Note: This article has been reprinted verbatim from the original article, including any grammatical errors.

Chapter Thirty-Five

November 15, 1924

As the trial loomed, Arline became more and more angry at the injustice of it all. What the gossip was doing to her, Rose, Blanche and Richard was criminal in itself.

Arline had a hard time holding her head high when she went into town, but she did anyway. In fact, she'd stare down anyone who dared to take too long of a look. Little Eldo didn't need their bad thoughts directed at them, and she wouldn't allow it.

All the while she shrugged off the gossip, Arline became more and more angry with Minnie. She thought back to when she saw the trouble brewing on the farm and wondered. Could she have done something to stop the runaway freight train between her papa and that woman? Likely not, but what if she had said something?

She remembered a day a few years back when she was watching them both out on the farm. Maybe Papa thought Arline wasn't old enough to know what's what, but she knew what was happening. He was lying with her, that's what. And Minnie was flouncing around acting so coy. It just seared Arline's blood, it did. Right under Rose's nose, too.

That day as Arline stood in the shadow of a tree, its leaves just starting to turn for the winter, she held her breath and watched the despicable scene unfold.

The two of them were standing outside the barn where Papa had his infernal still. He was grasping the she-devil by the wrist when she tore her hand away and wailed like a little baby. "You always do that—always pull away from me, Emil! And then you come back. Again and again. I'm done. I'm done with all your lies. I'm done with all your promises. I know what you want. And that's all you want from me."

"That isn't true, Minnie. You know how I feel."

"I've had it. Had enough of this. You promised me. I'm going to tell Rose."

Arline saw her Papa change then, swift as lightning. He turned into steel at the mention of Rose and grabbed Minnie's wrist and twisted hard, until she winced. His voice was low, Arline had to strain to hear him, but she got the gist.

"You say anything to Rose, ever, and you're a dead woman. You hear me. Dead to me. Dead to this world." Arline couldn't see her father's face, but she pictured his dark eyes warning Minnie he meant every single word.

Arline saw tears spring to Minnie's eyes. "Emil, please, let go! I was just mad. I won't do that. Ever. You know that. You know I love you."

He let go of her wrist, turned and walked back to the barn; probably to drink some more moonshine.

Minnie had stayed where she was, rubbing her wrist, tears streaming down her face.

Served her right, thought Arline. Messing with another woman's husband. A sore wrist was the least she deserved.

Chapter Thirty-Six

"Is Pupil of Zeno: Fricker Very Calm as Jury is Selected"

Edwardsville Intelligencer, November 17, 1924

Emil Fricker, Highland farmer, alleged slayer of Robert Kehrli and "mastermind" in the death of John Nungesser, went to trial this morning in the circuit court before Judge J. F. Gillham on the Kehrli death. For an hour, while attorneys were working on the preliminaries, Fricker sat in the courtroom with his head slightly bowed as the large number of spectators looked him over.

If his wife was in the courtroom, she was not recognized. His daughter is attending the trial and was sitting in a front seat.

It was said this morning that Fred Koehler of Belleville, Wis., a star witness for the state, arrived here this morning. Another important witness for the state will be Rudloph Kamuf, who lived on the Fricker farm for many years. He made a confession during September which implicated Fricker in the death.

For several days, there has been considerable talk about the courthouse that Fricker would ask for a change of venue from the county. One of his lawyers was engaged last week in a trial at Quincy and the filing of a notice ten days before the trial was overlooked. The change of going into another county was lost through the oversight.

There also was talk this morning of asking for a continuance. The motion was not filed and at 11 o'clock the attorneys for Fricker announced they were ready to proceed.

Quite a large number of women were in the courtroom, the number being so great that many were standing in the rear of the room.

Fricker would make an exceptional follower of the Greek philosopher Zeno. He would be in the A class among the Stoics. Nothing seems to get him very excited, and he sits calmly by as the various steps are taken. Some have wondered if he will warm up as the proceedings continue.

The selection of the jury may take all day, and it may be Tuesday before the twelve men are picked to pass upon the defendant's fate. The selections will be slow. The death of John Nungesser, a few weeks ago, was the beginning of a great deal of publicity on the two deaths and the affairs were generally discussed over the county.

Note: This article has been reprinted verbatim from the original article, including any grammatical errors.

Chapter Thirty-Seven

"Fricker is Bankrupt"

Highland News Leader, November 18, 1924

Emil Fricker is broke. It was indicated by voluntary petition in bankruptcy filed at the office of the Bankruptcy Referee at East St. Louis yesterday. The papers on file show that he has liabilities of $74,405.06 and assets of $47,000.00. The petition states that of the liabilities, $58,493.11 are in secured claims.

The assets show that he had 49 Holsteins, 49 heifers, 5 Jersey cows, 62 hogs, 200 chickens, 7 horses and 2 mules. Fricker owns a large amount of real estate in Madison and Clinton counties but it is heavily mortgaged, and the chances are when he settles on the claims against his property there will be nothing left. Besides the proceedings instituted yesterday, there are several assumpsit proceedings on file against him in the Madison County circuit court here.

Note: This article has been reprinted verbatim from the original article, including any grammatical errors.

Chapter Thirty-Eight

One thing was for darn sure, Fricker's family didn't deserve any of this. As the court proceedings went on, Deimling thought about his own children and wife and couldn't wrap his head around the idea of leaving them to shoulder such an enormous burden.

He didn't know much about Fricker's missus, but from what he could tell, she kept her head down and it looked to be on straight. He'd seen her at church studying her Bible while the pastor spoke and singing the hymns with a serious look on her face.

She hadn't shown up to court yet, and Deimling couldn't say he blamed her. Of course, the papers sensationalized her absence. Questioned whether she was culpable, even. That in itself was shameful. What God fearing woman in her right mind would want to sit through this maelstrom, which he suspected was about to get a lot more gruesome when the true details came out.

He looked over at Fricker sitting ramrod straight, no expression on his face. Did he give a rat's tail about his family? Did they ever cross his mind? And now his missus had to fend for herself and her children, thanks to the lawyers running through Fricker's estate. It was a crying shame.

Chapter Thirty-Nine

"Fricker Trial on Now"

Highland News Leader, November 18, 1924

The trial of Emil Fricker, on the charge of murdering Robert Kehrli in May 1920, began in Circuit Court at Edwardsville yesterday and a good many Highland people were in attendance there. The trial still continues today and at the time of going to press, no information can be given as to the probable outcome.

Relatives of Fricker's had been at work last week securing affidavits preparatory to asking for a change of venue to some other county and his lawyers were ready to make a motion to that effect when the case was called yesterday morning, but later changed their minds when they found out they had failed to give a ten-day notice. Their request for a continuance of the case was also denied.

It took several hours to select a jury, the final selection being the following men: Geo. Faulkner, Alton; Julius Gaertner, Pin Oak; Ben Prosser, Livingston; W.A. Lowe, Woodriver; Morris Hunt, Fosterburg; Ben Brickley, Alton; Christ Schuette, Alton; John Dunn, Alton; Frank Laugwisch, Edwardsville; Jos Mullane, Edwardsville; John Bergdorf, Glen Carbon and Tom Williams of Glen Carbon.

With the jury selected, the trial got rapidly under way. The first witness examined was Rudloph Kamuf, whose testimony was about the same in substance as his confession which appeared in these columns at the time it was made and which led to Fricker's indictment. Additional to the confession he also told of having purchased the pistol for Fricker at the latter's request.

Undertaker Louis Spengel was the second witness placed on the stand, and he told the position in which Kehrli's body was found and the circumstances surrounding it and of the coroner's inquest which followed. The last witness on the stand yesterday was Mrs. Minnie Nungesser, who was formerly Kehrli's wife. She told of her life over a period of years at the Fricker home and of how Fricker forced and intimidated her into submitting to unlawful relations. She also told of how she ran away from the Fricker home and married Kehrli and of how Fricker went to Edwardsville after them and persuaded them to return. She told of how later Fricker threatened to her that he would kill Kehrli. These threats being made during the few weeks that she was Kehrli's wife.

States Attorney J.P. Streuber is taking personal charge of the prosecution and Harold Bandy is the main attorney for the defense.

Note: This article has been reprinted verbatim from the original article, including any grammatical errors.

Chapter Forty

"Fricker Denies Murder, Going to Jury Late During Afternoon"

Edwardsville Intelligencer, November 17, 1924

Emil Fricker, Clinton county farmer, answering for the murder of Robert Kehrli, made a sweeping denial of the charges this morning when he took the witness stand in his own defense shortly before 11 o'clock. He was on the stand for exactly fourteen minutes and was not cross-examined by the prosecution. Questioning by States Attorney Streuber would have developed nothing but additional denials.

Fricker was calm and cool as he was questioned by the lawyer representing him. He said he was 44 years old and was born and raised on the farm, five miles east of Highland. He said his family was composed of a wife and three children.

Fricker said he was acquainted with Minnie Schlicht, later Kehrli's wife, and also knew Kehrli. He admitted going to the timber to cut wood with Kehrli on May 7. They worked all day. Fricker said that he and Kamuf went home about 5 o'clock.

According to Fricker, Kehrli remarked that he was not feeling very well, and Kehrli told Fricker to tell his wife he would be home about 9 o'clock that night or he would return to work the next morning.

Fricker said that he and Kamuf returned to the timber the next morning. When Kehrli failed to appear, Fricker and Kamuf began a search. Fricker testified that Kamuf found the body. Fricker said Kehrli appeared to be sleeping when he looked at the body. They afterward discovered he was dead.

Fricker denied that he ever made threatening statements, that he had Kamuf buy a revolver, that he shot Kehrli or saw him die. In fact, he denies everything.

He said that Kamuf had told him that he purchased the gun for Kehrli. Fricker denied the statement of Mrs. Nungesser "that there would be something doing" if she married.

Fricker admitted coming to Edwardsville and offered to give the two employment on the farm because it was the busy season and he needed help. He said that mention was made of $1,000 but that he suggested the two go to work, save that amount and have something to begin with for themselves.

Simon Frey of Marine was the next witness called for Fricker. He said he knew Kehrli. The defense wanted to show that Kehrli attempted to take his life seven years ago, but the evidence was ruled out.

Mrs. Mabel Federer of Pierron, a sister of Fricker, testified to offset Kamuf's testimony. She said that about four months after the death she had a conversation with Kamuf in the kitchen of her home. She declared that Kamuf remarked, "They are trying to lay the blame on Emil, but I know he did not do it."

A number of character witnesses were introduced just before the noon recess as the case was drawing to a close. There were indications at noon that the case would go to the jury before adjournment this evening.

The state completed its case this morning after offering two important witnesses. One was Fred Koehler of Belleville, Wis. He was living on the Hehling farm and overheard parts of the conversation in which Fricker and Kamuf figured on May 7. He bore out much of the evidence offered by Kamuf. He said that Fricker threatened to kill Kehrli at that time or a later date. He said efforts were made to discourage Fricker.

Mrs. Arline Fricker Wernle, daughter of Fricker, and whose husband is held in the Nungesser death, testified against her father. She said that her father made a remark that something would be doing if Mrs. Nungesser married.

Note: This article has been reprinted verbatim from the original article, including any grammatical errors.

Chapter Forty-One

Oh, the guilt! It started to eat away at Arline's insides as soon as she stepped off the witness stand. Rose had told her just to tell the truth in the courtroom, because it was the right thing to do. Arline had agreed—in theory. But she also knew it would look really bad for Papa.

In the end, she did tell the truth. Not because it was the right thing to do. No, she had told the truth because she was angry, and something even worse, jealous. She was as mad as a wet hen that Papa had on multiple occasions taken more interest in Minnie than he had in her—in his own flesh and blood. That's what drove Arline when she walked up in front of the judge and put her hand on the Bible.

But being mad and jealous wasn't something she could admit to people when they gave her a perplexed look about testifying against her own father. The fact was, if she admitted her anger and jealousy, she would fall in their eyes. And that was something Arline just couldn't do. Better to insist she did it to be truthful.

Rose knew, though. Arline could see it in her eyes. And the funny thing was, even though it could end up being one of the reasons she lost her husband, she didn't blame Arline.

That Rose—what an incredible woman she was! She had been shunned by much of the town the moment Papa went to jail. Yet she didn't appear to let that faze her. Instead, she went on doing what she could for Blanche and Richard and even Arline while running the farm. In the midst of this terrible hubbub, she made sure Arline was okay. She'd check in with her and give her space to talk about Papa.

It was hard to imagine sometimes that Arline and Rose were born on the very same day—November fourth. Not the same year, of course, but the same day. That perplexed Arline some and made her wonder. She hoped one day she could become as good a person as Rose. A woman with a heart truly made of layers upon layers of gold.

For now, Arline would concentrate on being the best mother she could be to Eldo, Jr. Her little boy was truly the pride of her life and the light of her eyes. Right then and there, she vowed she would do whatever it took to make sure he had the best life possible. And she would never, ever put another person in front of him. Most certainly not a man!

Chapter Forty-Two

"Fricker Denies Murder, Going to Jury Late During Afternoon"

Edwardsville Intelligencer, November 18, 1924

The other witness of yesterday afternoon was Mrs. Minnie Nungesser and alleged to have been a victim of another plot of Fricker's. She was the widow of Kehrli when she was married to Nungesser. Objections were raised to the testimony of Mrs. Nungesser on grounds that she had been in the courtroom. The judge ruled she might testify. Mrs. Nungesser answered every possible question by either "yes" or "no."

Mrs. Nungesser went to the Fricker home to live as a girl and had been there about sixteen years. She said she worked about the house and milked cows. She told of getting acquainted with Kehrli after he returned from the war. They were married on April 13, 1920. She said Fricker was a married man.

She told of a conversation with Fricker shortly before her first marriage. He told her not to get married, and if she disobeyed, "There would be something doing." She also told the reasons he objected to her marriage.

She said that the relations of man and wife began two years before her marriage. She left at midnight the day before they were to be married and came to Edwardsville the following day. They remained at the home of Mr. and Mrs. Albert Reutz of Edwardsville for a week after the marriage and Kehrli went to work at the plant of the United States Radiator Corporation.

Three or four days after the marriage, Mrs. Nungesser testified that Fricker came here and remarked that he would have given her $1,000 had she remained single. Fricker remained about two hours according to the witness and waited until Kehrli returned from work. An arrangement was made for the two to return to the Fricker home and they went back about a week later.

She testified of being told of Kehrli's death on May 8. She said she remained with Kehrli's folks for about six weeks and then returned to the Fricker place again. Kehrli was 31 years old according to Mrs. Nungesser.

Note: This article has been reprinted verbatim from the original article, including any grammatical errors.

Chapter Forty-Three

It just tore Arline's heart out to see her Papa sitting in the courtroom with all those horrid things being said about him. She wanted to break down right there in the middle of the courtroom and just sob.

How did her papa end up here? He was a strong man. Maybe not the nicest man in the world—but he certainly had a shrewd head on his shoulders. And he had always been good to her. Even now. After her testimony that morning, he had given her a quick smile, as if to say, it's okay.

She had visited him a couple of times since he'd been put in jail, and he always asked about little Eldo. During each visit, her heart tugged when she wondered if her father would ever be able to hold her son again and give him a kiss on the top of his head like he always did.

Oh, if Mama had just lived! None of this would have happened. She would have kicked that Minnie out on her behind the first time she lifted her skirt at Papa.

Arline would never fault her stepmother, though. When it came to men and their "ways," Rose was no match for Minnie.

How Arline hated the woman who had broken up her family. Sometimes she even daydreamed about shooting her. But that would do no good. Not now. Not ever. Look where losing your head got you. Sitting in a courtroom with a jury and crowd out for blood.

Arline looked from the jury and back to her Papa and wondered for the millionth time. Was this a conspiracy against a powerful man who had a weakness for the drink? Or was he truly guilty?

***

Later in the quiet of her home, Arline put little Eldo in his bassinet and threw herself on her bed.

"Mama, Mama, Mama," she cried out to an empty room. "Why did you have to leave us? None of this would have happened."

The sobs tore through Arline's body then—ones that had built up over the years since she'd lost her mother. As she cried, she thought about her testimony and knew that though Papa would never say so, what she said had to have torn his heart in two.

Why had Arline been honest on the witness stand? It wasn't like anyone else in this horrid mess was telling the God's honest truth—certainly not Minnie. What if her father was hung because of what Arline said? The thought made her heart seize.

She sat up and willed herself to stop crying as she stared at the dresser, still stuffed with Eldo Sr.'s clothing. The way things were going, he wouldn't be needing any of them anytime soon.

Little Eldo started to fuss then—probably from all her crying. Arline went over and picked him up, then held him to her breast and breathed in the innocent scent of baby. The one sweet spot in this whole mess was her son. He'd been so good in court today; not a peep from him.

"Mama's here," she cooed. "I'll take care of you. And I'll never, ever leave you."

Chapter Forty-Four

"Fricker Given Life – Juror Stood Alone: Jury was 11 to 1 to Hang Slayer of Kehrli"

Edwardsville Intelligencer, November 20, 1924

Emil Fricker, Clinton county farmer, is going away from his relatives and friends for a long, long time if a circuit court verdict returned against him this morning remains against him. He was given life in the Southern Illinois Penitentiary at Chester for the death of Robert Kehrli at Highlight on April 7, 1924.

Fricker can thank his lucky stars for not receiving orders for a trip into eternity. For several hours last night, the jury voted eleven to one for execution. He was saved by the stand of one juryman who declared that he would die before he signed a death verdict.

The action of the juror recalls a picture which used to hang in the sheriff's office of the old court house entitled, "The Obstinate Juror." The noise emanating from the jury room about midnight last night indicated that everything depicted in the picture was being enacted by the jurymen.

Jurors said this morning that the eleven who took the stand against the one had their associate near a nervous collapse during the deliberations. The juror is said to have wept before the compromise was reached to give Fricker the rest of his days in prison.

The juror who stood alone is said to have argued that the prosecution failed to ask him if he was opposed to the death penalty. State's Attorney Streuber said today that he used care in selecting the twelve men and is absolutely certain that each and every one of the twelve was questioned about his views on execution if the evidence warranted.

A number of ballots were taken. On the first ballot one juror believed Fricker should be given his freedom. Eleven voted him guilty. On the second ballot, the twelve were unanimous and found him guilty.

The next step was to fix the punishment. A ballot was taken, seven voting for the death penalty and five for a prison term. The two ballots which followed were without any changes. When the sixth ballot was taken, two more jurymen favored death and those for a prison term fell off to three. When the eleventh ballot was ordered, all but one voted to send Fricker to the gallows.

The ballot was the one which started the fireworks. Alone, the juryman took a stand for imprisonment. His discussions indicated that he favored a term of fourteen years, the least possible on a murder charge. It was almost 1:30 o'clock this morning when the eleven others agreed to sign a verdict of life if the lone juryman would change his opinion. The jurymen went to bed at 2 o'clock in the morning.

Upon convening court this morning, Judge Gillham was advised that a verdict had been reached. He arranged yesterday to receive the verdict until 10 o'clock last night. The prisoner was ordered returned to the courtroom. He sat motionless for several minutes while the twelve men were being brought to the courtroom. Not the least change in expression came over him upon hearing his fate.

Newspaper reporters attempted an interview as he was going back to the jail under guard of deputy sheriffs. "I'm not satisfied," was the only thing he had to offer. After leaving the courthouse Fricker said he had not received a square deal. He did not explain what he meant.

Fricker, it is believed, will ask for a new trial or possibly take an appeal in efforts to escape going to the penitentiary. One of his relatives said this morning that he was not satisfied. "It can't be any worse than what he has been given," said the relative. There is another murder charge against Fricker who may be held here for a few weeks to have the other case set and disposed of before he goes to prison. He is also under indictment with his son-in-law, Eldo Wernle and Jacob Landert for the death of John Nungesser, north of Highland on the night of September 15.

The hearing in the Kehrli death was completed yesterday afternoon at 3 o'clock.

Note: This article has been reprinted verbatim from the original article, including any grammatical errors.

Nov. 19th 1924

We, the jury, find the defendant, Emil Fricker guilty of murder in manner and form as charged in the indictment, and we find his age to be ~~44~~ years, and we fix his punishment at imprisonment in the penitentiary for his natural life.

Chris Schuette foreman
Ben Brickey.
Jno. Burgdorf.
James Mullane
Ben Prosser
Tom Williams
John Bunn.
Maurice Hunt
Frank Langwisch.
Wm. A. Lowe
Geo. R. Falconer
Jewett Smith.

Robert Kehrli Murder - Jury Verdict

Chapter Forty-Five

November 20, 1924

"All rise! The honorable Judge Gillham presiding."

Arline stood, the baby on her hip as the judge walked into the courtroom and sat down at what she considered his throne. She jiggled Eldo Jr. as if to keep him quiet, but the truth was, she had to move, or she might just lose her mind.

At first, she tried to avoid looking at her papa. If she did, she'd have to admit to herself this was real, and moments from now, he could be labeled a murderer. She couldn't help herself, though. She turned her head to watch his back as he stood there waiting for his fate to be announced. Though he appeared to be standing straight, Arline could see it. It was almost imperceptible, most certainly to anyone else, but she saw a slight hunch in his back. Did he know the verdict? Did he suspect already? Or was he just afraid of what they'd soon say?

The bailiff walked across the small courtroom and handed a slip of paper to the judge, who unfolded it and read the contents. He turned his head to the jury foreperson and asked, "Has the jury reached a verdict and sentencing?"

"We have, your honor," said the jury member.

"What say ye?" asked the judge.

"On the charge of murder in the first degree against Robert Kehrli, we find the defendant guilty and hereby warrant he be sentenced to life in prison in the Southern Illinois Penitentiary at Chester."

At the announcement, Arline felt like a sledgehammer hit her in the middle. She fell back in her seat, Eldo bouncing as she hit. A cry began to escape her mouth, so she slapped her hand across it. As her shoulders heaved, seemingly on their own, tears sprang to her eyes.

The silence that had settled in the courtroom prior to the verdict suddenly broke like ice and the room became abuzz with loud whispering.

The judge banged the gavel then and commanded, "Order in the court!" Then he instructed the bailiff to take the prisoner to his cell.

As they did so, Papa looked back at Arline, who saw through her haze of tears him mouth something. It wasn't until they had walked him out of the courtroom that she realized what he had said. "I love you."

Chapter Forty-Six

Funny how all these old memories, long buried deep, were resurfacing for Kamuf now. Must have something to do with the morphine they were pumping into him. Or more likely, because he'd finally come clean about the day that tore at him for so long. It was as if that day had been holding back all the other things he'd seen on the farm that sickened his soul.

Like the time Minnie came tearing out of the barn with her skirt all askew. And who should come running out after her, but Fricker.

Kamuf remembered now what Minnie shouted at him as he followed after her. "Never again, Emil! I'm done having your children only to watch them die inside of me."

That memory sparked another one. Them two in the pigsty burying something. Fricker dug a hole, and then she handed him a tiny package wrapped in burlap that he tossed in and covered up. All while the pigs snorted and carried on like they do.

At the time, Kamuf wondered what they were burying, but his gut knew. He'd seen Minnie getting sick under a maple tree, not three days before.

Remembering that now, Kamuf coughed long and hard, as if his lungs were trying to say something to him. Holy Mother of

God. How many children had there been? And what were the two of them doing in the barn that day? Back then he thought they were making a fool out of the missus again, but now he wasn't so sure. The thought sent a shudder throughout Kamuf's body.

Chapter Forty-Seven

"Rudolph Kamuf Died Friday"

Highland News Leader, December 2, 1924

Rudolph Kamuf, whose confession caused the indictment of Emil Fricker for the murder of Robt. Kehrli and whose testimony was the main factor in Fricker's conviction, died at the Madison County Home at 7:30 am Friday.

When Kamuf was taken into the courthouse two weeks ago, he was so weak that he could not walk. Deputy sheriffs and court attachés carried him to the witness stand and back to the ambulance after he had told his story. It helped give Fricker life in the penitentiary and nearly caused his execution.

At the time Kamuf testified, he was so weak he could hardly speak. Persons in the courtroom realized he had but a few days to live.

Kamuf was 69 years of age and was born in St. Louis, but for the last 30 years he had made his home first with Rud. Fricker, the father of Emil, and afterwards with Emil himself. So far as is known he had no relatives.

Kamuf was at the Clinton County Home when he heard of the death of John Nungesser on Sept. 15th, and of the arrest of Fricker in connection therewith. He consulted his physician and was told that he had but a short time to live. His confession of his knowledge of Kehrli's murder followed with the result that all of our readers know.

His death was due to asthma and heart trouble. He was buried Saturday in Woodlawn cemetery in Edwardsville.

Note: This article has been reprinted verbatim from the original article, including any grammatical errors.

Chapter Forty-Eight

October 1923

Why was it when Arline was out walking around the farm trying to clear her head, she had to run into them two? This time they were in the pigsty. That was a new one. She took cover behind a nearby maple and peeked to see what they were up to.

Papa had a shovel and dug around in the mud while Minnie watched. Unlike usual when they were either bickering or making up, this time they didn't say anything to each other.

Her father stopped digging then and gestured to Minnie for something she held in her hands. It looked like an object wrapped in cloth. Arline gasped when Minnie held the thing to her breast and started sobbing.

As Minnie cried, her father glanced around, which made Arline stop peeking and stay still against the tree. In the cold October air, vapor formed from her breathing. She prayed it wasn't visible. Something told her this would be a really bad time for them to see her spying.

Not until Arline heard the pigsty gate slap shut, did she check to see them leaving. Papa put his hand on Minnie's shoulder in a comforting sort of way as they walked toward the house.

After they became an inch tall in the distance, Arline left the shelter of the tree and went over to the pig yard and opened the gate. Once inside, she spotted where Papa had been digging; the ground was indented slightly. Her heart pounding at her forehead, she grabbed the shovel and tentatively dipped it into the slop. The pigs were in the other yard now, but Arline knew they'd be let in by nightfall and would eat whatever was in the muck by morning.

She felt the tip of the shovel hit something solid, which she scooped up and set on the muddy ground. After glancing around to ensure no one was watching, she squatted in the mire.

For one small second, she hesitated to open it but then continued. Not knowing what was wrapped inside would haunt her to her dying day. She unfolded the cloth; her head dizzy like after she fell off the horse last summer. It took her eyes a second to adjust as she looked at the small item lying there. It was only a half-inch long, but Arline knew when she saw the tiny arms and legs what it was. She gulped several breaths as her stomach churned and threatened to expel her lunch. Once she felt steadier, she stood and used the shovel to rebury the tiny being, not bothering to cover it with the cloth. As she hurried out of the pigsty and ran for the stand of trees where she often spent time alone, Arline wondered, would that have been a brother or a sister?

***

Arline never had nightmares. She figured her psyche just rejected them as stupid. The way she saw things, life was confusing enough without filling her head with a bunch of nonsense. So, when she woke up in the middle of the night after finding what she had in the pigsty, she was shocked to discover herself shaking.

Had the pigs eaten it already? The thought brought bile to her throat, so she reached for the glass of water Rose was so kind to put on her nightstand earlier that evening when she noted Arline's pale complexion.

As she swallowed, the liquid pushed the horrid tasting concoction from her stomach back down again, and she thought about the irony. Rose worrying about Arline when her father and that woman.... She shook her head to fling out the vision. Certainly, it was a one-time occurrence. The poor little baby probably died in Minnie's belly. Talk about an inhospitable host.

Just then, Arline thought she heard a sound coming from the hallway. She carefully made her way to her door and peeked out. It was Papa, sliding into the room he shared with Rose. Where had he been at this hour? As if Arline had to ask. Her head lit up like a firework. With that woman again? What was wrong with them both!

Chapter Forty-Nine

January 1925

"Mom, how are you?" asked Richard one day after school.

They were waiting on the date of Emil's second trial, and the tension had been thick. In many ways, it felt like Rose and her children were tiptoeing around each other, as if not saying anything might change the course of things, but of course, they all knew better.

"Son," said Rose, who was in the kitchen deciding what to make for supper for the three of them. Over the last few months, she had let go of all the help, due to the estate being drained by Emil's lawyers.

Rose eyed her son as he towered in the doorway. He had taken on the role of man of the house and tried hard to care for her and his sister. She smiled at him. "My dear son, you're becoming such a handsome and caring young man. I know you hear awful things just about every day at school. I so wish that I could change that for you. I hope your day was okay?"

Richard interrupted her. "I asked you first, right as I came through the kitchen door, how are you, Mom?"

Once again, she looked intensely at him and saw the boy as well as the man. Without thinking, she blurted out, "You're far too young to carry such a heavy burden. Get rid of it. It only gets heavier and heavier."

Without a moment of hesitation, Richard replied, "You know I do the things I do because I want to help. I love you and Blanche and try to ease things for the two of you. I don't expect any thank yous but telling me to not help makes me feel terrible. Actually, worthless. Please don't keep doing that. Now, how are you, Mom?"

Taken aback by her son's candor, it took Rose a few moments to arrange the words to answer his question.

"I'm alright, son. Today, I felt pain combined with fear, anger and sadness, all at the same time. I probably had other feelings mixed in but couldn't say exactly what they were. But here we are all three of us together. I'm a blessed woman."

Richard smiled and approached Rose, then gently wrapped his arms around her.

Chapter Fifty

"Local Events in Brief"

Highland News Leader, February 3, 1925

A baby daughter was born to Mrs. Minnie Nungesser on Wednesday. The father was killed last September 15. The trial of Emil Fricker for complicity in the murder of the father had been set for January 19th, but was postponed on account of the approaching maternity of Mrs. Nungesser, who is one of the prosecuting witnesses. It will likely be held in a few weeks now.

Note: This article has been reprinted verbatim from the original article, including any grammatical errors.

Chapter Fifty-One

"Fricker Trial Starts Today"

Highland News Leader, February 24, 1925

When Circuit Court convenes at Edwardsville this morning, one of the first cases called will be that of Emil Fricker who will be tried on the charge of planning and conspiring the murder of John Nungesser on last Sept. 15th. The case has been set to come up twice before, but was postponed the first time at Fricker's request, and the second time at the request of the state on account of the approaching maternity of Mrs. Minnie Nungesser, widow of the murdered man, and one of the chief witnesses against Fricker.

Eldo Wernle and Jacob Landert Jr. have each been sentenced to life imprisonment for their part in Nungesser's killing and have been held in jail at Edwardsville to appear as witnesses against Fricker.

Fricker at present is under a life sentence for the murder of Robert Kehrli in May 1920, but is to be tried on the other charge before entering upon that sentence.

A large number of Highland people are in Edwardsville today attending the trial, many of whom are relatives and friends of those directly interested, and some others are attracted there just by the salacious details the case promises to bring out.

Note: This article has been reprinted verbatim from the original article, including any grammatical errors.

Chapter Fifty-Two

"Jury Did Not Agree"

Highland News Leader, March 3, 1925

The trial of Emil Fricker for the murder of John Nungesser occupied the attention of the Circuit Court at Edwardsville for several days last week. All day Tuesday was consumed in getting a jury, there being more than a hundred talismen examined before final selection was made. The jury, as finally completed late that evening, consisted of the following:

- Charles Agies, Sr., Edwardsville, bricklayer
- Henry Delbert, Alhambra, clerk
- Jos. M. Pyle, Edwardsville, bank officer
- Henry Finke, Nameoki, farmer
- Arthur Crittenden, Alton, retired
- Philip Best, Ft. Russel, farmer

- J. Gruenfelder, Nameoki, foundry worker
- John Harbig, Nameoki, farmer
- Irving Hittner, Edwardsville, farmer
- Theodore Finke, Chouteau, farmer
- William Fones, Alton, retired
- Roy McMichael, Edwardsville, radiator worker

The case was given to the jury Thursday evening and after forty-eight hours of deliberation, they were unable to agree on a verdict and were discharged.

It is claimed that the jury was agreed as to Fricker's guilt, but could not agree on the penalty, 8 of them being in favor of hanging and 4 in favor of life imprisonment. Their failure to agree makes necessary another trial of the case which we understand will be held sometime this month.

The trial attracted more attention than any held in this county in recent years, the courtroom being literally jammed with people during each session.

Large numbers of people from here attended, being interested in the central figures of the case.

The opening statements to the jury were made Wednesday morning and were followed by evidence for the prosecution which took up all of that day. The evidence for the defense and the arguments of the lawyers were heard Thursday.

Mrs. Nungesser was on the witness stand for about half an hour, just before the prosecution closed. The state did not show through the witness any of the details on the death of her first husband, Robert Kehrli. She testified, however, that she was married to Kehrli in April 1920 and lived with him about four weeks. He was killed on the afternoon of May 7, 1920.

The witness went into some of the details on her relations with Fricker and told of being at his house after Kehrli's death. She told of one visit of two or three days during November 1922, and said she went there to get some money due for work on the farm. She remained until Sunday night, leaving during the night and walked into Highland several miles away.

She told of numerous threats made by Fricker for her not to marry anyone after Kehrli's death. Asked how frequent those threats were made, she remarked, "So often I can't tell."

She testified that she had known Fricker since she was 15 years old, and that she had been in his employment several years prior to her marriage to Robert Kehrli in April 1920. Kehrli was slain on May 7, 1920. Classed by a Coroner's inquest as a suicide, the Kehrli case did not assume the proportions of a murder mystery until the murder of Nungesser.

"My second marriage was on October 2, 1922," Mrs. Nungesser said.

In answering to questions by the State's Attorney, Mrs. Nungesser admitted visiting the Fricker farmhouse less than two weeks after her marriage to Nungesser. She called for some clothing which she had left there, she testified.

It was following this statement that Mrs. Nungesser related her relations with the defendant. Questioning developed that Mrs. Nungesser spent three days, between November 22 and 26, 1922, at Fricker's home being forcibly detained. Before leaving the witness stand Mrs. Nungesser identified the hat which her former husband wore on the day that he was murdered. At that sight she burst into tears.

Declined to Participate

The feature of Eldo Wernle's testimony was the latter's explanation how he and another man had been asked by Fricker to lure Nungesser from his home and then shoot him on a lonely road. The plan, Wernle said, was abandoned when it developed that the other man in question declined to participate. Later, Wernle testified, he and Landert were to have induced Nungesser to join them on a fishing trip, in the course of which Nungesser was to have been thrown into a pond. Wernle also testified that Fricker, Landert and he had discussed and planned the murder of Nungesser. Landert, who took the stand later, gave a similar version.

Nungesser was driving a four-horse team when he was slain. Wernle said that he and Landert, armed with a revolver and an automatic pistol supplied by Fricker, stopped Nungesser on the road and shot him without warning. Wernle said that he was engaging Nungesser in conversation and that Landert fired the first shot at the victim, who fell from his wagon.

The other important witness of the state Wednesday was Jacob Landert, under sentence of life in connection with the death. He said he had known Fricker for about 10 years. Landert repeated a long line of testimony previously published at the time he entered a plea of guilty. He said that Fricker suggested he get down low in the automobile on the day of the killing so he would not be seen by anyone.

Arthur Huehne, a farmer living near the Fricker Farm in Clinton County, said that Fricker had talked to him about giving Nungesser a couple of blue eyes. It was during October, 1923.

John Ackerman, a half-brother of Mrs. Nungesser, testified of a conversation he had with Nungesser.

He said that Fricker made remarks of wanting Mrs. Nungesser and added, "I got to have that woman and I'll get her some way." Fricker talked of getting Nungesser out of the way and made remarks of having Wernle and Landert do the job or that he would get a negro in St. Louis.

All of the evidence was completed Thursday morning about 11 o'clock. The defense had its day in court and Fricker was the principal witness. He made a sweeping denial of everything. Fricker was followed with several character witnesses. The taking of evidence was concluded by introduction of a court record showing his conviction for the death of Robert Kehrli. Lawyers for Fricker objected. The court ruled that the record was permissible.

Fricker was on the stand for an hour or so. Frequently he looked straight at members of the jury when he denied parts of evidence against him. One arm was laid along the rail of the witness stand and the other hung carelessly over the back of his chair. There was little or no change of expression.

He declared that he was opposed to his daughter, Arline, marrying Wernle but said they "made up" during July 1924. He admitted under cross examination he wanted the daughter to marry John Ackermann, a half brother of Mrs. Nungesser.

Fricker said he remembered September 15 and recalled it was on Monday. He said he learned of Nungesser's death the same night. He denied having anything to do with a plot in which others were to take Nungesser fishing, get him drunk and throw him into the water.

He said that on Sunday before the killing he was plowing with a tractor in the field, eager to get the work finished so that a silo could be filled during the coming week. He said Landert and Wernle were at the house that day. He said Wernle talked about some pigeons stolen from a farmer and wanted his father-in-law to help get him out of the trouble. Fricker said he signed a note to help satisfy the claim. It was introduced.

Fricker admitted owning a 32-caliber automatic gun introduced Thursday. He said it was one loaned

Landert during the middle of August and in exchange for a shotgun belonging to Fricker's son. He said Landert wanted a gun for protection. Fricker said Landert was in the field the day he took the gun to the place and left it on Landert's trunk.

Under cross examination, the prosecution did not question Fricker on the alleged intimacy of the defendant with Mrs. Nungesser. It was brought out by Mrs. Nungesser and when not denied through questions of Fricker's lawyers it was permitted to stand for what it was worth.

The state completed its case Wednesday afternoon about 4 o'clock, the introduction of the three guns and Nungesser's hat being the final move of the prosecution. Mrs. Nungesser, while on the witness stand, testified that her husband wore a khaki hat. She was shown the one offered earlier in the day and identified by Wernle and said it was the same one. No objections were offered.

Note: This article has been reprinted verbatim from the original article, including any grammatical errors.

Chapter Fifty-Three

March 25, 1925

It was early afternoon when Rose walked out to the barn. She stopped in at the tack room, clean and well organized thanks to Richard, the sole caretaker nowadays of this room, the stables, horses, and her buggy. She took several deep breaths, savoring the splendid mixture of leather mixed with hay. Then she gathered the gear she needed to hitch the pair of chestnuts to her buggy. A ride would do her good today—help her escape, at least for a little while, the shambles of her present life.

She went to gather the horses, such beautiful animals. Emil had given them to her early in their marriage. She liked the feeling of control the chestnuts gave her. It was good to know she could always hitch them up to her buggy at a moment's notice. She guided them both out of their stalls, the rest now empty. The dairy portion of the farm was also shut down. Only one old milk cow and two laying hens remained. There were no pigs anymore. It was so very quiet everywhere.

When she allowed herself to focus on the emptiness, Rose found the silence overwhelming, and tears would gather in her eyes. The barns, pens and pastures, as well as the buildings, had no life in them. Even the once perpetual smell of manure had greatly faded. She knew ghost towns existed, and had even been through one many years ago, so she could call her barns ghost barns. She lived on a ghost farm.

As she slipped the bridle over the first chestnut's head, she gave it a hard yank, immediately regretting the action. Sure, she was angry—madder than a wet hen—but taking it out on this poor animal was something Rose thought she'd never do. She reached into her apron pocket and pulled out an apple for her grateful horse.

With Helen, or was it Victoria, securely hitched to the buggy, she went around and did the same with the other horse. Blanche had named the pair long ago, and no matter how Rose tried, she was never certain which was which.

The horses and buggy were ready. She had a canteen of water with her, but as she took an appraising glance at the sky, she decided to walk back to the house to exchange her hat for a bonnet and get longer gloves to protect her skin from the sun's harsh rays on this unseasonably warm March day. She knew she would never have the pale delicate porcelain skin of true beauties, but she'd not allow hers to become brown or splotchy.

Finally seated in the buggy a few minutes later, she flicked the reins, indicating to the horses to start out slowly. A couple of miles later, she allowed the pair to increase their speed. The buggy was heading away from town, traveling toward nothing, as the next town in this direction was several hundred miles away.

If only today was before her life had become a shambles and she was going to visit Suzy in town. How she wished she could go back to those days. Though she worked hard back then, she enjoyed working. But the main thing she had a few years back that was nonexistent today was a sense of security. Security for her children and herself.

With that thought, her anger boiled up to the surface and spilled over into the beautiful day. In addition to the anger, she identified an enormous amount of guilt, and regret. Not about her own actions, but about what she didn't do. If only she had spoken up more and demanded Emil stop making moonshine. And then there was Minnie. She should have protected her family and insisted the girl leave the farm.

As she continued to move along in the buggy, Rose felt the enormous jumble of emotions wreaking havoc within her start to calm and separate. This allowed her to examine the anger, guilt and regret, and she came to the same conclusion she always did. She could not and obviously did not control her husband and his actions. This knowing of not being in control made her feel a sudden overwhelming fear.

Forcing her mind into the present, Rose noted how the two steed pulling her buggy had slowed. She looked at the sky and the lowering sun. The children would have been home for at least an hour by now. She would stop so the horses could take a short rest and then skedaddle back.

Rose motioned for the pair to stop on the path, then looked as far as she could see in three different directions at the supremely flat Illinois landscape—not a rise in the land.

She had brought sliced apples for a snack and ate several pieces, then shared what remained with the horses. After they had feasted, she lugged a big dairy can out of the buggy to water the pair, watching as they drank as if it was their first taste of water. After returning the dairy can to the buggy, she lifted her skirts and climbed up into her seat in one fluid movement, then directed the chestnuts to make a wide half-circle and head back the way they had come.

Some of Rose's church friends said her buggy was old-fashioned. Even Suzy teased it was an antique, although with kindness in her voice and a twinkle in her eye, so Rose could never be offended by her words. Rose's reply whenever anyone mentioned her horse and buggy being antiquated was, "It gets me to church every Sunday and anywhere else I fancy."

The truth was, Rose loved her beautiful carriage, along with the two chestnuts that pulled it so deftly. Emil had the buggy made for her as a wedding gift. He had listened to what she wanted her carriage to look like and ensured it exactly matched her desires. Each time she climbed aboard, she'd caress the supple leather of the tufted seat, and she never tired of looking at the grandeur of the solidly built carriage. She truly felt safe in it, and it never gave her a moment's worry, even with her precious babies on board.

"Those motor machines are death traps," she said out loud. "I'll never drive one."

The chestnuts moved forward at a rapid pace now toward Highland as Rose bounced along behind them in the buggy. She really didn't like the rough ride but knew her horses rarely moved forward in a smooth manner with matched strides. The trail was also filled with stones and rocks, and a fair number of miles contained many unavoidable potholes. As they rode along, she thought it strange she hadn't noticed the poor condition of the road when traveling in the opposite direction.

After a while, Rose noted she had gone further into the middle of nowhere than she had previously realized. It was time to really hustle toward home. A quick flick of the reins and she was heading back to the farm even faster than before.

For a moment Rose shuddered at the word home. Not for much longer. Where would she and her children call home in the future? The attorneys had taken everything away, except the clothes they wore. At that thought, she felt panic rise within her. Then she reminded herself to slow her breathing and block the thoughts. This resulted in her body relaxing, and she followed it with a prayer.

"Dear Lord, I know you are with me, protecting us. Wherever we are sent; whatever you guide me towards, it will be your plan. Thy will be done. Amen."

She thought then about what she'd cook for dinner, and how she would check in with her children's lives and do her best to meet their needs.

As she continued on the path, Rose felt somewhat renewed thanks to the day she spent with herself. If only she could carve enough hours out of her life and get back to writing poetry. In past years, many of her writings had been published by the *Highland News Leader*. Since the day Emil was put in jail, though, she had not had a single poem request from the *Leader*. Additionally, no one else, including the church, had made any requests of her.

Sadness enveloped Rose about this disappointing turn of events until the farmhouse appeared on the horizon. When she spied it in the distance, her heart lifted to see light coming from the windows. Richard's doing, she was sure.

Right at that moment, Rose felt like the richest woman on earth.

Chapter Fifty-Four

"Court Records"

Edwardsville Intelligencer, March 31, 1925

People vs. Emil Fricker. Case called for trial. Defendant is furnished with list of jurors. Defendant presents application for change of venue from county which is denied. Defendant excepts. Defendant thereupon requests he be allowed to reserve the matter of challenge to the array which is denied and defendant excepts. Selection of jury begun.

Note: This article has been reprinted verbatim from the original article, including any grammatical errors.

Chapter Fifty-Five

“Jury is Given Case: Emil Fricker’s Fate is Again Deliberated. Denies All of the Charges When Questioned Yesterday”

Edwardsville Intelligencer, April 2, 1925

Emil Fricker’s fate in the killing of John Nungesser north of Highland last September is again in the hands of a jury in the circuit court. The evidence was completed at one day’s session of court yesterday, the arguments of the lawyers being presented during the morning session today and the afternoon meeting opened with the instructions from Judge Bernreuter.

After a lack of interest in the early part of the trial while the jury was being chosen, the courtroom was packed with men and women yesterday who were eager to hear and see.

The evidence as a whole was the same as that offered at the previous trial. Some presented by the state over the former relations between Mrs. Minnie Nungesser, widow of the dead man, and Fricker was slightly changed.

Mrs. Nungesser took the witness stand as the principal witness for the state and told of her younger life on the Fricker place. Eldo Wernle, Fricker's son-in-law, and Jacob Landert, who have taken pleas of killing Nungesser, related the story they previously told.

Fricker took the witness stand in his own defense. He made a sweeping denial of the charges. He repeatedly answered, "I did not," when asked about the alleged planning of the death.

Note: This article has been reprinted verbatim from the original article, including any grammatical errors.

Chapter Fifty-Six

"Death Penalty Given: Jury in Fricker Case Gives Him Extreme Punishment"

Highland News Leader, Tuesday, April 7, 1925

Emil Fricker was found guilty of murder Friday for the second time by a jury in the circuit court at Edwardsville. The jury fixed his punishment at death for the murder on September 15 of John Nungesser, the second husband of his former dairymaid. He already was under a life sentence for the murder in 1920 of Robert Kehrli, the woman's first husband.

Only a few persons were in the courtroom when the jury filed in with its verdict at 8:50 a.m., and Fricker, who had displayed no emotion at any time since he first was arrested charged with the two murders, apparently was unmoved when the clerk read the verdict sending him to the gallows. He faced the verdict alone, none of the members of his family being in the courtroom.

Walter Scott, foreman of the jury, which began its deliberations at 2:30 p.m. Thursday, said the verdict was reached shortly before midnight.

He declined to say how many ballots had been taken, saying that the members of the jury had decided not to make public anything which occurred in the jury room.

"We believe we have done our duty," said Scott, "and we do not feel that the public is interested in how many ballots were taken or what the vote was on each ballot."

The death sentence will as a matter of course take precedence over the life sentence as the only object of the state in trying him in the second murder was to impose the death penalty if possible. No appeal has been taken by Fricker's attorneys from the life sentence, but they will ask a new trial in the present case and probably will appeal if a new trial is denied.

This was the second trial of Fricker in the murder of Nungesser, the jury having been unable to agree on a verdict at the previous trial. The former jury reached an agreement as to guilt on the first ballot, but stood eight for death to four for life imprisonment after two days of deliberating and was discharged.

A single juror saved Fricker from the rope when he was tried last November for the murder of Kehrli, who was thought at the time he was killed to have committed suicide. This juror held out until the other eleven men agreed to a life sentence.

Fricker fired the actual shot which killed Kehrli, but when he wanted to put Nungesser out of the way he induced his son-in-law, Eldo Wernle and Jacob Landert, a farmhand, to ambush Nungesser and shoot him down on a lonely road near his home.

Wernle and Landert pleaded guilty to the murder of Nungesser, and both have been given life sentences. They were the chief witnesses for the state against Fricker in that case.

Rudloph Kamuf, 68, a farmhand who had worked for Fricker and his father before him for nearly half a century, came forward after Fricker was arrested for the Nungesser murder and told how Fricker had lured Kehrli into a patch of woods and shot him and then had instructed him to testify at the coroner's inquest that Kehrli committed suicide.

Kamuf, seriously ill, said he wanted to clear his conscience before he died. He testified at Fricker's trial and died in less than two weeks after the life sentence had been imposed on Fricker.

The form of verdict used by the jury follows:

"We, the jury, find the defendant, Emil Fricker, guilty of murder in manner and form as charged in the indictment, and we find his age to be (44) forty-four years and we fix his punishment at death by hanging."

- Walter Scott
- Alvin Pflugbiel, Sr.

- James Fitzgerald
- Cecil Hendley
- James Moore
- Jake Dressel
- John A. Isert
- W.I. Lee
- Verner A. Cherry
- Robert J. McDonald
- Alexander Weir
- Hilbert C. Brockmeier

Note: This article has been reprinted verbatim from the original article, including any grammatical errors.

April 3rd 1925

We, the jury, find the defendant Emil Fricker, guilty of murder in manner and form as charged in the indictment, and we find his age to be (44) Forty four years, and we fix his punishment at death by hanging.

Walter Scott
Alvin Pflugbiel Sr
James Fitzgerald
Cecil Headley
James Moore
Jake Dressel
John A. Isert
W. E. Lee
Verner A. Cherry
Robert J. McDonald
Alexander Weir
Hilbert C. Brockmeier

Jury Verdict for Nungesser Murder - Death by Hanging

Chapter Fifty-Seven

April 3, 1925

When Blanche returned home from school, Rose heard her daughter well before she saw her.

"Mama, Mama, oh, Mommy!" The ten-year-old emitted a keening cry that revealed deep, raw pain.

When she found her mother, Blanche ran to her and clasped her arms around Rose's waist, repeating, "Mama, Mama," but it had become a soft whisper now.

Rose led her little girl to a nearby sofa, then pulled her baby close and waited for the soft wailing to abate. After she had quieted, she gently smoothed her daughter's wiry corkscrew curls away from her face, then looked into her eyes, which held so many emotions for a young child. In addition to the overwhelming pain, Rose saw anger and fear. Surprisingly, though, no tears, not even one. This was most unusual, because for Blanche, tears almost always flowed over the tiniest of things. But right now, Blanche remained dry-eyed.

"What's the matter, sweetheart?" Rose asked.

The words tumbled out of her daughter, not necessarily in order. "They said he's gonna die...cuz he's a bad man. And they'll put a rope around his neck and KILL him. Those boys in school said—" The high keening returned until Blanche managed to finish, her voice low and pained, "They're going to stretch and stretch and stretch his neck. That's what they said."

Rose pulled Blanche's delicate body toward her and waited while she continued to speak. "My papa, my papa, he's going to come home. He has to come home. He loves me. And us. I love him. He can't die. That's forever, isn't it, Mama? Those boys are wrong, aren't they Mama?" Not waiting for an answer, she continued. "They kept saying Papa's a murderer. That's not true. That's not true. He's my papa, and he loves me!"

Rose herself was feeling every possible emotion, all at the same time. Or was it nothing she was feeling? She took a few deep breaths and looked upward, her lips struggling to form words as she asked for help from above, but no sound came out. It was then she realized she was angry. There had been talk about the death penalty, but the lawyers assured her they would personally deliver her husband's punishment directly to her before it became public knowledge. That certainly didn't seem to be the case.

As Rose held her precious daughter tight, Blanche continued to whimper, yet her small, fragile body remained stiff. Her baby was in tremendous pain, Rose thought. She drew the tortured, confused child even closer, as if doing so could absorb some of her little one's suffering and anguish.

Anger continued to well from deep within Rose. Why had those ruffians learned of Emil's fate before his wife and children? She knew which boys taunted Blanche. The three of them were a couple of years older than her daughter. They were mischievous and always seemed to be involved when something was doing. All three were cruel troublemakers. She wondered why the schoolmarm had not put a stop to those bullies. Was she paying attention and doing her job?

Then Rose wondered why Richard wasn't home yet. Was he enduring similar taunting from school classmates? He never told Rose anything about what occurred daily since his father was arrested. His best friend had shared with her the vicious cruelty inflicted upon her son by some of his classmates, though. When she asked Richard directly about this, he assured her he ignored the terrible things said to him and added that the offending teens were simply stupid. He claimed he'd be fine.

When Blanche's breath finally relaxed and moved into a more normal rhythm, Rose loosened her arms from around her child. She wanted to say something to her little girl, but what would be best at this time, she wondered?

Before Rose could even open her mouth, though, Blanche looked directly into her mother's eyes and exclaimed, "I'm never going to church again. The day after the sheriff took Papa away, I told God I'd be a really good girl and work even harder on my studies if they would let Papa come home. I was good every single day, and my marks are so much better. If what those boys say is true, God just doesn't love me anymore."

Rose returned her daughter's intense gaze, looking deeply into her child's dry, brown eyes and opened her mouth to speak, but Blanche interrupted, almost shouting, "No, Mama, no! If God lets them hang Papa, I'll never go to his house again!"

***

Later that night when the children had settled down as best they could, Rose sat in her rocking chair and sighed. She picked up her Bible but kept it in her lap and stared into space, thoughts rushing about in her head.

What had caused her life to crumble? Her husband, the man who slept in bed with her, the co-creator of her two perfect babies—they were going to murder him. The man she was to love and cherish until they were both old and gray. The man, who until about two years ago when they arrested him, had provided for Rose and her children so generously.

Her heart ached when she thought of Blanche, who Emil loved dearly. Unlike many fathers, he actually spent time with his little girl. Often, they walked out to the barns as he talked at length about the needs of his dairy cows, explaining how he kept his producing the best in the county.

Blanche would skip and hop alongside him, knowing she could not slow to a walking pace and still keep up with his long strides. Her eyes would sparkle as she hung on his every word, her expression one of fascination that broke frequently into excitement. She loved when he came home during daylight hours and called out over and over for his "favorite girl."

When he did this, Blanche would immediately stop whatever she was doing and stay perfectly still as a large, beautiful smile broke out on her face, her eyes projecting anticipation and delight. Then she'd break into a run toward her father, the giant of a man who would stoop down and snatch his daughter up into his oversized arms. It was one of the few occasions in which Rose saw a smile on Emil's face. Then he would ever so gently place Blanche down by his side and they'd begin to walk. Rose could tell Blanche felt these times with him were the happiest moments of her life. In fact, she told her mother that.

Rose would watch them walk; Blanche's face upturned as Emil talked. She would become ecstatic and almost grin and giggle, allowing her happiness to overflow. However, Rose saw that she would stop herself in order to appear demure. She suspected her daughter didn't want to appear to her father frivolous or as if she didn't care a whip about his cows.

Blanche did care about the cows and even named a couple of them. Emil had tried several times to teach her to milk a cow without success. Rose could tell Blanche hated to disappoint him, so she kept trying.

The fifth time she tried milking Betsy, a prized dairy cow, and failed once again, Blanche looked over at their sheep and exclaimed, "Sheep have milk, too." Rose watched as their daughter grabbed a bucket and little stool and approached a sheep. Within moments, the squirting milk was pinging against the sides of the pail.

Blanche was so proud as Emil remarked to Rose, "I didn't notice how tiny her hands are."

Then Rose's mind wandered back to the day Blanche turned seven years old. Emil had come home quite early that day and called his girl in the usual manner. They headed for the barn together. Soon, Blanche squealed, and Rose knew it was with delight. She was so loud, everyone in the fields, the house, and even on the road heard her.

Her daughter came shooting out of the barn and ran toward the house, eagerly calling out, “Mama, Mama, a pony!” Rushing into the kitchen, she grabbed Rose’s legs, hugging her mother tight. Then she let go and jumped up and down, saying, “Papa got me a pony!” Repeating this over and over.

Seeing her daughter’s joy and enthusiasm, Rose’s heart grew with love for Emil.

“Mama, come see my pony. Come to the barn.” Blanche grabbed her mother’s hand and pulled her with all her strength toward the doorway. Rose grabbed a dishtowel and wiped her hands while still moving toward the door. Her daughter’s enthusiasm was infectious, and Rose found herself almost running toward the barn with her.

Chapter Fifty-Eight

When the word came about Papa's sentencing, delivered to her by Abe, Arline, who had answered the door with little Eldo on her hip, nodded and thanked him, then shut the door.

At first, she felt a deep, dead silence within her, like she stood in the eye of a storm right before a tornado came ripping through. She took little Eldo to his crib in the bedroom and set him down, smiling and tapping the tip of his nose with her forefinger. Then she left the room, gently shutting the door behind her, ignoring his whimpers of protest about being left alone.

In the living room, she sat down and gripped the edge of the couch, steeling herself as waves of heart-wrenching despair swept through her. She had heard about your life flashing before your eyes when you died. She felt like she was dying—literally dying at that moment. She had never felt such deep-seated pain. It was anguish, pure and simple.

Though she wanted to cry out and scream at the injustice of it all—at Minnie for coming into their lives and at her father for being so stupid and greedy—she stayed silent. The walls were paper-thin, and she didn't want to scare an already confused little Eldo. Instead, she sat there for some time as the tears streamed down her face, soaking the front of her dress, until she had run out of tears. She wasn't sure how long she sat there. It was as if a heavy lead weight bore down on her lap; she couldn't move.

No sounds came from the room, so little Eldo had apparently decided to sleep. That was good, because Arline wasn't sure she could trust herself to pick him up right now. She was pretty sure her arms and legs were inoperable.

Her thoughts ran through the last few years—how Papa had slipped further and further away from her the closer Minnie came. But she knew it was more than that. In reality, it was the demon drink, as the pastor at church called it. And in this case, it was a demon. She'd seen her father change when he started brewing and guzzling what he made. Right before her eyes, he became a man she never, ever imagined he could become, and that tore at her heart, at her soul.

Finally, after she had no idea how long, Arline felt the lead weight lift. She nearly gasped when this occurred, because she'd been breathing at a limited level. Once she caught her breath and wiped stray tears from her face, she got up and opened the door to the bedroom to peek in on her son, who was awake after all. She walked over and reached down for her little angel, pulling him to her breast and inhaling the scent of innocence, permanence, love.

She might have lost her mother, husband and father, but she had this precious little soul right here, right now, next to her breast. She thanked the Almighty for this priceless gift. She'd be the best mother possible to little Eldo. She would never leave him and never fail him. That was a promise she made to herself, to God, and, yes, to her father.

Chapter Fifty-Nine

"Taken to Penitentiary"

Highland News Leader, April 25, 1925

Eldo Wernle and Jacob Landert were taken to the Cheater Penitentiary Friday by Sheriff Deimling to begin their life terms for the murder of John Nungesser near Highland last fall. The trip was made in an automobile and required only three hours. It was previously planned to take the two men to Cheater Saturday, but the plans were changed. After being sentenced for the killing of Nungesser, in which Emil Fricker was also implicated, Wernle and Landert were held in the county jail as witnesses against Fricker who was tried and sentenced to hang for his part in the murder.

Note: This article has been reprinted verbatim from the original article, including any grammatical errors.

Chapter Sixty

"Fricker Seeks New Trial To Save His Life"

Highland News Leader, May 12, 1925

Arrangements are being made by Emil Fricker's attorney to appeal the circuit court orders of hanging in regard to Nungesser's murder. His first move, when taken into court for judgment, which has not yet been rendered, will be to ask for a new trial. If denied, he must either pay the death penalty or look to the supreme court to be saved.

The law provides when judgment may be passed upon a man who is to be executed, and the convening of the supreme court is an important factor in this. Judge Bernzeuter has not given out the least intimation on his plans but Sec. 749 of the 38th chapter of the Illinois Statutes gives information on what may be done.

From that petition it seems that June 12 is the earliest possible date for execution, but it may be set for a number of days after that date. The next term of the supreme court will convene on June 2 and the execution cannot be set for at least 19 days after court opens. Checking the other provisions of the law, it seems possible that the judgment may be passed on Fricker between May 19 and May 29.

Criminal lawyers of Chicago who were acquainted with the section, realized that Loeb and Leopold would be hanged when the trial announced a date for judgment that conflicted with the requirements.

Note: This article has been reprinted verbatim from the original article, including any grammatical errors.

Chapter Sixty-One

In the days following the news her husband would hang, Rose kept herself busy. She worked on packing up the house for their inevitable, impending departure and tried to put out of mind, at least for now, how her children would react once Emil paid with his life. They were at school on this particularly pretty spring morning, and while Rose really should continue working, she was truly going stir crazy.

So, she hitched up the chestnuts and set out for town to visit Suzy. As the team began to canter along the road, Rose looked to the left and right to take in the sights and sounds of spring growth, but within minutes her thoughts turned toward Blanche. A child that smiled most of the time, she used to be so carefree and always so well-mannered. Especially when she spent time with her papa. Rose's heart hitched when she thought about how Blanche loved and idolized Emil. Now he was incarcerated and soon to be.... Rose's heart broke over and over as she thought about what her little princess had become—more and more unhappy and angry. Rose tried repeatedly to get Blanche to share her feelings with her, but that didn't happen.

As if her little girl wasn't hurting enough about Emil's fate, an incident at school the prior day cut her to the core and was almost unbearable for Rose to witness. Apparently, Blanche's two best friends were instructed by their mothers to "stay away from anyone named Fricker." Both girls told Blanche they couldn't play with her anymore. Then once they dissolved their friendship on the school playground, they turned and walked away, leaving Blanche alone and stunned.

Later that day after school as Blanche told the story, Rose saw not even a hint of a tear. Rather, rage burned brightly in her brown eyes. Rose was almost frightened that anyone, much less her baby, could experience such overwhelming, all-consuming anger. She found herself blinking back tears as she listened to her daughter's sad tale.

Lost in her thoughts of Blanche, Rose was surprised to see the carriage enter town then. She said a short prayer for both of her children and asked for help conveying her love, understanding and acceptance to them.

When she stopped the buggy at Suzy's house, she looked up at the sun, noting it was probably about noon. She got out of the buggy, stretched her legs, and led the horses to the side area of Suzy's home. Her friend's late husband had cleared the area for the temporary housing of travel animals whenever guests came calling. That was quite a while ago when the only transportation was by horse or mule. Today, because of motorcars, the space wasn't used as much. Regardless, Rose was grateful to have a place to rest her pair of chestnuts.

As she walked up the path to Suzy's house, the door sprang open and there stood her friend. She wore a large sunhat and looked as if she was ready to go out.

"Rosie, I didn't expect you today," Suzy said, a surprised look on her face that turned to concern. "Are you okay, my dear?"

Rose walked up to her friend and nodded. "I'm doing okay, thank you, my dear friend. I just needed to get out of the house. I was feeling so restless."

Love passed over Suzy's face and she took Rose's hands. "I've been thinking of you nonstop since..." she trailed off for a moment, then finished the sentence, "the verdict." Her eyes searched Rose's face. "Are you sure you're okay?"

Rose took a deep breath. "I would be lying if I told you I was doing fine. To know that your husband, the man you laid next to and made children with, is going to hang for murder is a terrible thing, but I'm doing my best. I keep reminding myself about my dear children, and I have you."

Suzy smiled. "That you do. I was just going out on a walk. Care to join me?"

"That sounds like a wonderfully refreshing idea."

Suzy closed her front door, and the two women set off. At first, they walked in silence, until Suzy spoke up. "Besides the obvious, what's troubling you my dear friend?"

Rose sighed and shared her concerns about Blanche. As she talked, Suzy reached out and squeezed her friend's hand, a gesture that made Rose feel better somehow.

"You know," said Rose as they walked, "I think Emil became so close to Blanche because he was trying to make up for the years he was absent in Arline's life."

"Really, I didn't know that," said Suzy.

"It seems that Emil's first wife was raised with firm conviction that girls were kept very close to their mothers when they were young. Except for unavoidable situations, such as school," she stopped and laughed, then resumed. "They kept company only with female family members and other little girls. Emil told me he wanted to play games with Arline and rock her to sleep when she was little, but he believed it would have been improper. He added he felt a little guilty to want that. When he told me that, Blanche was just a few weeks old. I had just finished feeding her, so I got up and plopped her on his lap and told him I never heard such things. 'You spend as much time as you want with her,' I said. Then I left the room and went to take a nap."

"You really just left her there with Emil?" asked Suzy.

"I did," replied Rose firmly. "In fact, he brought her to me, wet diapers and all, about three hours later. She was content and ready to eat and nap again."

"Were you ever envious of them—of their close relationship?" asked Suzy.

"Lord sakes no! The way those two were together—they brought out the best in each other. Watching them gave me enormous joy." Rose's heart hitched once again when she thought of her little girl and the impending terrible loss she would soon have to face.

Suzy, who always seemed to know how to say the right thing, asked then, "I'm sure you and Blanche have had some special times together, too."

Rose's heart lifted at her friend's words. "As a matter of fact, we have. I've never told you about those wonderful times. One memory in particular stands out. You want to hear it, dear girl?"

"Certainly, my friend," replied Suzy, who glanced at Rose, her eyes twinkling. They had been moving along at a brisk pace, but

Suzy stopped then and looked around at the quiet landscape. "Why, we're officially no longer in town. We're in the outskirts of Highland. I'm sure tuckered out right now. How about you? Would you like to take a brief rest so you can tell me about your and Blanche's time together?"

Suzy appeared to be searching with her eyes and seemed to locate the subject of her quest when she took Rose's arm and began guiding her off the road.

"What on earth are you doing?" Rose asked. "Where are you taking us, pray tell?

Suzy pointed to a grouping of large rocks. "I'm hoping we can find a comfy boulder to sit on for just a bit."

Each woman began to test a few.

When Suzy remained seated on a gray-colored boulder, Rose inquired, "Found yourself a soft, fluffy seat, did ya?"

From her perch on the large rock, Suzy replied, "Don't you think you should find a place for your derriere and use it? You keep running from one rock to another, and it will be time to hightail it for town before long."

Both women were grinning from ear to ear when Rose said, "It's a good thing no one is around a listening to us. We have a strange sense of humor, and we're clever."

Suzy laughed. "That's what we are, clever. I believe we can banter so well, because we're super intelligent."

Rose came to rest on the boulder next to Suzy. The women sat in silence for a while gazing upward into the expansive blue sky, peppered with many white, semi-opaque, fluffy clouds. Rose noted the position of the sun revealed it was early afternoon. She continued looking up and said, "I just can't tell if we're to have rain today or tonight. When clouds float to obscure the sun, I almost feel the cold that results."

"Rosie," Suzy said loudly then.

"Yes, my treasured friend. I certainly can't ignore that volume." Rose tried to keep a bland expression on her face as she spoke without success, and instead grinned.

Suzy cleared her throat and said, "You were going to tell me about your special times with Blanche."

"Thank you for asking me to tell you about the outings Blanche and I took when she was younger. I hope by telling you about our mommy and me excursions they'll remain 'alive' longer in my mind."

Rose smiled as she pictured her and Blanche together, then spoke. "As we began each outing heading into the back acres of the farm, we said little to one another, but our eyes met frequently. She would dance and twirl about when she was ahead of me. Without a single word, her body conveyed messages of unspoken love. Watching her antics during a 'magic adventure,' as Blanche called them, my heart filled with so much love and gratitude. I was certain I would just burst open from all the wonderful feeling building up inside of me. Of course that didn't come to pass."

Rose closed her eyes for a few moments, then continued. "One afternoon was quite memorable—magical and delightful. We left the house in the late morning and brought our midday meal with us. As we walked, Blanche skipped forward and far ahead of me, her curly tendrils springing and bouncing as she went. She stopped frequently, turning with an enormous smile and waving to me. It seemed that each smile entered my heart a little further.

"The weather was beautiful. Not too warm, not too cool. The sky was clear—a perfect day. It was uplifting, that's what it was. Blanche was darling. She looked lovely. She had pleaded with me that morning to allow her to wear the fabric dress I had sown for her earlier in the year for Easter. She was breathtaking in the soft blue fabric of the dress. It was so gentle and rich looking. With the ruffled pinafore, her curly curls atop her dress seemed at home. Honestly, Suzy, her smile was just beautiful that day. Everything about her was soft and gentle, you know. She appeared almost angelic."

Suzy smiled and nodded, as if to urge Rose to continue.

"After a while, we found a big tree and Blanche chattered on as we ate in its shade. When we finished and felt rested, we continued our journey, Blanche's doll-sized hand tucked in mine until we encountered a field of white flowers. Then my beautiful child took her hand from mine and ran into the flowers. She was so happy, Suzy. I watched her twirl and dance through a blanket of white, her smile perfect, almost as if it was sent from Heaven.

"Suddenly she ran back to me and said while gently clasping my hands, 'Oh, Mama, I saw the most beautiful dresses in a magazine. All of them were white and had pearls, and shiny beads on them with a lot of beautiful lace. They were so fancy and delicate. How can anyone make something so beautiful? I mean, Mama, there were real women wearing the dresses. Why have you never shown me your wedding dress? How did it feel to be so beautiful?' She looked up at me with great expectation, so I motioned for her to sit with me amongst the flowers and told her that I didn't have a white, lacy wedding gown. I explained that I wore a long, black dress."

Rose adjusted her seating on the boulder, then said, "My daughter's smile was replaced with confusion. Looking deep in my eyes, she asked why I wore an 'ugly old black dress' when I could have worn a beautiful white one. I explained that I am a farm wife, and black was a proper color. I had never been told about a farm wife wearing white lace and pearls. My darling daughter looked as if she might start to cry, so I gathered her into my arms and assured her it was truly a beautiful black dress. I also explained that her papa had a wife before me and one of the reasons he married me was to provide a mother to his child, Arline. I really never thought about wearing white, especially since her papa was marrying again."

"How did our dear girl react to that?" asked Suzy.

"Blanche finally gave me a soft smile, and then I shared with her the celebration after the wedding. As you know, my dear friend, it was a small affair. However, I embellished my story, making it seem like a grand party. Within moments, her eyes began to twinkle, and she got a dreamy look on her face. She started to describe again the elegant bridal gowns she had seen in the magazine. The more she talked about thick lace and pearls and beading, the more excited she became. Then she looked into my eyes and said, 'Oh, Mama, I'm going to wear the most beautiful long, silky wedding dress ever worn by a bride in this county. My wedding dress will be so lovely, with yards of lace and tiny beads, and it'll sparkle like diamonds. And guess what, Mama, I can get white shoes made from dress material. They will match the dress. And there will be lots and lots of petticoats, and a long veil that covers my face, because I'll also be a mysterious bride.' Then suddenly she stopped, put each of her little hands on her own cheeks, and announced, 'I plan to be the most beautiful bride ever.'

“It was then she jumped up and began twirling around in the white flowers and laughing. 'I’m in a field of beautiful, gorgeous, white wedding gowns. There’s white as far as I can see,’ she shouted. She pointed to the white flowers and said they were the lace and satin for her wedding dress and a part of her wedding veil. Then she began taking small staccato-like steps. It seemed she was playacting some sort of processional. She held her arm up as if being led by someone. Goodness, Suzy, the look on her face as she gazed upwards was truly magical.

"I then commented to my precious daughter, ‘Your young man must be unusually tall to capture your gaze up so high.’ Her face conveyed confusion for a moment but then quickly transformed into one of mystical beauty. With an enormous smile, she replied, ‘Oh, silly, Mama, it’s Papa’s arm I’m a-holding. You know how tall he is. Isn’t it proper that he walk me down the aisle and give me to the man of my dreams? I do want a young man who is tall like Papa. Someone handsome and brave.’ Then a serious expression flooded her face and she came over to me and asked, ‘Mama, do you think anyone will want to marry me?’

“She seemed rather desperate, so I gathered her into my arms and told her when she gets old enough, it will be no problem finding the perfect man. Her brow un-furrowed with that comment, and a smile returned to her face. Then she gave me one of the biggest hugs I’ve ever received. Suzy, that was the most memorable outing she and I have ever experienced.”

Rose swallowed over a lump in her throat and frowned.

That prompted Suzy to reach out and put her hand on Rose's and ask, "What is it?"

"I'm remembering another outing some time after the one I just described."

"Not such a good memory?"

Rose sighed. "It was a beautiful day, weatherwise, but the conversation wasn't so happy. We had our midday meal and were resting in the sun when Blanche suddenly said that her papa was different than he used to be. I asked her what caused her to believe that. She replied in a matter-of-fact manner about when he came home and couldn't walk properly. She added that he usually said some really bad words a-coming up the stairs, and it looked to her like he might not get all the way up."

"Oh, my dear friend, were you able to find words to respond to her?" asked Suzy.

Rose continued staring straight ahead for a time before replying. "I was in a state of shock at her words, but I did manage to find out what condition her father was in after midnight. She said that some nights she tries to fall asleep but is unable to when she hears anything that might be a-doing. Then she silently goes to a hiding place and watches. I was taken aback, as I never suspected she was out of bed, much less observing activity in the house. I felt so sad, because I thought I'd sheltered her and Richard and even Arline from those ugly scenes of Emil's."

Rose paused and pushed stray hair into her chignon. "As Blanche and I continued to share a look, she told me how much she missed the games he used to play with her and how he would promise to spend time with her but instead would leave or go to sleep. She appeared dejected and forlorn, and seeing how deeply wounded she was just broke my heart. She even asked if she misbehaved or if he didn't love her anymore. I assured her he did and always would. Then she mentioned that Richard told her he had changed because of the drink from his still. She asked quite rationally why he just couldn't stop drinking from the still. I explained what a still was and told her about the moonshine made there. I also shared that I had asked him to stop repeatedly and that he said he'd drink less."

Rose stopped for a moment. Though this was a difficult story to tell, sharing it with her good friend seemed to be lifting the burden a bit.

"Blanche never took her eyes off me as she listened to my every word. Then, after a few minutes of silence when I thought the subject was closed, she gave me an almost pleading look and said she thought he'd been drinking more of the moon stuff, not less. She then inquired as to why he didn't just stop going to his still and not drink even a drop of the moon drink. I wasn't certain what I should tell her. Finally, I explained that some folks just couldn't stop drinking, even when they tried. I added that it could be a sickness. Suddenly, her little face revealed a look of alarm as she wailed, 'No! My Papa can't get sick. I'm his princess, you know.'"

Rose swallowed over the lump in her throat, then continued. "I took hold of her and held her tightly until she calmed down and could hear me. Then I explained it could be a sickness, but I wasn't sure. I encouraged her to tell Emil she wanted him to stop drinking the moonshine. The very next day when he came home from work, she was waiting for him. She slipped her small hand into his large one and was so grown up when she led them both to his desk and sat down next to him."

Stopping for a moment, Rose put her hand to her heart, then continued. "I really didn't listen to what transpired between them. However, because he has such a booming voice, I heard him say princess more than once. Also, he declared he'd never hurt her and there was even a sorry or two."

Rose glanced at Suzy. "You know, he did actually seem to stop with the moonshine for a few days. It was wonderful. He was pleasant and kind, like our first years. As I expected, though, he eventually returned to visit his still. Gradually, he came home later at night. When he came home full of drink, he was angry and sometimes went into a rage. However, after that, anytime he arranged to spend time with Blanche, he was true to his word."

Chapter Sixty-Two

"Stay of Execution Expected"

Highland News Leader, June 9, 1925

It is expected in Edwardsville today that a stay of execution in the case of Emil Fricker will be received there sometime today. It is thought the stay will be granted by the Supreme Court or any judge thereof in order to give the lawyers more time to perfect their appeal to the Supreme Court. Although everything is in readiness, it is the conviction of all in Edwardsville that a stay will be granted.

Note: This article has been reprinted verbatim from the original article, including any grammatical errors.

Chapter Sixty-Three

"May Have Thought of Escape"

Highland News Leader, June 16, 1925

According to the daily papers of Saturday, Emil Fricker is believed to have laid plans for possible escape from the county jail with the finding of a steel saw on the outside windowsill of his cell late Friday afternoon and he was transferred into the main building the next day and the quarters recently occupied were carefully searched by Sheriff M. H. Deimling.

John Drall of Fosterberg, who is serving a jail sentence for wife abandonment, found the saw. He has been a trusty for the past few days and was mucking near the gallows when he made the discovery.

Fricker has been in the boys quarters the past several weeks, occupying a cell on the lower floor and within

150 paces of the gallows. Whether the saw was left with the hopes that Fricker would be able to get it or that another would pass it in is unknown. The saw was lying on the windowsill.

Fricker's cell is about three feet from the window, a passageway separating the cell from the window. The confederate, if he had one, would have been required to slip the saw through the window grating and Fricker might have received it on a broom.

It was not until 10 o'clock Friday night that Fricker was officially informed that the execution would not take place Saturday. The Supreme Court writ was delivered to Sheriff Deimling that night at 9:30 o'clock by Attorney H. J. Bandy. When the Sheriff went to Fricker's cell, the prisoner was lying face down on his bed and was sound asleep.

Note: This article has been reprinted verbatim from the original article, including any grammatical errors.

Chapter Sixty-Four

Ghost Farm

Early September 1925

Rose slowly walked around the quiet farm, recalling how she and Emil had traveled through a ghost town early in their marriage. She couldn't remember exactly when that occurred, or why, but it had definitely been an abandoned town. Now her home was almost empty.

Most all the livestock, cows, pigs, chickens and sheep, had been sold at auction. A handful of chickens were in the henhouse. They produced just enough eggs for the three of them—Rose, Richard and Blanche—to eat. One of the dairy cows was all that was left of the prize-winning herd. The livestock sale included the horses, but she still had her chestnuts in the barn, thank goodness. She was grateful for them, as they provided her only transportation.

Rose never saw any of the money from the sale of the livestock. Emil's attorneys arranged for the auction and told her the money recovered what was due to them for the attempted appeals and his defense. Defense, humph! Even though Rose didn't attend the trials, everything that got back to her made it apparent that few words were said in Emil's defense.

Rose stopped at the large elm tree where a single swing dangled from its mighty branches. Emil hung it when his little princess asked and would push Blanche for many hours—especially when it was new and a novelty.

There were some good memories on this ghost farm, once so busy with farmhands and household help. Rose thought back to her favorite employee—Cook. When Rose arrived at the farm as Emil's new bride, the woman, who had worked on the farm for several years by then, was with child. When it was time for the baby to arrive, Rose assisted with the birthing of her daughter.

At the time, Rose had wondered if Cook would be able to keep up with the cooking and care for her infant daughter. It turned out the young woman seemed to work harder than ever after giving birth. She amazed Rose, who made a point of stepping in to take over the cooking several times every day so she could go nurse her child. The two women became close friends, and Rose truly missed her now. In fact, she missed many things. Not objects like the fine linens and china, but she did miss the people.

It was a good thing Rose didn't miss the things, like some people might, because Emil's attorneys had come in and taken just about everything. She turned toward the huge farmhouse, deciding as she did so it was time to pack up the remaining tired, old items left. She didn't know as of yet when they would have to leave, but she wanted to be prepared when the time came.

Once inside, she looked around and truly took note of her surroundings, tears forming in her eyes. She felt indignant. She could cry. She should cry, if she chose to. The children were in school and there wasn't a single person there other than Rose. She, Richard and Blanche were the only ones who lived on this enormous spread. She really couldn't call it her home anymore. Emil's lawyers had her sign the farm over to them for payment for his defense. A lot of good they did defending him. Short of a miracle, she'd become a widow soon. Either way, she had to vacate the farm. Moving, leaving the house was alright, but where was she to go?

Fear bubbled within Rose as it did every time she thought of the future. How would she provide for Blanche and Richard? Her brothers and sisters attended college, not Rose. Elise was teaching school and Samuel was becoming known as one of the leading trap shooters in the region. No matter what her siblings were doing, none of it was going to repair her present predicament.

She could maybe find work at an orphanage, but often they were run by nuns and the workers were also nuns. Besides, there wasn't an orphanage nearby. So, she and the children would be forced to move. All she'd heard from others who came to settle in or near Highland was that a pack of problems came with moving. Besides, Richard and Blanche were losing so much—their father, their home, their pets—everything that had made them feel safe. Moving away from Highland just might be more than she and they could bear.

Rose swallowed down the lump that had formed in her throat. She saw every day the effects of Emil's arrest and sentence grinding her children down. They had both left a carefree childhood behind and were now serious people in children's bodies. Blanche no longer hid around corners and bounced out at someone as a lark. No longer did Rose hear her laughter, giggles, and whispers. Her daughter didn't cry, but she no longer bounded with joy.

Although Richard's relationship with Emil was quite different than Blanche's, he did love his father. Whenever Richard had gone to Emil for help, the man did good by his son, and Richard knew he could count on him. Rose had also noted that when Emil was home, Richard seemed relaxed and at ease and smiled a bit. She surmised that Emil made the boy feel safe. Now her son seemed stoic and hypervigilant all the time. This did not change, no matter what Rose told him. She knew he felt responsible for the welfare of his mother and sister.

Through all her thoughts, Rose continued packing. Currently, she was in the kitchen. Most of the pots, pans, skillets and bakeware was still there and needed to be packed. Not so in the dining room, where all the beautiful cut glass and every single piece of silver the lawyers had removed from the home. Long before this had occurred, Rose had a premonition her house would be gutted in the name of "Emil's defense." So, she had hidden some items in her petticoat drawer. Goodness, she had thought, these few pieces will never be missed.

There were four different sets of silverware, plus odds and ends. And she had also secreted away a couple of small serving dishes, a creamer and sugar bowl. The utensils had the initial "F" engraved on the handle, and all were beautifully ornate. She recalled how she had truly enjoyed polishing the silver, running her hands over the smooth, cold metal and watching the gleam and shine of them when she finished. The silver on a particular sunny day, freshly polished, glistened so brightly it made one squint to gaze upon the pieces.

Rose surveyed the kitchen articles in various states of containment. More than half were tied up and ready to move. A few were in a state of incompletion; partially ready for transport. She remembered how fatigued she had been the last night she'd been gathering up this room. She'd put nothing out of the way or stacked anything neatly the way she usually did most everything else. Tidy with an organized plan had always served her well.

That past night when fatigue set in, she had simply left the kitchen in a shambles, walked to her rocking chair and collapsed into it. She loved the small chair that had been her mother's and found it her refuge. When she was young, her brothers would chant, "baby rocker, baby rocker." She would pretend their chanting upset her and she didn't like hearing it, but the truth was she enjoyed their playfulness and agreed that many babies had been soothed in that chair.

Today, she wasn't tired, though. In fact, she felt almost energized. She suspected her present state was a combination of stress and worry, along with a healthy dose of fear. She looked at the task before her and said out loud, "Best use this strange force in me to accomplish something." Rose began packing with precision and speed.

When finally nearing completion a few hours later, she stopped to rest and get a drink of water. After draining the glass and placing it next to her favorite small black skillet, she picked the pan up, noting how the weight was just perfect in her hand. Then her mind turned to some of the wonderful spices and seasonings she'd cooked up in the skillet over the years. Some were mixed and made as her mama had, while many of the concoctions were ideas of her own.

Cook always followed Rose's lead in the kitchen. There were a lot of farmhands, house help, family and friends to feed, and the woman appreciated Rose's help. She also expressed awe when she watched Rose plan meals and use in-season foods from the gardens. In fact, Cook called Rose the "conductor" in the kitchen.

She could make meals feed extra people, if need be, and everyone enjoyed them.

Rose remembered fondly the myriad compliments she had always received on her cooking. They made her feel accomplished and like a true contributor. Rose set the pan down and ran her hand back and forth in a caressing manner over a huge, heavy brown bowl. It felt so smooth and cool. She smiled as she thought of the many flavors of cakes and cookies that had originated in the bowl.

Cooking meals gave Rose enjoyment, but she had to admit desserts were her forte—where she shined. Her mouth actually began to water as she mentally listed some of her desserts, especially her pies. Oh, yes, she thought, baking was a love of hers.

She picked up the bowl and started to pack it up, as time was running short. Richard and Blanche would soon be home from school. At the thought, panic about how she would take care of her children once again overtook her. Stopping and standing quite still, Rose took several deep breaths as she unconsciously clutched the big mixing bowl to her chest.

When she finally felt her emotions return to manageable, she realized she was still holding the bowl.

At that very moment, she said loudly, "A cook, a baker! I can work for anyone who needs one!"

Still clutching the bowl in ecstasy at the thought, Rose twirled around in the kitchen, her skirts flowing.

Chapter Sixty-Five

When I was twelve years old, I found a chest in my parents' bedroom. I'd seen the chest before that day but hadn't thought of opening it and checking out the contents until then.

Part of me knew I wasn't to be looking at my mother's things. But the other part of me thought the contents might shed light on the secrets shrouding our home. So, on that day, I decided to put caution aside and open the trunk.

It was an overcast Saturday in Southern California. Pop was at work at the butcher shop, and I was home with my mother and grandmother, who were in the kitchen making lunch.

The room was quiet, except for the slow tick of a clock as I unlatched the trunk and lifted the lid. What lay inside intrigued me. Beautiful white linens and a small amount of silverware I had never seen before, as well as some clothing, including christening gowns.

I lifted a silver spoon and held it up to take a closer look, noting an engraved letter on the handle—an F. Within the stash was a couple of candlesticks, a silver ring, also with the initial F, and some small silver cups.

Just then, my mother called out to say lunch was ready. I gently closed the chest lid and hurried to the kitchen, where they had set out bowls of chicken soup and crackers.

After my mother waited for my grandmother to say grace and we began eating, I started to wonder. Dare I ask about the contents of the chest? Would my mother answer, or shut me down, and the house would grow silent, cold, and tense again?

When I finished my chicken soup, however, curiosity finally overtook me. I cleared my throat and spoke. "The chest in your room, Mama."

My grandmother and mother looked at me and waited for me to continue.

I swallowed. "I looked inside the chest. Whose things are those?"

My mother and grandmother met each other's gaze, seeming to silently communicate. Then my mother spoke. "The items in the chest were from our home in Illinois."

"Oh," I said, waiting for a few moments to see if she would elaborate. When she didn't, I asked, "Is that all there is?"

"Yes, your grandmother wasn't able to carry any more than that when we left the farm."

"Why did you leave?" I asked, looking from her to my grandmother, who sat silent.

"It was time," said my mother simply. Then she changed the subject. "Help your grandmother clean up the dishes. I've got some studying to do."

Pushing down the disappointment at being so close to an answer, I nodded.

Chapter Sixty-Six

September 1925

It was midmorning and Rose was finishing the farm chores in a leisurely manner. Actually, she was not paying any attention to the task at hand. Rather, her mind was racing as excitement grew within her and ideas followed.

Had it only been a few days since she realized she most likely would be able to provide for her children after she became a widow? To cook and bake in a well-stocked kitchen again thrilled her tremendously. Now, she thought, I just need to locate the path that will take me to a job that will pay enough for the three of us to live on.

As she continued with her chores, Rose's mind made lists, which included every person she knew who might know of potential cooking positions. As she finished her chores, she admitted to herself she might be forced to cook in some rich people's homes. There was no good reason for her to be opposed to such a work setting. She had run this home and overseen Cook, although she had always felt like they were working together. In some homes, the mistress looked down on all hired help. Rose believed that any situation in which a person or some people were considered better than others is not a Christian home. She shook her head. No good reason to fix her thoughts on that.

It was approaching noon and empty hours stretched out ahead. Rose was certain she could not bear another afternoon holed up out here all alone, when she felt such overwhelming excitement and a bundle of other emotions. She might simply burst if she didn't do something to help herself toward getting a job. She desperately needed to release some of the spirited energy pressing at her seams.

That decided things for Rose. She was a-going to town to see Suzy. No matter what the issue, her dear friend always had a helpful idea or two.

Rose removed her white muslin apron and looked down at her dress. Composed of a lightweight, blue, cotton fabric, the frock fitted to her small waist and draped perfectly to her ankles. The sleeves covered her elbows, a personal preference of hers. While she had a local girl sew her and the children's clothing, she had a professional dressmaker sew her this dress, along with a few others. The dressmaker had clearly understood color. The first time Rose saw herself in the bright periwinkle-blue fabric, she had to blink back tears, as she saw for a moment her young bride self from so long ago. The dress had a flattering oversized collar that paired nicely with the dress color. It would do just fine for her trip to town.

Her decision to go to town now firm, Rose quickly washed and dried her coffee cup and a small breakfast plate and put them in the only cupboard containing a few dishes. Her attention shifted to the loaves of bread she had baked the day before. She picked out the most perfectly shaped loaf. Usually, she would wrap the loaf in a towel and tie it with string. But she had some decorative paper she'd been saving for something special. "Well," she said out loud, "my best friend Suzy is very, very special."

After wrapping and tying the bread and placing it in a basket, Rose ventured to the deep part of her pantry and chose a small jar of peach preserves to go with the bread. At that moment, it hit her that she had almost forgotten these many jars of food put up over the past few years. Apricots, cherries, strawberries, peaches, beets, green beans, peas, pickled beets, and other fruits and vegetables from her garden lined the shelves. She even had some cured and pickled meat. It would have been a disaster to forget all these canned goods. That night or the next morning would give her adequate time to pack all of this up.

In the barn a few minutes later with her riding cape over her dress, Rose hitched the chestnuts and got into her carriage, then signaled them to head out. As she rode the buggy toward town, Rose's excitement elevated.

When she arrived at her friend's house, she tied up the team, grabbed the basket and headed toward the rear of Suzy's home, where she tapped on the small window in the back door. Within moments, Suzy came into view and began walking slowly toward the door. When the light of recognition filled her eyes, though, her friend hurried over and yanked the door open, exclaiming, "Rosie, what a great surprise."

She smiled and gave Suzy the basket. "Some fresh baked bread and the peach preserves you like."

Suzy beamed as she took the basket and set it on the kitchen counter. "Thank you! Come on in and have a seat in the parlor."

Once they reached Suzy's parlor, she gestured for Rose to sit in one of the beautiful, burgundy, brocade-covered winged back chairs.

When both were seated comfortably, Rose's cape hanging in the closet, Suzy asked, "Why this surprise visit?" Despite the twinkle in Suzy's eyes, both women felt the seriousness of the visit.

Rose replied, "I've come to believe I will be able to care for the children and me when I'm widowed. To accomplish this, I truly need your ideas, opinions and support, my dear friend."

Suzy bounced forward in anticipation, "Don't keep me in the dark, Rosie, what will you do? You and I have picked each other's brains and discussed a plethora of ways you could manage to support yourself and found not a one that might be possible, so tell me, tell me."

Rose gave Suzy a mischievous half smile that proved to heighten the other woman's excitement. After a few moments, Rose calmly replied, "I'll be a cook."

Suzy's eyes widened as she took in her friend's quiet proclamation. She immediately replied, "Of course, why didn't we think of it sooner? You are a wonderful cook. When I think about those pies and desserts you make, my mouth literally waters." Suzy sat more upright in her chair, pressed her palms together and looked directly and deeply into Rose's eyes. "Don't keep me waiting, tell me. Exactly where have you procured a cooking job?"

Rose looked down and began studying the large pink and red flowers woven into the parlor carpet. She felt ashamed she didn't have a job, nor had she even gone looking for one.

Watching her friend's reaction, Suzy said a bit too loudly, "Silly me, that's what we're a-doing today."

Rose looked up at Suzy with grateful eyes and replied, "Well, I was hoping..."

"Don't say another word," interrupted Suzy. "Let's get busy. I'll go get paper and something to write with so we can keep our ideas straight." Her friend got up and bustled out of the room, returning with paper and pencils.

The two went to the dining room table, pulling two wooden chairs next to each other.

As Rose sat, she said, "I think we do best when we actually put our heads together."

Suzy chuckled and grabbed her friend's hand and gave it a gentle squeeze. Then she asked. "Rose, where do you want to work? You know, in a perfect world? A restaurant? At someone's home? An institution like a hospital?"

Rose replied, "I've been thinking about this for days. I loved my own kitchen and working with Cook, however, I truly doubt it would be as enjoyable as my kitchen if I were to work in a home. Usually in a home, there is one single bedroom for each servant. Could the three of us survive in one small room? Would an employer allow it?"

"Good points," said Suzy. "There is an upside working for a family. Most folks are good, decent people. And the way you cook, they would keep you forever. Also, many who have cooks are in town, so you'd have no need for your horses or carriage."

Rose immediately bristled at the last comment. "I'm not getting rid of my transportation, my sanity. Sometimes I hitch them up and just go for a quiet, peaceful ride with myself."

"It's alright, things will work out." Suzy assured her. "We're just beginning the search. A private home doesn't seem really promising for several reasons, like where would you board your horses? But we'll keep it on our list."

"Beggars can't be choosers," replied Rose as she blinked back tears.

"Aww, come on, Rosie, like I said, we're just getting started. What about the restaurant in town, and there's food served in the lodge now. Even the old bakery could use your talent."

"All good possibilities," replied Rose. "We might want to put the lodge first on the list, as it shouldn't be hard for them to include a couple of rooms for us to live in."

"Yes, yes," said Suzy as she put a large number one on the paper next to that option.

"Oh, Lordy," interjected Rose. "What is the time?"

Suzy squinted as she looked across the room at the beautifully carved, old grandfather clock, which Rose knew to be one of her prized possessions. "Around 2:30. Are you hungry?"

"I'm really too excited to be hungry, but I need to go fetch the children at school. If Richard prefers, he can go home, but I want to bring Blanche here. I decided to visit spur of the moment, so they don't know I'm not home."

The word home stuck in her throat for a moment as she stood. "If it is about 2:30, I have plenty of time to reach the school." She went to retrieve her cape from the closet. "I'll come back directly with the two or three of us, if that's okay with you."

"That's more than okay," said Suzy. "I'll make us something to eat. Anything your children don't like?"

"These last few years have been difficult," Rose said. "Both learned to eat whatever was prepared."

Suzy exclaimed, "My best and dearest friend, I truly had no idea there might have been a shortage of food for you. I'll feed you all well."

Rose smiled. "Thank you, Suzy."

As she left the house to gather her horses and buggy, Rose's heart brimmed with gratitude at having such a thoughtful and loving friend.

Chapter Sixty-Seven

On my eighteenth birthday, my mother told me she felt I deserved an explanation about her father. As I sat there waiting for her to speak, I felt a mix of anticipation and trepidation.

She proceeded to tell me how her father loved her dearly—that she was his princess—and that he was very good to her, no matter what terrible things others might say about him.

"My father played games with me and bought me a pony and showed me how to ride it. He wasn't like other fathers who had children so they could have farm workers. He didn't make me work. Instead, he spent time with me and really listened to what I had to say. He loved me and made me happy."

When she said this, I saw a softer side of my mother I'd never seen before. I waited, curious, expecting to hear more. Afterall, I was essentially an adult. Surely, she could finally tell me the secret.

But that's all she said. As I sat there waiting for more, I wondered, should I ask something? And if so, what would that be? I recalled at that moment how I had asked several questions when I was four about my grandfather and how he had died. Those questions were met with silence and a change of subject.

I cleared my throat and opened my mouth to speak, although I had no idea what I would utter. The look of apprehension in her eyes turned to relief when I asked, "Was my Grandfather Emil a tall man, like Pop?"

My mother smiled. "Yes, he was. Although Pop is a bit taller."

Hoping that she would add to that, I waited, but when she said no more, I wracked my brain for something else that felt safe. Finally, I asked, "The farm sounds very nice. Did you like playing outdoors?"

Another smile from my mother, who didn't give out smiles freely. "Yes, I had free reign to roam wherever I wanted on the farm, which was one of the biggest in the county. Your grandfather hung me a swing from the branches of an old maple."

What happened to that large farm? I couldn't help but wonder. I waited for her to add more, but she didn't. Instead, she said, "I'm going to get dinner started now." Then she left my room, leaving me with a multitude of questions. It became clear at that moment that I was to hear nothing more of the secret. What came through more than ever was the idea that I should also bury what little information I had about the secret in a deep, dark, obscure location.

Chapter Sixty-Eight

Blanche burst into the parlor straight to Suzy, who threw her arms around the little girl and exclaimed, “I’m so happy to see you. It has been such a long time.”

“Richard sends his love. He plans to visit soon,” said Blanche.

Suzy immediately asked, “Is there food for him at home?”

Rose smiled softly. “You know how important my children are to me. Would I allow either to go hungry?”

“I’m sorry, Rose. Silly me. Of course, you left food for him. However, we’ll have leftovers when we finish eating here. I’ll just pack them up, and you’ll take them home.”

Suzy unentangled herself from Blanche’s embrace and smiled at the girl. “Young lady, please go wash up, and we’ll eat.”

As soon as Blanche left the room, Suzy said, “I had a terrific idea while you were gone. It’s much better than anything we wrote down.”

Before she could share her idea, however, Blanche returned and announced, "All washed up."

“We’re going to eat in the kitchen where it’s nice and cozy,” said Suzy, leading the way.

Both Rose and Blanche sat down at the kitchen table while Suzy filled bowls with a delicious smelling soup and carried them to the table. Then she sat and the three of them joined hands and said grace. It was quiet as they started eating their soup.

Before long, the silence was broken when Blanche began chattering almost nonstop, Rose and Suzy joining in at times. When they finished the soup, Suzy handed out sandwiches, and they even laughed a few times.

Then Suzy, who completed her meal before the other two, got up and poured cream into a bowl and beat it until it became light and fluffy. She slowly added in sugar, then took out delicate, glass dessert dishes and placed large peach halves into each bowl. After drizzling on sweet nectar, she topped each bowl with whipped cream and set them before Blanche and Rose.

"This looks so yummy," said Blanche, who quickly dove in.

Rose took a bite and nodded in agreement. All three quickly ate the delicious fruit with gusto.

When they had finished, Suzy rose to clear the dishes, but Blanche stopped her. "I'll do the dishes, Aunt Suzy. I'm plenty old enough. I do them at home lots."

Suzy looked to Rose, who said, "Just remember these aren't the old, cracked dishes we've been eating off of. Be careful with them."

Blanche stood a bit taller. "I'll make them sparkle and shine."

"Thank you," said Suzy. "I know you will."

Rose, now impatient to hear her friend's idea, took Suzy's arm and quickly walked her to the parlor.

After both took their respective chairs, Rose urged, "What's the good job idea?"

"You know that cute restaurant just outside of town across from the hospital? Well, it seems the owners were having such a hard time of it, they disappeared in the middle of the night and have never been seen since. They left most everything in the restaurant. And rumor is there's a little apartment in the back."

Rose took interest when the apartment was mentioned but said what came to mind first. "So, I would cook in a place that has a poor reputation?"

"Everything you make is delicious. Word will get around. It'll be perfect."

"Hold on now," said Rose. "Do we know who owns the building, the contents, even the land? How much money will they ask me for? Is there enough space for my horses and buggy?"

Suzy stood abruptly from her seat on the couch. "Those answers are at the courthouse, and anyone can go in and find out." She squinted at the grandfather clock. "And it just so happens the courthouse is still open. Let's go get some answers."

Rose glanced at the clock. "We'll get into the courthouse only minutes before it closes. Shouldn't we wait and go another day?"

Suzy headed to the closet for their capes. "We're a-going now."

Rose knew her friend was right. She truly didn't have any time to spare when it came to figuring out her future. Taking her cape from Suzy's outstretched hand, she shrugged it on, then went into the kitchen and announced, "We're going to the courthouse. Would you like to come?"

Blanche shook her head with great energy, her numerous curls bouncing as she did so.

Rose gave her daughter a serious look. "You must stay in the house. Do not answer the door should someone come knocking. And complete your schoolwork. When you're done, Suzy has many wonderful books in the parlor."

With a pout and a whine, the child retorted, "You know I hate to read. But can I look at all the books that have photos?"

Suzy had just entered the room and said, "Of course you can look at anything in the parlor. You're always so careful."

Rose went to give Blanche a peck on the cheek, and the two friends left and climbed into Rose's carriage and headed to the courthouse.

As they made their way into the heart of town, Suzy said, "I've heard that Mazie, who runs the records office, stays late if a person is a-needing some information. Rumor has it she's very helpful. No matter what a body needs, Mazie finds it or at least something related to what a person needs. Also, she spends her lunch hours visiting the shops and businesses along Main Street. Consequently, she talks to courthouse patrons passing on the current gossip. So, they all think she's wonderful. No one has ever said she was cruel or hurtful. She just reports things as they are. I heard her myself when Emil was her topic. She related facts as she knew them when he was arrested, denied change of venue, and other such stuff."

Rose slowed the chestnuts as they approached the courthouse. "Seems to me she has a good thing going getting paid to chat."

"From what I heard, when she was hired about eight years ago, the salary she agreed to was a mere pittance. That probably goes a long way with all the councilmen."

They reached the courthouse then and both women hopped out of the buggy. After Rose tethered the horses to a hitching post, they climbed the stairs to the imposing building and pulled open the large door and entered.

"The records office is right over there," said Suzy, pointing to a nearby open door.

They went over and entered. As they did so, Mazie appeared behind the counter and gave them a big smile. "Welcome ladies. May I help you?" Then she turned to Rose's companion and said, "I believe you to be Suzy Saunders. You live here in town, correct?"

When Suzy nodded, Mazie turned her attention to Rose. "You look so familiar, but I can't quite place you."

Rose returned the woman's smile and said, "Our paths have crossed at church. I'm Rose Fricker."

Recognition sparked in Mazie's eyes. "You're Emil Fricker's wife."

Rose held her head high. "Yes."

Mazie's expression softened, and she seemed to radiate sincerity and kindness. "How are you and your children, my dear?"

"Some days seem unbearable and others not so bad," Rose answered quite honestly.

The woman didn't reply but gave her a slow nod. Then she said, "Well, you didn't come here to chat. What can I do for you two?"

After Rose explained what she needed, Mazie got right to work, pulling out paperwork and relaying what she found.

Suzy, standing ready with paper and pencil, wrote down all the pertinent information regarding the abandoned building. As she did so, Rose read much of each document, at one point apologizing. "I'm sorry, we know it's past closing time. We're hurrying. I don't want to miss anything important."

"Nonsense," replied Mazie. "It's my pleasure to gather your information. Of course, now I'm curious. Are you planning on opening that restaurant?"

Rose hesitated, feeling the enormity of her plan. Then she said, "I'm sure going to try. I'll be the proprietress, chief cook, and bottle washer."

"I'll bet you cook just as well as you bake. I'll never forget the rhubarb pie you brought to the church get together. It's the best tasting pie I've ever had. Words just can't explain how delicious that piece of pie was."

Rose was embarrassed by the praise, however, it also felt good to hear. "Thank you. I love to bake and cook. It's hard work, but I enjoy it. You know, Emil's lawyers took everything, the farm, our home, all the livestock, even the china, cut glass, and silver. I need to put a roof over my children, and feed them, too. That building has a couple of rooms in the back that we can live in."

Mazie said quite seriously, "We don't know each other, but if I can help in any way, tell me. I want to be your first customer when you open the place. I'm going to try every one of your pies."

"Thank you," said Rose. "Your kind words have given me more courage to make my plan work."

Mazie responded by moving from behind the counter and giving her a gentle hug. That startled Rose, who thought hugs were for family and best friends only. Her parents, both of staunch Swiss German lineage, rarely, if ever, gave hugs. Usually, such affection was reserved for infants and small children. However, as Mazie continued to hug her, Rose didn't pull away. Human touch was nice, she decided.

They said their goodbyes then and armed with all the necessary information recorded on paper, headed back to Suzy's house.

While Blanche gathered her things a few minutes later, Rose quietly said, "I'll come to see you in the morning after I see those worthless lawyers and get my cafe."

"You are such a good person, Rosie. You deserve a happy life. I'll be a-praying for you."

"Thank you, my very smart friend," said Rose as Blanche bustled into the room, her schoolbooks in hand.

They took their leave, waving to Suzy as they made their way to the place Rose had called home for more than 15 years, but would soon be vacating.

Chapter Sixty-Nine

Except with babies, my mother and grandmother rarely showed physical affection. When I was growing up, I felt the absence of that—sometimes profoundly—which was why I told myself I would be different with my own children, and in many ways I was.

At the same time, though, I found myself repeating generational patterns. I wonder now if I had known about my mother's and grandmother's struggles—of what they had endured during their lifetimes—would I have treated them both differently? Would I have treated my children differently?

Often it seems we don't realize the generational fallout—the profound significance of what and who came before us and what they endured—until later in life. At that point, we can't turn back the clock knowing what we know, but we can change what we do, think and feel moving forward.

The more I discover what happened all those years ago, the more it explains the woman my mother became. She was a harsh disciplinarian, shaped no doubt by the consequences of her father's choices. She did not use physical punishment but rather withheld privileges for extended periods of time. No matter what punishment she doled out, she always told me the same thing.

"We had you because we wanted and loved you. This restriction is for your own good because we love you."

Though I didn't see it then, I see now, so many years removed from girlhood, the many ways my mother did indeed show her love for me. Knowing what I know now—that she had been a carefree child until horrifying events trampled her girlhood—I realize what occurred could have caused her to withdraw from the world, and yet she didn't.

At the same time, I can't help but think about the generational fallout stemming from the actions of one man—the ripple effect created. From a clinical standpoint as a therapist, it's clear that alcoholism played a significant part in all of this. It's also clear to me there were personality disorders at play. The obsessed Emil I read about was much different than the father my mother described to me.

I felt the effects of a secret I knew so little about in so many ways over my lifetime. The pain and suffering borne out of one man's choices is overwhelming—nearly suffocating. My hope by writing this book and telling my family's story is that I've broken the cycle. That my children, grandchildren, great grandchildren and their children can rest and move forward without a secret looming over them.

Chapter Seventy

It was early morning when Rose awoke to the sound of Blanche's little bare feet on the wood flooring. Within moments, the child and her head of curls bounced into her mother's bedroom. Rose's heart warmed at a sight she hadn't seen in months—a look of excitement on her little girl's face.

"Mama, Mama, you still gonna get us a new home close to the hospital near town? You gonna do that today? Are you? Are you?"

Rose laughed. "Goodness sakes, girl, you're a-bouncing so fast I can't rightly see you."

Blanche stopped jumping and carefully climbed up onto her mother's bed. She sat down very close to Rose, her small legs tucked under her body as she rested a hand on her mother's shoulder. At the simple gesture, Rose's heart brimmed with love. Staying toasty under the bedlinens, she pulled her daughter close. "Yes, Missy, I'm a-going to try to get us a restaurant and a place for us to rest our tired heads. All in the same building."

Blanche's face became animated again. "I just knew you would, Mama. You take good care of us. How could you sleep? After I woke up and came in from the buggy and put my nightshirt on, I was just too excited to sleep right away."

It was then Rose realized how good and rested she felt. As soon as she had gotten into bed last night, she had fallen asleep. Usually, the feeling of impending gloom and tragedy cloaked her at bedtime, making it difficult to rest. These wretched feelings usually followed her into her dreams, but today they were totally gone, and her heart felt almost light. She was grateful as she took hold of her daughter's small hand and said, "Let's thank the Lord for this help," and then they prayed together.

Rose directed her children to dress quickly, and she planned to do the same. She went to her closet and began looking carefully at each frock. Shaking her head, she called out, "Blanche, please come help me."

Again, her little girl bounced into her mother's bedroom, her curls doing double-time. "Yes, Mama, how can I help you, my queen." The child had an impish smile accompanying her question.

"You know where I'm a-going this morning. What would be best to wear?"

Her daughter's eyes gleamed as she replied, "I know the perfect outfit to wear."

Rose cleared her throat and said, "Now, my sweetie, remember, I'm no fashion plate, and I don't take to wearing outrageous things."

With a large grin on her face, Blanche said, "Oh, dear, is my Mama fearful of the clothing choices I'll make? Just look at what I put together before using words like outrageous. Besides, you have nothing outrageous in your closet."

Rose already wore her undergarments, so Blanche took a crisp white blouse from her closet and handed it to her mother. "Please put that on."

Next, the child plucked a navy blue, long and lean skirt from her mother's clothing and handed it to her. Together they adjusted the items until both were satisfied. Rose looked at her reflection in the mirror and was surprised at the businesslike effect of the clothing.

Blanche then handed Rose her black high button shoes, increasing her height by some three inches. Thinking she was done dressing, she exclaimed, "My, my, Blanche, you arranged the perfect outfit for me to go meet with lawyers. I'm truly grateful for your assistance, but now I must prepare the oatmeal for you and your brother and get you both to school."

"Mama, we're not done a-dressing you."

"Oh, goodness, we must head downstairs soon," said Rose, who called out, "Richard, please go down to the kitchen and prepare the oatmeal for you and your sister."

Richard came and paused in her doorway, carrying books in his arms. "Sure, Mom, anything special I need to do with the oats?"

Rose noted his books and said, "We're not keeping you from finishing your schoolwork, are we?"

"No, you know me, all was done last night."

"Just heat the oats in water like I showed you, and when they're tender, you can add a splash or two of milk."

Richard nodded and ambled down the stairs in his usual thoughtful manner as Rose and Blanche turned their attention to completing the task at hand.

As Rose met her daughter's eyes, she saw mischievousness. "What else could I possibly wear? I'm all dressed and today is unseasonably warm. No need for a coat."

Blanche turned to her mother's bureau and pulled out a scarf Rose had received as a gift but had never worn because it shrieked of the color red.

"Missy, you expecting me to wear something that bright? It could cause a body to go blind," stuttered Rose. No longer able to maintain a serious demeanor, a large smile broke out over her face. "Pray tell, where would you have me put this? My head?"

Appearing put out, Blanche said, "Why, your neck, of course."

Rose took the silky scarf and tied it loosely around her neck, then moved to the looking glass to see.

"Mama, I think you look beautiful. What do you think of the red scarf now?"

Rose took her child's hand and smiled at the two of them in the mirror. She gave Blanche's hand a squeeze, and said, "I look perfect. Just perfect. Now let's go downstairs. Your brother should have the oatmeal ready."

A few minutes later, Rose and her children were settled in the buggy heading to town. Richard had a somber look on his face. Just before leaving the farm, he had told her, "I'll drive, Mom, so you can relax or think."

"No, siree, young man, this is one drive to town that I'm controlling," Rose had replied.

Now as they bumped along in the buggy, Rose realized the error and apologized. "I'm sorry I spoke so sharply to you, Richard. I appreciate your help. I'm just nervous about exactly what I'll say to those lawyers. There will be three or four of them and only one of me. Getting that restaurant means everything to us. It's our survival."

"It's okay, you'll do fine," said Richard.

When they were a few minutes from school, Rose said to Blanche, "Little girl, I think you chose the very best clothing for me today. When I saw how the red scarf looked, I actually felt the power it gave me. It was like every part of my body became super strong. I do admit the scarf looks wonderful. I think anyone I encounter will be aware of the strength radiating from me and my scarf. I'll get whatever we need today."

"You'll get nothing," said Richard in his soft, slow drawl, "if you don't slow down. We'll all be a pile of smashed junk and won't need a thing."

Rose quickly released the hold she had on the reins, signaling the horses to slow down. "Goodness gracious, how true. We'll all be history if I keep going so fast." The horses pulling the buggy returned to a reasonable gait.

They arrived in town well before the first school bell. Rose had stopped the pair of chestnuts in front of the main entrance. Blanche gathered her things, gave her mother a peck on the cheek, and her eyes twinkling, said, "You're the strongest woman in the whole world, Mama."

As Richard descended the carriage, he said, "You'll get the building. You're invincible. You're my mom, you know. See you later." Then in almost a whisper, added, "I love you."

After watching her children enter the school building, she started her horses with a flick of the reins.

The next thing Rose knew, she was seated in the outer office of Emil's defense lawyers. At the moment, she was alone in the luxurious space filled with furniture upholstered in plush velvet and rich-looking tapestry. If Rose remembered correctly, the enormous rug covering the floor was imported from Europe. Exquisite oil paintings adorned each wall, and several tables built of generous pieces of wood filled the room. The surfaces of each table gleamed from polish—not a single scratch or scrape visible. Rose knew the home she was losing was elegant, especially the dining room, but the understated elegance of her home did not hold a candle to this opulent space. She ran her hand along the satiny cover of the pillow next to her on the settee where she sat.

Suddenly, an inner door burst open, and a man dressed in a gray business suit stepped into the room and came toward her. He held his hand out, and Rose stood and shook it. He introduced himself, but she didn't make out his name, as her heart was beating loudly from the shock of the door suddenly opening. In a few moments, however, her heart slowed to a more normal rate, and it was then she noted how calm she felt. Unlike the anxiety and fear she had expected, she felt keenly alert and mentally sharp. Observing the man's solemn face, she thought he did not look kind, but no evil was revealed there, either.

"Mrs. Fricker, please come with me to our inner conference room."

"Will it be just the two of us?" inquired Rose.

Rather than answering, he simply led her down a hallway past closed doors until they entered a room with chairs surrounding a large, elegant table.

Two men seated at one end of the table stood when she entered, both wearing what appeared to be forced half smiles. They were clothed in bland colored business suits, and the shorter of the two was bald. Both wore glasses and appeared to be in their fifties and sixties.

Rose thrust out her hand as she approached them. "I'm Rose Wilhelmina Jenny Fricker. Thank you for seeing me."

The two men appeared surprised at her forward manner, both reaching out and taking turns shaking her hand. Once they finished, the bald man motioned to a chair near them and said, "Please, Mrs. Fricker, have a seat." As she did so, the young man who had accompanied her took a seat as well.

After she settled in the chair, the other lawyer said, "We filed another stay of execution with the governor."

The bald man looked at his colleague, then met Rose's eyes and said, "I'm sure you know your husband has no money left to pay us, but we generously completed the request for a stay." After his pronouncement, he sat back and smiled like a cat that just swallowed a bird.

Angered by his condescending statement, Rose shifted in her chair.

Immediately the man next to him said, "We've tried over and over to help Emil, despite his inability to pay Mrs. Fricker. Do you have funds to cover our costs?"

That question boiled her anger over. She sat up straighter and said, "Pay you? When not one of you has done anything to help him. You didn't pursue a change of venue in time and knew that if he were tried here, it would become a witch hunt. You never spent any energy showing the jurors what that harlot, Mrs. Nungesser, was capable of. That much of what she said was not the truth. You didn't tell of her scheming and setting up others to take responsibility for her wrongdoing. Not to mention how she..."

Rose stopped. "I'm not here to discuss my husband. What I'm here to discuss is how you and the other lawyers in your firm have left me penniless with two children to clothe, feed, and shelter. I need financial help from you. Consider it my portion of Emil's estate."

"Now, Mrs.—," started the bald man.

"Stop," she replied. "I plan to explain everything."

Ignoring Rose, the other man said, "We don't give to charity cases, so you must leave."

"If I leave without a way to feed my children, I'll sue you for attempted murder and make certain the *Highland News Leader* gets all of the information," replied Rose.

"Please stop talking and listen quietly," he replied, but the bald man held up a hand and said, "Please, ma'am, excuse his bad manners, and say what it is you seek."

Rose cleared her throat and continued. "You know after the day I become a widow, my children and I must leave our only home. This business of yours actually owns my home, all my livestock and land, including all the homesteads. You even helped yourselves to my crystal, silver, and dishes, and your representative even confiscated my jewelry. I'm surprised my undergarments were left for me."

The bald man cleared his throat. "Perhaps some coffee before we continue." He motioned to the young man, who stood and left the room.

While he was gone, Rose and the two men sat in total silence until the younger man reappeared carrying an ornate silver tray with a beautiful matching creamer and sugar bowl. The cups and saucers on the tray were made of the finest porcelain. While Rose studied the tray and what it held, he placed a cup filled with dark aromatic coffee in front of her, along with sugar and cream. Rose poured cream into her coffee, then stirred it with a delicate, sterling silver spoon. She took a sip and smiled at the young man. "Delicious, how did you brew it so quickly?"

He smiled back and replied, "I started it just before you arrived. Thank you."

All were drinking coffee when Rose resumed. "I'm a very good cook, and I've been called a superior baker. There's an abandoned restaurant at the edge of town, and it is for sale at a real bargain price. I need that building and the entire lot it sits upon. So, what I'm asking is that you purchase the restaurant and sign it over to me. Then I'll be able to feed my children and me, and we will have shelter. There are rooms and a complete bath at the back of the building."

"How do you know this place will prove successful? And the edge of town, not a plethora of customers out there," said the bald man.

"I've no doubt I'll make enough to pay for our needs, because I'm a really good cook. Many, if not all, of the people in this county know my name in association with pies and delectable deserts. Being directly across from the hospital, I expect many of the employees to enjoy my food. I've heard that most who visit patients are forced to eat the hospital cafeteria food that has a poor reputation. The visitors are often unable to go into town and must eat there or go hungry."

The bald man asked, "I'm curious as to why you need the entire lot."

Rose smiled. "My transportation is a buggy and two horses, and they require space. I also must provide a place where customers can hitch their horses and put their cars while eating."

The bald man's colleague piped in then. "Do you know how much or approximately how much money the bank expects to fetch for the entire properties?"

Rose stood and pushed the small stack of papers she'd brought with her toward the men. "Everything you'll see in the papers was copied directly from official records on file at town hall."

"Ma'am, will you please go to the outer office and give us time to read the papers and discuss everything?" asked the bald man then.

"Of course," answered Rose as she started toward the waiting room in a gracious manner.

"I'll fetch you as soon as we make a decision," said the young man.

After only a few minutes, the young man was guiding her back to the conference room. As soon as she sat in the chair, the bald man informed Rose, "Our unanimous decision is to deny your request."

Rose sat stunned, not so much because of the denial, but because of the satisfied smirk on the man's face as he delivered the news.

For a few moments, she drew her attention inward. The anger welling within her was enormous and overwhelming. She knew when she replied, her words must be chosen carefully. She mustn't allow her rage to be released.

The three men were staring at her waiting for a reply, and Rose complied. "That would be foolish for you to do. I've lived here all my life—my parents, brothers and sisters, as well. We're all held in high esteem."

"Excuse me, I doubt..." started the other older man.

"Quiet," Rose interrupted him. "You men have done a lot of talking. It's my turn now. I have also written poetry for many years, and the *Highland News Leader* has published my poems. I have lifelong friends working there. How do you think this headline would look? 'Widow and children starving due to cruel lawyers.' The article could include how greedy this firm is and how your only concern is making money. You all know Emil had a small fortune; much of it passed on from his father and grandfather. The Frickers worked hard to make Highland what it is today. Furthermore—"

The bald man interrupted, "Please stop, Mrs. Fricker, I'm sure we can do what you need. We'll complete the papers right now and file them in the morning."

"Thank you. Let's begin the papers now. I would like them filed today, so that the deeds for the land and building are in my name as soon as possible. I can wait while you take care of the paperwork and do the filing."

Without a word, the three men produced forms and began writing.

***

It wasn't until Rose was in her carriage and holding the reins an hour later that she realized the enormity of what she had accomplished. She was now the sole proprietress of the building and the land. Without direction, the horses had started for home, but Rose said out loud, "Suzy." She then turned the chestnuts in the direction of her friend's home. She could hardly wait to share the events of the morning.

When she knocked on her friend's back door, Suzy pulled it open and exclaimed, "I'm so glad to see you. I was beginning to worry. It's after noon. Did they make you wait? Tell me, I'm really excited. You're not crying, so some good must have happened."

When Suzy stopped talking, Rose said, "I'll tell you every morsel of what happened. But first, could I sit down?"

Suzy motioned to the kitchen table. "Oh, gracious, I'm not being polite. Please sit. Could I get you something to eat? Coffee or tea?"

Rose went to pull out a chair. "Something to eat would be wonderful. I was so excited this morning that I didn't eat my oatmeal. I'd love some tea, and do you have any of those little pastries from the bakery?"

"I've got some chocolate cake. How about that and some tea?"

"That would be perfect," said Rose, who had removed her cape and bonnet and set it on the chair next to her.

"Okay, lady, I'm getting your tea and cake, so start talking," said Suzy.

"I left the lawyers offices with everything I need."

"More specifics, please. You know I always need to hear it all."

"I was so nervous and scared when I first walked through their door, but I walked out of it with every single thing on the list."

"You, Rosie, afraid," she said. "I've always known you to be the strongest woman I know."

"At first, I forgot that about myself and just listened to what they had to say. I must have looked deaf and dumb to them. There were three of them, by the way. One young, and two that looked to be fifty or sixty. The fools started out by telling me that Emil was out of money, like I didn't know that. They justified everything they did like the change of venue and not checking out Mrs. Nungesser before her testimony. They were defensive and at the same time condescending. The more they talked, the less fear I felt and the bigger my anger became. Once I had apprised them of all my needs from our list, they seemed to reject everything."

Rose spent the better part of an hour telling a rapt Suzy every little detail, such as what the men were wearing and about the highly decorated offices. She also drank every drop of the tea and ate every morsel of the large slice of decadent chocolate cake. As she ran her fork over the plate, she said, "Suzy, you've always baked well, but this cake is fantastic, really delicious. I'll have to have you do some baking when the restaurant opens."

Suzy was beaming as she said, "Thank you, Rose, that means so much coming from you, the queen of desserts in this county."

"I'm not any sort of queen, but I do make a good pie or two."

"Oh, Rose, you are always so modest. Please finish telling me all."

Rose continued describing her morning. When she began talking about going to the courthouse, Suzy interrupted, saying, "The legal work and papers for buying are already done?"

Rose gave her friend a big smile and pulled the deed out of her cape pocket. "It says free and clear that I, Rose Wilhelmina Fricker, am the proud owner of the restaurant and land."

"My dear, dear friend, I'm so happy for you," Suzy squealed. "You are so deserving. Why not call it a cafe with you baking, cooking and running the place. It'll be a great success." Suzy paused, her expression becoming serious. "Oh, dear, I've never thought how hard this may be on you. The physical work alone is tremendous. Have you thought of that?"

"Too late to worry now. I'm the sole proprietress. The good news is I have control over when I'm open. And if the cafe is a success, I can hire some help."

Suzy said quite earnestly, "You know I'll help if you're ever in a pinch, or even a couple of days a week to get started. I've always wanted to waitress."

"Thank you, Suzy, you could help me determine the best foods to serve and maybe teach me how to manage money and set up the books. Maybe you'd make up the menus. Could you start on some of that in the next few days? I want to open my cafe as soon as possible."

"Of course, I'm here to help any way I can. How does the building look? Lots of damage, or does it just need a good cleaning?"

"I've never been inside, but I did take a quick look through the windows before my meeting with the lawyers. Not surprisingly, it looks a bit dirty. I do know there's indoor water and plumbing and even gas ovens. One of the building's best things I saw was the lamps on the walls. I'll be able to do more work at night. The furnace is probably coal."

Suzy sat perfectly still and stared at her friend as she continued.

"I'm really hoping all those services work well. Guess I could go to the companies and see what to do to get them working. I'll gather the children from school and take them to the cafe."

"At first the cafe sounded like something different and fun, but now I'm frightened for you," said Suzy. "It's so much work, and more importantly, responsibility. Plus, your young ones depend on you for everything."

Unfazed, Rose continued, "I'm pretty sure the gas and electric companies will require money from me. The lawyers gave me a small amount when this nightmare started that they put in a bank account in my name. I've been taking money out every week, but there's some left. It's enough to pay for what's necessary for the water and others. Suzy, do you know how much they'll ask for? You know Emil always did this kind of stuff. I'm really lost here."

"I wish I could help," said a concerned Suzy. "I have an accountant who takes care of all money matters."

"Oh, well," replied Rose. "I'll leave a small amount in the bank account and take the rest out to get everything working or fix what's broken."

Suzy had a half smile on her face when she said, "After you collect Blanche and Richard from school, they can come home with me, and you can finish paying those folks."

"Thank you," said Rose.

"I'll make supper for us all and Blanche can help. Richard too if I need anything from my cellar."

Rose felt overwhelmed then by gratitude. "Thank you, dear friend, I couldn't have done this without you."

"Oh, sure you could have," said Suzy. "You're the wisest, strongest, kindest person I know. But I'm glad I could be here to help."

"I don't know about kind," said Rose after a few moments. "I've had a lot of troubling thoughts and feelings I haven't shared with anyone."

"You can tell me. What's troubling you?"

Rose sighed. "I want to live with a heart of love, but I'm so angry. At everyone who found Emil guilty and sentenced him to hang. I'm really filled with rage and even want to hurt the townspeople that keep passing untrue gossip. They make up outrageous stuff that's all lies. It doesn't hurt me, but Blanche and Richard have been wounded deeply. Needless to say, those lawyers feed my fire of anger often. I'm praying to release and forgive but it's so hard. Sometimes I think Emil will pay for his transgressions when he dies in a few weeks, but despite everything, I still love him. The worst, most awful part is bearing my guilt. At times, I'm certain I caused the pain that others have."

"How on earth could you bear any responsibility?" asked Suzy as she took Rose's hand and held it.

"If only I'd spoken up when Emil came home filled with the drink acting mean and cruel to everyone he encountered. I feel so guilty for not even trying. I should have taken my children to my father's home to live right after the first time Emil started drinking too much and started acting so cruelly. I'm responsible for everything. I'm continuing to pray for all involved and ask for forgiveness."

"Stop!" said Suzy. "You're a good, loving person. No one alone caused all the mayhem."

Rose took some deep breaths and said, "You're so right. That harlot also had a lot to do with this. She should be punished, too. But all I've heard over and over is 'poor girl, how will she survive?' Likely she'll survive by getting herself a third husband to manipulate." Rose frowned. "If only I insisted he stop going to his still and drinking himself silly."

"Now wait a minute," said Suzy, her voice becoming sterner. "You did all you could, but things were out of your control. I remember you coming well after dark one night, your lovely, wavy hair pouring over your shoulders and down your back. You said Emil had come home from the still looking for an argument. When you got here, you were mad as a wet hen but also frightened. The fear was so strong, I could see it almost surrounding you. You must remember. It happened in late winter the year before Emil was arrested. You were freezing and hysterical when you arrived. I bundled you up and put you near the hearth and gave you a cup of hot tea. You sat a long, long time before saying something that chilled me to the bone. 'He might have killed me,' you told me. You said, 'He came home from the still and acted like he had drank lots more than ever before. I told him he must stay away from the still, and even more importantly, no more drinking. He looked at me and his face contorted into someone evil I didn't recognize. Then he came toward me and demanded I never speak to him that way again. But before he got to me, he fell down, his face twisted and ugly.' You said you ran from the house and hooked your horses onto the carriage in a heartbeat. I was thankful there was a full moon that night to help you find your way to town. You returned back home in the wee hours of the morning before he woke up."

Suzy stopped for a moment, then continued. "You said to me, 'Oh, Suzy, what will I do if he keeps doing this? I can't make things right—not when he keeps filling up on the Devil's drink. I fear for me and my children.'"

Chapter Seventy-One

"Fricker Came Around Before Supreme Court"

Highland News Leader, November 1925

Four reasons why Emil Fricker, convicted to be hung for the murder of John Nungesser, should be given a new trial, were presented to the Supreme Court at Springfield by his attorneys Saturday. After hearing the arguments, the case was taken under advisement, and a decision is expected at the December term.

Harold Bandy and Maurice Johnson represented the convicted man in the oral arguments and State's Attorney Brown argued for the state. Bandy, who occupied most of the time before the seven justices gave four reasons why, he said, Fricker should be granted a new trial.

1. The motive the state showed for the crime—that Fricker wanted Mrs. Nungesser to return to him—was prejudi-

cial.

2. The Circuit Court erred in not allowing a change in venue and not granting a new trial after the first one, resulting in a hanging.

3. The state's attorney made improper remarks to the jury, calling the defendant to task for demanding a jury trial.

4. The jury was not impartial; one juror having stated before the trial started that he would hang Fricker.

Note: This article has been reprinted verbatim from the original article, including any grammatical errors.

Chapter Seventy-Two

"Emil Fricker To Hang: Supreme Court Has Set April 16th As Day for Execution"

Highland News Leader, February 23, 1926

The long delayed decision of the Supreme Court in the case of Emil Fricker was received Thursday and upholds the verdict rendered by a jury in the Circuit court at Edwardsville and sets April 16th as the day for his execution. The complete decision covers eleven typewritten pages and comments on the four principal issues raised by Fricker's lawyers.

Fricker himself was not officially notified of the verdict yet Saturday, but Sheriff Deimling changed his location to a different part of the jail and he likely has been informed ere [before] this time.

In rendering the decision the Supreme Court makes the following mention, "In State vs. Reed, 53 Kan. 676, the court said, It has been universally conceded since David wrote to Joab, 'Get you Uriah in the forefront of the hottest battle, and retire ye from him, that he may be smitten and die, that the man who covets his neighbor's wife has a motive for desiring the death of his neighbor.' "

Continuing in the decision, the court quotes a statement made by Attorney Brown in his brief. It says, "Illicit connections may be proved to show a motive where the defendant is charged with murder of a husband whose existence was an obstacle to the complete gratification of the defendant's wrongful desires with the wife."

The decision in the Fricker case was rendered by Justice Frederic R. DeYoung. None of the justices dissented in making the decision unanimous. It is the first time that the Supreme Court has affirmed a death penalty from Madison County. Those hung were without necessary funds to appeal their judgments. The court has reversed at least two judgments for execution and those were in the Gavrilovich case.

If Fricker is executed on April 16, it will be the first hanging in Madison County since January 16, 1893. On that day, thirty-three years ago, Patrick Boyle paid with his life for the death of a stranger he met at Mitchell. They had a drink together, Boyle's associate having $1. Boyle killed the man and robbed him of the change.

There have been but few hangings in the county, considering the great number of murders.

Nikola Gavrilovich stood in the shadow of the gallows on three occasions but lost his mind while the charges pended and was sent to the hospital for the criminal insane at Chester. With financial assistance from countrymen, he fought the case through court. The men who were executed lacked necessary money to take appeals.

The late date for the execution of Fricker was also explained by Attorney Brown last week. His life cannot be taken until at least ten days after the convening of the next term of the Supreme Court on April 6th. The date fixed is the earliest possible day. The Criminal Code makes that provision to give doomed men a last chance to file a petition for a rehearing.

Four principal points were used by Fricker's lawyers to get him a new trial. They lost all of them. The lawyers contended that statements made by Attorney Brown were improper and prejudicial. The court held them to be proper arguments.

Change of venue on account of prejudice was another question. The defense filed six affidavits from persons about Highland. They were offset with thirty-seven from the county in general, being obtained in the more densely populated sections of the county.

Statements made by John Isert, a juror, were raised but the court held nothing irregular had occurred. Testimony on the illicit relations of Fricker and Mrs. Nungesser was attacked. The court admitted it as proper.

Note: This article has been reprinted verbatim from the original article, including any grammatical errors.

Chapter Seventy-Three

"Will File A Motion for A Rehearing"

Highland News Leader, March 2, 1926

Emil Fricker and his relatives and friends will continue the fight to save his life to the very last.

Next week a motion for rehearing will be filed in the Supreme Court at Springfield asking for a new trial. Attorney H. J. Bandy, one of three who represented Fricker at the trial, said that the motion for a rehearing is now in the course of preparation. Under rules of the court, the lawyers have until March 15th to file the petition, and it will probably be acted upon on April 6, the date the court will convene.

Through a reliable source it was learned also that relatives and a few others are making plans to go to Governor Len Small and ask that the judgment be commuted to life in the penitentiary. Just what points will be laid before the governor are unknown.

Note: This article has been reprinted verbatim from the original article, including any grammatical errors.

Chapter Seventy-Four

"Fricker Case Will Be Carried to Governor"

Highland News Leader, April 6, 1926

The Supreme Court meets at Springfield again today and it is likely that the application of Emil Fricker for a new trial will be one of the first questions to confront that august body. Attorneys for Fricker are not very hopeful of a favorable decision from the supreme court and we are told they have so informed Fricker and his relatives.

With that prospect in view, we understand the attorneys and relatives are preparing to carry the fight for his life to the State Board of Pardons and Paroles and will petition that body to commute the death sentence that now hangs over him to one of life imprisonment.

Note: This article has been reprinted verbatim from the original article, including any grammatical errors.

Chapter Seventy-Five

April 14, 1926

Rose realized she was shaking, and given a mirror, she was certain she was white as a ghost. Cloaked in the darkness of early morning, she had just left the jailhouse. She truly believed she'd never again see her husband alive. That thought brought tears to her eyes. More tears threatened to spill over as she saw Emil in her mind's eye. He was no longer the tall, confident person he once was. That man commanded attention, simply with his presence. He looked smaller now, broken down and beaten, the courage once shining brightly in his eyes no longer there. He'd lost weight, and Rose startled herself when she mentally compared him to a skeleton.

Once the buggy was a good mile from the jail, Rose took a deep breath of relief. During the last nineteen or so months, she had secretly made her way into town to the jailhouse. Every visit was late at night or in the wee hours of the morning. She feared being recognized and becoming a headline in the newspapers. Should that happen, she believed the townspeople would judge her even more harshly than they did Emil. Before her first visit, she decided she would take no chances to be seen. Never would she risk adding yet another burden to her children's lives.

On this last visit, she and Emil really didn't speak much. He told her she was lovely, as he had almost daily since they first met, and inquired about his children—his pain more than evident as he said their names. When his enormous hand swallowed up her slender, small one, he said, "My beautiful, Rose, I never meant for you or the children to be hurt. Much less this whole debacle. Remember to give them my love. Tell them they deserve better."

Momentarily, Rose felt her heart go out to the big man. Then she pulled her hand out of his and said, "Carrying on with Minnie. You knew that nothing good could come of that." She looked directly and deeply into his eyes and added, "Losing almost every single possession, being shunned by most of the townspeople and knowing that me, Blanche, Richard and Arline are the main topics of gossip—it truly hurts. Taking up with Minnie right under my nose. There are no words to express my pain. I feel you were telling me I wasn't enough for you."

Rose's voice caught and she took a moment, then resumed. "I am the mother of your children, and I always tried to do everything and anything you desired. Then you tryst with Minnie. Minnie, of all women!" She fought tears now, and her thoughts raced back in time to the broken dish. Almost in a whisper, she said, "That woman is a liar and quick to cause others pain."

They both looked away from the other in complete silence, and Rose immediately felt ashamed of her outburst. She knew forgiveness was the only path for her to take, but total resolution was a long way off. Rose believed keeping anger and resentment, possibly even hate, within, turned her into an ugly, cruel woman. She reached for his hand then and said quietly, "I love you." And she did.

Sitting in the near blackness with Emil, Rose stared at the splashes of blue light the moon spread across the wall of his jail cell. She looked around at the dingy little room surrounded by bars and more bars. She knew the cell wasn't clean, yet not quite filthy. Emil had never mentioned the poor conditions he'd been forced to live in all these months. She hadn't wanted to remember him behind bars, but that's what she saw as she folded up the image and tucked it away deep in her heart.

After some time in silence, he asked her, "Is it time for you to leave?"

"I need to go before the sun rises, but I want to stay with you a few more hours."

Emil started to speak, but the words seemed to catch in his throat. Eye contact between them became deep and intense, and for a moment, she was given a glimpse of an Emil she never knew existed. "Thank you, my Rosie Posy," he said, finally, using a nickname she had last heard before Richard was born. He was sincere and even humble when he told her, "You've no idea how much this means to me."

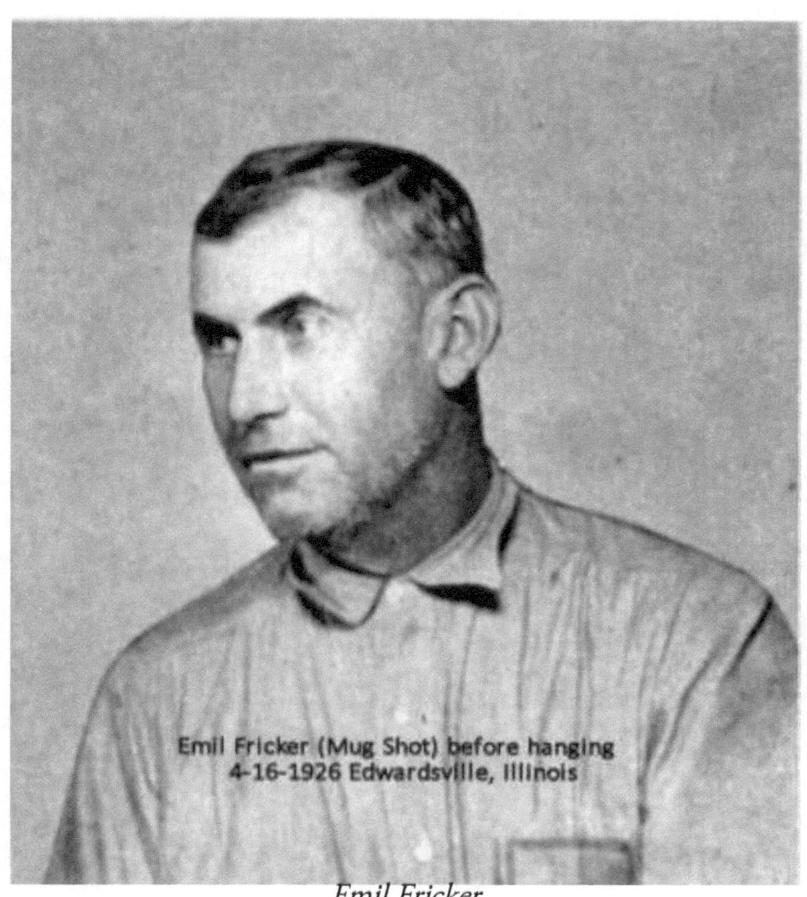

Emil Fricker

Chapter Seventy-Six

"Fricker Must Die: Pardon Board Refuses To Disturb Verdict. Hears Fate This Morning Without Least Emotion."

Highland News Leader, April 15, 1926

Emil Fricker was denied his plea of clemency by the Illinois Board of Pardons and Paroles at Springfield this morning at 10 o'clock.

Unless there is some legal interference before tomorrow morning at 9 o'clock he will be sent into eternity for the death of John Nungesser, former Highland farmer on the evening of September 15, 1924.

Newspaper reporters told Fricker his fate this morning. He maintained his former stoical composure.

He refused to talk although several questions were asked.

Fricker was found lying on the cot of his cell. His hands were carelessly thrown across his breast. He appeared to be sleeping and was probably awakened by the click and clang as the doors were unlocked and opened.

Fricker was told by one of the reporters that the state board had denied his plea. He listened while the few words were spoken. He was laying flat on his back and did not as much raise his head as he listened to the several words. His eyelids dropped and during the several minutes the reporters remained he did not speak a single word.

Everything for the execution has been completed. Philip Hanna of Epworth, Ill, an expert in adjusting the noose, arrived here last night. Hanna has officiated at fifty executions and tomorrow he will add another.

Sheriff Deimling will operate the lever which springs the trap. Hanna will simply adjust the knot in the noose in such a manner that death will be produced by breaking of the neck instead of strangulation. Hanna's work is to make the death of the doomed men easier.

Hanna arrived here last night. This morning, he gave a few final instructions in regard to the gallows. He wanted everything in perfect adjust to avoid a serious hitch tomorrow. Fricker weighs about 185 pounds. The rope will stretch a foot or fourteen inches.

Sheriff Deimling said this morning that Fricker's meals of today and his last breakfast will include anything he wishes. Fricker had not made special requests for dishes for supper or breakfast.

Fricker has been visited during the week by Rev. E. J. Eckhard and taken the sacraments of the Catholic church. He will receive the last rites Friday morning, a short time before going to the gallows.

For two or three days Fricker has had very little to say, either to the death watch or others about the jail with whom he came in contact. Whether he will maintain his stoical attitude to the last minute and not make a statement is problematical. In his latest conversations about the Nungesser death he maintained that he was not guilty of the charge.

Fricker's last appeal to escape death was made to the pardon board yesterday afternoon when two other death verdicts were reviewed. Fricker's case was the last taken up and held under advisement by the board until this morning. His mother, sister and brother attended the hearing yesterday.

He was represented by Attorneys H. J. Bandy of Granite City and H. J. Johnson of Carlyle. They argued that the two men who actually killed Nungesser were given life in the penitentiary and that Fricker's punishment is too severe. The plea for clemency was received by States Attorney J. R. Brown.

Note: This article has been reprinted verbatim from the original article, including any grammatical errors.

THIS TICKET WILL ADMIT
MR.
To witness the Execution of
EMIL FRICKER
at the County Jail at Edwardsville, Illinois, for the murder
of John Nungesser,

4-16-26 SHERIFF.

Ticket to the Execution

Chapter Seventy-Seven
"Emil Fricker Paid for Murder With Life Today"

Edwardsville Intelligencer, April 16, 1926

Emil Fricker today paid with his life for the murder of John Nungesser at Highland on September 15, 1924. He was executed at the county jail yard, Sheriff E. R. Deimling springing the trap at 9:11 o'clock. The fall broke his neck, and he died within fourteen minutes without a struggle. He was pronounced dead at 9:25 o'clock.

It was just nineteen months ago this morning at 4 o'clock that Fricker and two associates in the crime were landed in jail. Nineteen months passed last night since the crime was committed.

Fricker mumbled something as he was escorted to the gallows. As the straps, cap and robe were being adjusted he mumbled again, "I am not guilty of what I am charged with."

All of the details for the execution had been completed at 1:30 o'clock this morning when the death warrant was read. It is a lengthy instrument of several hundred words. Mrs. Rudolph Fricker, aged mother of the doomed man, and other relatives visited with her son last night. They left at 11 o'clock. Fricker was more or less restless until 2 o'clock and then settled down to sleep.

About 200 persons were in the enclosure and fully 1,000 stood on the streets, hoping to get a glimpse of Fricker. Fifty sheriffs and deputies were here for the execution.

Four men fainted but were revived in a few minutes. One man reeled ever after the execution was over. The others were in the enclosure and collapsed within a few seconds after the drop.

Fricker's last few hours on earth were restless. He talked with persons in the cellhouse. He asked one something about hangings and did not get more than two hours of sleep.

This morning, he was awake bright and early, the sun being partly obscured by clouds.

At 6:45 o'clock this morning he took communion with Rev. E. J. Eckhard for the last time. Later in the morning he was asked what he wished for breakfast. "What's the use of breakfast," he remarked. At 8 o'clock he drank a glass of milk.

Some of the first arrivals in Edwardsville reached the jail yard at 7 o'clock but it was an hour or more before the majority assembled. Everything was conducted with best of order. Men stood around in groups.

Gus Reickert, a brother-in-law, arrived here this morning at 8:30 o'clock. He had spent the night at Springfield hoping to get an interview with Governor Small and ask for clemency. Governor Small could not be seen. Reickert was permitted to have a few words with Fricker, shortly before 9 o'clock.

It was a few moments after 9 o'clock when Rev. Eckhard arrived from St. Boniface's church where he had conducted his morning services. He and the prisoner had a few words, the priest attempting to console Fricker.

At eight minutes after 9 o'clock the party filed from the building. Rev. Eckhard led the way, followed by Sheriff Deimling, Phillip Hanna and Fricker, who was accompanied by Deputy Sheriffs T. C. Dooner and Paul Taylor.

Fricker was told to step upon the trap, and he complied with the command. Rev. Eckhard gave him the last rites. In the meantime, the deputies were adjusting the straps and a moment later the cap was drawn down. In the twinkling of an eye the noose was adjusted around his neck.

Mr. Hanna raised his right hand. It was the signal for Sheriff Deimling to pull the lever. The doors swung open and it was all over. Death followed without the least struggle.

"He died game," was the answer Hanna made when asked a question by a reporter. "It is my fifty-first, and I really believe it will be the last," he added.

The body was taken to the funeral home of Straube & Schneider. After being hurriedly prepared, it was taken back to Highland.

Five doctors were present. Those who were present and made observations of the pulse were: Drs. E Wahl, H. E. Wharff, J. R. Sutter of Edwardsville; Dr. C. E. Moulden, Troy and Dr. J. J. Walsh.

As provided by law twelve men constituted the jury and they signed the death verdict in connection with the doctor's certificate. The twelve on the jury were: Fred L. Leadley, George Daubo, Norbert Hotz and James Stallman, Edwardsville; John F. Deimling and Thomas A. Taylor, Troy; William Feldwisch, Alton; Joseph Healey, Livingston; Gustave Wisnansky and John Willman, Alhambra; A.H. Winter, Highland and Fred Henke, Fruit.

Fricker went to the gallows today for a crime that has been widely published in newspapers, the publicity being due principally to another murder for which he was given life in the penitentiary and more or less suspicion through the finding of some bones in a cistern at his place during January. [The bones found were purported to have been of an infant from seven years prior.]

He was a son of the late Rudolph Fricker, former and highly respected resident of Highland. His father was a member of the County Board of Supervisors. The son was held in high esteem as a young man.

From a very reliable source it was learned today that Fricker became a bootlegger shortly after prohibition went into force. About the same time, he became very careless. Fricker is said to have been an early producer of liquor.

His relations with a woman who had spent years in the Fricker home were his downfall. Back in May 1920, he killed Robert Kehrli, according to the circuit court jury. The woman in the case was then Mrs. Kehrli.

Later she married John Nungesser, a promising young farmer. Fricker had a desire to get him out of the way and spent months in planning the death. His plans were finally put into effect by his son-in-law, Eldo Wernle and Jacob Landert, a farmhand. The two entered pleas of guilty, turned state's evidence against Fricker and principally on their statements the state developed a case that led to the death verdict.

The verdict was returned just a year ago on April 3 and since that time Fricker and his lawyers have had a hard fight in the Supreme Court and before the Board of Pardons and Paroles to get a new trial or a commutation to life in the penitentiary.

Fricker lost at every turn in the road. First the Supreme court denied a new trial. Next the tribunal refused a rehearing of his petition and finally the Board of Pardons refused to commute the sentence in spite of appeals for mercy from his aged mother.

There was a day that Fricker had considerable power in his community. Some of his acquaintances had more or less fear for him. He owned some fine farming lands and operated a dairy farm. When a bankruptcy proceedings was instituted at East St. Louis some months ago, the papers placed his liabilities at $74,405.06 and his assets were listed at $47,000. The assets included 54 cows, 49 heifers, 62 hogs, 9 horses and mules.

Fricker was married twice. His first wife has been dead for some years. His widow was formerly Miss Rose Jenny. The children who survive are: Mrs. Wernle, Blanche and Richard Fricker. He is also survived by his mother, two sisters, Mrs. Flora Reickert, Highland; Mrs. Mabel Foedder, Pierron and a brother, Victor Fricker, Highland.

One of those who attended the execution this morning was Adolph Wernle, a well-known resident of Highland. He is the father of Eldo Wernle and was satisfied with Fricker getting his death penalty.

According to information today, Fricker carried life insurance of about $8,000. It was said the policies are made payable to his widow.

Wednesday night his mother asked him several questions that could not be heard by the guards. He gave an affirmative answer to them and after each the mother patted him on the shoulder. Whether they were relative to his spiritual duties or pertained to financial matters will never be known.

Fricker has always maintained his innocence. The first time the writer visited him at the jail in company with Sheriff Deimling, shortly after his arrest for a statement, the doomed man remarked, "If I knew anything sheriff, I would tell you." Fricker would talk on any subject but the killing.

He has always maintained the stoical attitude of a follower of the Greek philosopher, Zeno. It was not until this morning that he weakened to any great extent and then the change was very noticeable.

For a time some were under the impression he would end his own life. Borne up by a belief he would not be executed, the days passed and under the watch of guard, Fricker did not have the chance, if thoughts of suicide entered his mind.

Plans for the funeral had not been made this afternoon, according to statements from some sources at Highland, while according to other information, Fricker's body would be laid to rest this afternoon with simple services to avoid as much publicity as possible.

Louis Spangle, Highland undertaker, and distantly related, took the body to Highland this morning. He said that funeral plans had not been made and declined to discuss any of the arrangements.

Through another source it was said that members of the family would not see Fricker in death and that arrangements had been completed for the private burial late today.

Note: This article has been reprinted verbatim from the original article, including any grammatical errors.

Edwardsville

Emil Fricker Paid For Murder With Life Today

IS SEVENTH TO DIE

Stops Robber

CERTIFICATE OF EXECUTION.

STATE OF ILLINOIS)
COUNTY OF MADISON) SS.

In the matter of the execution of EMIL FRICKER, condemned at the March Term A.D.1925 of the Circuit Court of said Madison County, to suffer death by hanging, We Edward R.Deimling, Sheriff of the County of Madison, in the State of Illinois, and the Officials and persons whose names are subscribed to this certificate and who were selected and invited by said Sheriff to be present, all being Citizens and residents of the County of Madison, in the State of Illinois, do in conformity with the provisions and requirements of Chapter 38 of the Revised Statutes of the State of Illinois hereby certify, That on Friday April 16th 1926, between the hours of Nine (9),O'Clock in the fore-noon and Four (4) O'Clock in the afternoon, the said EMIL FRICKER, was executed by being hanged by the neck until he was dead.

That the said execution took place within the walls of the prison yard, of said County, in the City of Edwardsville, said yard having been enclosed by a high fence, That we Were present in said yard and witnessed the execution, and that such execution was in conformity to the sentence of the Madison County Circuit Court, as affirmed by the Supreme Court of the State of Illinois, at the February Term A.D.1926, and the provisions of the Statutes of the State of Illinois.

Given under our hands at Edwardsville, Illinois, this 16th day of April A.D.1926.

Ed R. Deimling Sheriff.
[illegible], County Judge
Rev. O. J. Eckhard, Pastor St. Boniface Church, Edwardsville
Thos. C. Dooner, Deputy Sheriff. Edwardsville
Paul C. Taylor Deputy Sheriff Troy
[illegible] Glass, Deputy Sheriff. Edwardsville
Dennis [illegible] Deputy Sheriff Granite City
M. [illegible] Welch Asst State Atty.
[illegible], Asst State Attorney
[illegible] Talley, Deputy Sheriff Alton
[illegible] Deputy Circuit Clerk
[illegible] Recorder

Certificate of Execution Performed

Chapter Seventy-Eight

April 16, 1926

How did you do this? How did you live through the day your father would be taken from the earth in such a cruel, harsh way? One foot in front of the other, Arline told herself as she got out of bed after a restless night. She checked on little Eldo, still resting comfortably, curled up with his little blankie Rose had crocheted him.

Arline was so grateful he didn't understand any of this. Especially since she saw the devastation this had rained down on Blanche and Richard. How Arline's heart ached when she saw little Blanche's once happy-go-lucky face. The little girl looked like a shell of her old self. Arline hoped the Blanche she once knew would return one day when the shock had worn off, but she wasn't so sure. Richard had always been shy and reserved, but now you could barely get a word out of him, or even a half a word.

And then there was Rose. Her stalwart stepmother, who stood tall throughout all of this. Arline wished she could be like Rose—so kind and strong. But she just couldn't help herself. Especially when it came to the things she thought and said about the hussy who started all of this.

Anger and pure hate switched to despair then. Arline knew her heart would never, ever be the same after today when Papa was gone from the earth. She had thought about going to the hanging but decided in the end not to go. Not because she couldn't take it. Because she could. She knew she could. No, she didn't go because she knew it would hurt her papa's pride something awful to see her there, or even to sense she was out there in the crowd somewhere. This was something he had to do alone.

Chapter Seventy-Nine

April 16, 1926

Traditionally, most every woman in the 1920s did laundry on Mondays. Rose was no exception. There seemed to be no dramatic reason for this activity to be done at the beginning of the week, although it had been postulated that throughout the coming week, the clean clothing could be mended and/or ironed and readied for church attendance and other Sunday events.

Another theory was that a particularly large meal was prepared on Sundays, and this usually created a plethora of leftovers. Because doing the family wash required women to work at it from sunrise to sunset, leaving no time for cooking, leftovers sufficed on Mondays.

However, this week in April 1926, Rose abandoned tradition. She felt she had to do laundry on Friday, because moving to the cafe would be mandatory by Monday.

She was outside hanging her just washed laundry on the clothesline when she stopped the chore at hand and gazed up at the blue sky above her. It was a clear, almost cloudless blue. She saw a few white, fluffy clouds in the far east. As she continued to look up into the sky, she murmured, "My Dear Lord, thank you for keeping me strong through all of this. Today, especially, I need to be stronger than ever before in my life. Please don't let my Emil experience severe pain today. Support him into your fold. Also, God, be with my children and keep them safe from the cruel words of others. Thank you for all you do for us. Amen."

She then turned back to her task at hand, clipping a pair of Richard's trousers to the line. She noted the size of them. They were large enough to fit almost any man of average build. Her baby boy was rapidly becoming a man. She knew manhood was forced upon him as he faithfully carried out his father's duties every single day. Her boy protected his mother and sister in an admirable way.

Tears threatened to spill from Rose's eyes, but she blinked rapidly. Then she concentrated on hanging each article of clothing in a careful manner that would minimize wrinkles and result in smooth fabric. As she pulled on a pair of trousers, an extremely uncomfortable feeling entered her body. She bent forward, holding her abdomen and didn't seem to notice the clothing as it slipped from her hand and landed in the grass. Rose felt an overwhelming pain. As tears sprang into her eyes, she again looked up to the heavens and asked out loud, "God, is this the beginning of the end of my pain? Thy will be done. Amen."

She straightened her stance and slowly walked to an enormous old tree. Several swings dangled from its mighty branches. She grabbed the rope attached to a seat and sat down. Rose knew when the feeling had swept into her body, she had become an instant widow.

As she sat on the swing, tears poured down her face and she sobbed loudly. After a while she began to weep softly. Once again, she spoke to her God. "Oh, Father in Heaven, you must already know my heart, and you know I'm not crying for myself. Rather,

I cry for Emil, who you put into my life so that Blanche and Richard could be. My precious children, who have been through hell and now must grow up without a father. God, today I'll no longer cry for my husband. These last couple of years have been so dark. I will enjoy life again and bring my children on a journey to happiness."

***

"Mama, are you okay?" The small voice caused Rose to stir. She was still sitting on the swing and almost fell before remembering where she was. Rose raised her arms up and wide, and Blanche flew into them. Squeezing her mother tightly, her daughter said, "You have to be okay."

Rose gently pried her daughter's arms from around her neck and looked into the girl's eyes, bright with anger, the wrath nearly palpable.

"I'm okay, and I love you forever," she said quietly. "Tell me, why are you so angry?"

"All the kids in school said that it's good Papa died today, and other mean stuff. What was good about Papa being hanged and dying, Mama? Are they right? Is that true?"

Rose kept her voice steady as she replied. "Oh, my baby, my lovely little girl. I guess sometimes dying can be good, when death is the only way a person suffering can be helped. You know, like when a person is terribly sick and doctors, healers, just nobody can help them. Then it can be good, as it stops the pain and sickness from getting even worse. But sweet girl, there was nothing good about your Papa dying today. As we've talked about before, some people in town think your father killed a man for no good reason. Never once did your papa say he killed someone. He always denied it."

"But if he didn't kill anyone, Mama, why did he get hung?" The anger in her daughter's eyes had started to subside, and now Rose saw tremendous fear in them.

"Because my sweet girl, some men at his trial didn't believe him. They were jurors. Remember when I explained what a trial is and the judge and everybody involved in it?"

Blanche nodded slightly, the fear in her eyes mixing with extreme sadness. "Now that he's really never coming back, I miss him. I really, really miss him."

"I do, too, and we probably always will. Tell me, why are you so afraid, child?"

Blanche spoke, almost frantically. "You, Mama, you can't go away and leave us. Those same men, could they say you have to be hanged to die, too? Can they do that?"

With a firm grip on her little girl, Rose replied, "I've said this before, and I'll say it as many times as I need to. I'll always be here for you. There's nothing I've ever done, nor could do that would call for a trial. I promise." She pulled her daughter close and before long could feel her little body relax.

After a few minutes, Blanche began to wiggle and squirm. "Mama, my tummy wants something to eat. What shall I eat?"

Rose let go of Blanche, who slid off her lap as she answered. "We've no fresh fruit, but I made bread yesterday. Put some berry jam on a slice and enjoy it."

"Yummy! Those are the berries I helped with last summer," said Blanche, who turned and walked toward the house, her head down, feet shuffling, sadness clinging to her entire body.

Rose followed her daughter toward the house, pausing to look back at the clothesline. She hadn't checked the security of the articles clipped to the lines as was her usual habit. From where she stood, she saw linens moving about in the soft breeze. "Perfect drying weather," she said out loud.

In the kitchen, she found Blanche already eating her bread and jam, and decided to go upstairs and check on Richard.

When she got to his door, she knocked lightly.

"Come in," he called out.

Rose entered to see her son sitting at his desk, a book in front of him. He turned to look into his mother's eyes. "I saw you with Blanche, and I didn't want to bother you. Is she okay? Are you okay?" he asked, his eyes reflecting so much more pain and sorrow than any sixteen-year-old should have to experience.

"She'll be alright, and I'm okay," she said. "What about you? Did the other children say the usual hurtful things today?"

Richard closed the book in front of him and fully turned to face her. "You know, Mom, I actually shouted at a bunch of them when they started with their cruel remarks. I said, 'Yes, my father was found guilty of murder and today's the day his life will be taken. He's a human being made of flesh and bones, just like you. No matter what he's done, he's my father, and your ugly words simply make things worse. So just STOP!' I said it real loud. I didn't plan to shout. It just happened, and every single one of them became quiet and stared at me."

"I'm glad you gave them a piece of your mind," said Rose. "They deserved it. Maybe they'll think before they speak in the future. Either way, I'm proud of you."

Richard appeared surprised. "You are?"

She entered her son's room and sat down on the bed facing him. "Your father was always proud of you, too."

A mixture of emotions crossed Richard's face when she said this.

"You were never really able to get to know your father and spend time with him," she continued. "He and I talked the week before he went to jail about the two of you. He loved you so very much. He just didn't know how to show his love for you while maintaining his and your masculinity. He was troubled by that for years. Why, before you were born, your father was very polite and protective of me. He was so careful and gentle, I thought he wanted to put me in a glass cabinet to keep me safe. When I told him we were expecting a baby, he was ecstatic, like over the moon happy. He had not truly believed he could once again father another child."

Rose stopped. "Do you want me to stop talking about him?"

Richard shook his head. "Please don't stop. I like hearing the good stuff about Pa."

Rose felt glad Richard didn't want her to stop, because the truth was sharing happier times was making her feel better.

"When I found out I was pregnant, your father asked if I thought I was carrying a boy. He said he had given up on his dream of having a son. He had imagined hundreds of things that he'd do with a boy if he had one, and he got so excited when he told me this. When I looked into his eyes, there were tears. He told me, 'My beautiful, Rosie, I feared that because you'd been essentially required to tend to your brothers and sisters until they went to college that the work might have made you opposed to any babies of our own.'"

Rose remembered how ecstatic she had been to see Emil's happiness and to know her dream of parenthood matched his. She continued, "Your father was so happy when I became pregnant with you that he swept me off my feet and began humming a song, and we danced for a spell." She recalled the feeling of euphoria being in his arms had given her as she gazed up at his goofy grin.

"When we finished dancing, he guided me to a chair and made sure he didn't hurt me. He didn't want to be careless," she said.

"He didn't hurt you, did he?" asked Richard. "You can dance when you're pregnant, right?"

Rose laughed. "Yes, you can do a lot of things." Then her tone became more serious. "Just like your Pa had given up on having a son, I had nearly given up on ever having children."

"Because you had to help out with your siblings on account of your mother dying," commented Richard, frowning. "How could you go on without your mother? I couldn't do a thing if you were gone."

"We all do whatever is presented and do the best job we can. Now, back to the subject at hand. You and your Pa. I've never seen or heard of a man more excited about becoming a father again. He made sure I ate a lot—really too much. He wouldn't let me carry anything more than about 2 pounds. I had to wait for him to leave before I could take the clean wet clothing to the clothesline. He went overboard as they say. He was so very happy and kind and gentle, too. I allowed as much of his overprotection as I could handle. I got cranky from time to time, as having a child beneath one's heart kicking and rolling around can be really uncomfortable. But not once did your father even raise his voice to me. Then when your projected date of birth neared, he added pacing and fidgeting to his love and care of you and me."

Rose stopped and asked, "Do you want to take a break and eat something?"

Richard shook his head. "I'm not hungry right now. I'd rather you keep talking."

"The night I went into labor, once the midwife and nurse came along to help, your father left my side, saying my pain made him too anxious. Actually, he went and got himself liquored up. Something he rarely did in those days."

Rose stopped and ran her hands along the front of her pinafore and continued. "My labor with you, young man, proceeded in a timely manner—that was what the midwife said over and over. Now son, if you ever have a wife who gives you a child, remember the labor portion of birthing is truly labor and quite painful, while at the same time it is so wonderful to bring a new life into the world. So, if you become a father, be grateful. I was exhausted once you had entered this world howling at the top of your lungs."

Richard's eyes widened. "Was I crying cause it hurt to be born?"

"No, son, you were unhappy being squeezed out of a place you'd been for a long time. It had been warm and safe and quiet in there, and you suddenly entered a room where the air on your bare skin was a new sensation, and then there were hands on you. It all was new to you, and it seems you didn't like it. I held you as you continued to protest, though, and I fell in love with you at first sight. The nurse took you to the nursery to clean you and wrap you up, and then she returned soon. You were swaddled in blankets and sleeping. Your cute, little monkey face was all that wasn't wrapped in blankets."

"I looked like a monkey?" asked a shocked Richard.

Rose smiled and said, "No, you just looked like a newborn baby, because you were. I was filled with so much joy holding you. I carefully removed your blankets as you continued to sleep and counted your fingers and toes and marveled at your perfection. You, my perfect son, Richard Rudolph Fricker, overwhelmed me. Your beauty brought tears to my eyes. How on earth could I have created such beauty? I remember thinking. Just as tears started to spill from my eyes, I heard a soft knock on the bedroom door, and then your father's head appeared. Sheepishly, he asked if it was alright that he come in. I smiled at him, partly because he looked rather silly with only his head in the doorway, and because he was so perfectly happy. I nodded to him to come in. When he took a look at you, I asked, 'What do you think of our little man?' He coughed and replied, 'He's so little. I've never seen any person so little.' That surprised me, and I proudly stated that all your fingers and toes were accounted for. Your father again looked at you in amazement and asked, 'Is he okay, really? I mean, isn't he too little?'"

She cleared her throat, then continued. "I didn't like your own father saying you were a little puny, so I said loudly, 'He's more than seven pounds, a respectable weight. Besides Arline, was probably smaller than Richard. Pick up your son. You are his father.' But he was afraid he would hurt you. I immediately bristled and said, 'No sir, not good enough. You need to hold him close and wrap your love around him, so he feels safe.'"

"Did he pick me up?" asked Richard.

"First, he protested. He said that Arline's nanny only let him look at her a couple of times a week. They didn't let him get close because of germs. I guess I must have sat there with my mouth open for a minute or so before I said that I'd never heard such a story and that my father came right into the room where my mother was birthing. He'd wrap the babies in towels and walk and talk to them, even if the baby was screaming. He also held my mother's hand and told her how she made him so proud. He would say that birthing had to be left to the women. Men just ain't strong enough."

"Was Pa surprised at your words?" asked Richard.

"He was even more surprised when I placed you in his arms. He looked so terrified, and he had an awkward hold on you. I gently repositioned you in his arms, and soon you began to fall asleep. It was clear you felt safe with him. He looked at me questioningly, and I told him sleep during the first months of life was exactly what you needed to grow strong and healthy. In response, he shushed me. But I told him most newborns could sleep through a hurricane. Then he really surprised me and said, 'I'd like to hold him for a while.' He walked over to my tiny rocking chair and slowly lowered himself to seated. I must have been holding my breath, because I took in a large amount of air when the chair didn't break. I had to suppress a smile, actually a giggle, at the sight of you two. Your father, such an enormous man, sitting on the small chair holding a little baby. Of course, you were a good-sized, healthy newborn. It was simply your pa's oversize that made you appear diminutive. Goodness, one of his large hands almost covered your entire body."

Rose stopped and watched Richard's face, so content at the thought of his father holding him. Before he could remember about the day's events, she continued. "I must have fallen asleep soon after he took to the rocking chair. Later I awoke to the sound of you squalling. You certainly had a set of lungs. As I rushed to get out of bed, I thought you'd wake everyone in the house. I quickly picked you up and held you close. You quieted immediately, and I fed you. I continued in that room for several more days, and every day, your father came in for an hour or even two hours to hold and rock you."

Rose stopped for a moment, her heart feeling like it might break in two at the next memory. She took a deep breath. "About a week or so after, we were all back in our own beds. One night, I had awakened, wondering why you weren't crying or at least fussing, since it was time to feed you. I was surprised to find your father in the nursery with you cradled in his arms. He was singing to you. How shocked I was, as he never sang. Even in church he moved his lips silently during the hymns. When I entered the room, he looked embarrassed and told me you had been making small sounds and he thought you might wake me, so he picked you up."

Richard smiled. "That's a nice memory, Mom."

She returned the smile. "As time moved forward, you turned one and then two and on and on. Your father spent time with you almost every day. You always screamed with delight when you heard his footsteps. No matter how many people were walking around, you knew exactly when he entered the house. Naturally, the older you got, the more the cuddling was abandoned, and games and toys were the activity. Do you remember playing with him? Any memory from that time at all?"

Richard's brow furrowed, and he met Rose's gaze. "I recall a bear, no, a ball, that wouldn't bounce. It looked old and in bad shape, because it had sewing on it. That's all, just a sewed-up ball."

Rose replied, "It really doesn't matter exactly when he played with you until he stopped. One day, your father didn't come looking for you. It was the same day after day. Finally, I asked him why he didn't spend time with you anymore, and you know what he said, 'My dear Rosie, our son has some problems in school.' I was taken aback, as I'd not heard any of this. Your father continued to explain that a child at school said mean stuff about our family. You told your pa, 'I'm going to punch his face in, is that okay?' Your father told me that whatever he told you would be wrong and could get you hurt and that he must stay away from you to keep you safe. No matter how I tried to convince him that you needed him in your life, the more firmly he became entrenched in his belief to never again engage you in a game. As you know, he was always one of your biggest supporters. You've heard him tell others how proud he always was of you."

Silence settled between them for a few minutes, and then Richard spoke. "I know Pa loved me, and he was always there when I needed him, even when his work required tending to. As I got older, I felt something filtering out our feelings toward one another, and now that you've explained what happened, it makes more sense, so thank you. Everything about him used to make me feel safe, protected, and loved."

Rose leaned toward Richard and took his hands in hers. She looked into his exceptionally tired eyes and said, "My dear, dear young man, thank you for sharing. My heart fills with pride and love as you continue to help every single day. If you have any more questions about your father, please ask. I'll tell you what I know."

Richard yawned. "Thank you, Mom. There's going to be some mysteries surrounding Pa forever. I know I'll eventually work through this, but I've got to start planning ahead and living my life. That's what's important for me. The other stuff will take care of itself."

Rose stood. "I'm going to make us something for supper. I'll send your sister up to fetch you when it's ready." She motioned to leave his room, then looked around and said, almost to herself, "These walls are no longer our home. When the sun rises, a new chapter of our lives begins."

Chapter Eighty
"Farm of Emil Fricker's Widow Sold for Taxes"

A forty-acre farm belonging to Mrs. Rose Fricker, widow of Emil Fricker, former dairy farmer of Highland, Illinois., who was hanged for murder on April 16 last, was the first piece of property sold yesterday morning at the opening of the Madison County delinquent tax sale at Edwardsville. City Treasurer Martin is conducting the sale.

Unpaid taxes totaling $33.63 were due on the property which passed into the hands of L. Hoskins of Kansas City, Mo., for that price. The farm is mortgaged to $2,000.

Note: This article has been reprinted verbatim from the original article, including any grammatical errors.

Chapter Eighty-One

July 18, 1926

They didn't have a proper funeral. That hurt Arline, maybe even the most. Not being able to say goodbye to Papa the way she should have been able to. Arline had her own funeral, though.

First, she thought about it for a few weeks. Sat there at night after he'd gone and thought and thought. How to honor him? Was he a good man? No, not really. Was he an honorable man? He could be. Was he a good papa? Always. That realization, that deep knowing, gave Arline the idea she had for how she would honor him. Honor his being her father; honor his walking the earth; honor him—those good parts of him.

Papa loved the land at the dairy farm. Loved to look out over the land. And he especially loved the trees. They were strong and stoic, he'd say when he came across an oak in the field that stood straight and tall, yet gnarled in its own good way. He'd reach over and pat the tree even, as if he wanted to let the tree know it was doing a good job just growing and being a tree.

Arline knew Papa's favorite tree. It was out by the south forty, down in a knoll. "A right mighty, strong tree," she'd heard him say once. Just like him, she thought, now heading for the tree with little Eldo on her hip.

As she walked toward the tree towering in the sky, she felt like it was reaching into Heaven for Papa. To pull him down and bring him here for this special ceremony she'd devised in her head just for the three of them. Her, Papa, and little Eldo.

How proud Papa had been of little Eldo. He'd confided in her when Eldo was born that though he loved being a father, he felt his heart swell with the most pride when he thought about how Arline had brought him a grandson. She remembered that day now, and though tears threatened to nip at the edges of her eyes, she willed herself to stay dry-eyed. It was important right now to honor Papa without breaking down and falling to pieces. And his birthday seemed like the right day for that. Honor him and his birth, not his death.

She sat down under the tree with little Eldo in her lap and leaned against the tree. As she did so, the tree seemed to move. Was Papa communicating with her? Did he want to tell her hello, or that he forgave her? She hoped it was both. How she hoped it was both.

The tears started and she wiped them away with her fingertips. Dagnabbit, she didn't want to cry! But they just wouldn't stop coming. Oh, well, there was no one here at the farm anymore, so she didn't need to worry about someone seeing her sitting under a tree bawling her eyes out like a baby.

She had brought a photo of Papa and her. She wasn't sure what she was going to do with it. She just had the urge to bring it. She took it out of her skirt pocket and looked at it. It was taken some months after Mama's passing. Papa had his arm around Arline, tight, like he wouldn't be able to let her go if he tried.

She felt bad thinking about it now, but she wished that things had remained just like that. Her and Papa. No Rose and the other children, and certainly not Minnie. They could have lived a good life just the two of them, and then Papa would still be alive. Although, who knows if she would have little Eldo now. Her heart filled with the purest, sweetest feeling ever when she thought of the little treasure on her lap. She kissed the top of his head and noticed through her misty eyes that she wet his head good with tears.

Laughing a little as she stroked his head in an attempt to dry it, she remembered what her papa used to say to her when she threw a fit as a youngster. "Cry me a river; I'm not changing my mind, Arli."

No one had ever called her Arli but Papa. How she longed to hear him call her that now. She put her head against the old tree and sighed, and at that moment she swore she heard, "Arli." Was it the wind? No, it was still. Was it a bird? Not a one in the sky. No farmhands around. They had moved out long ago.

"Happy birthday, Papa," Arline said and smiled as she absorbed the energy of the tree while she stroked little Eldo's moist head.

Epilogue

Rose (November 4, 1879-May 17, 1976)

Rose opened and ran the cafe, which proved very successful, until 1945. At that time, Blanche gave birth to her first child, Lynn, the co-author of this book. Blanche and her husband, Mike, had moved to South Bend, Indiana and needed help with Lynn's care, so Rose, sixty-six at the time, decided to sell the cafe and move in with them.

Rose's cafe, September 1929. She is standing behind the counter. Rose enjoyed running the cafe, where she was able to share her baking and cooking with satisfied customers. Blanche and Richard helped out when they weren't busy with their studies.

Rose next to her cafe, 1930s

Rose, late 1930s

Rose, Arline and Lynn, 1947

In 1957, Rose, Blanche, Mike Sr., Lynn, and her younger brother, Mike Jr., born in 1951, moved cross-country and settled in Tustin, California. There Rose enjoyed a life close to her heart, which included caring for her grandchildren, gardening, cooking for the family, doing needlepoint, writing poetry, and being an active member of her church.

Rose and Lynn going to church, South Bend, Indiana, 1947

Rose and Lynn, South Bend, Indiana, 1946

Rose died in Tustin, California at the age of ninety-six and was buried in Highland Cemetery in South Bend, Indiana next to Richard. Services were also held at Waverly Chapel in Santa Ana, California on May 19, 1976.

Blanche (August 11, 1914-January 5, 1999)

Blanche on farm, 1916

Blanche in buggy with farmhand

Blanche, 1916, 2 years old

Blanche graduated from Highland High School in 1932. She did eventually meet and marry her prince charming, Zeno (Mike)

Sackett, who was born in St. Jacob, Illinois on May 25, 1912, not far from Blanche's place of birth in Saint Rose. The two had met as children when they were in the same one-room schoolhouse, Mike then nine and Blanche seven, and Mike never forgot her. They married on September 14, 1940, in South Bend, Indiana and after five miscarriages over five years, Lynn was born on their anniversary on September 14, 1945.

Blanche (Fricker) Sackett, early 1940s

Mike (Zeno) Sackett, husband of Blanche, early 1940s

Lynn Sackett, 3 years old

A career woman at heart, Blanche enjoyed working during her adult life. She earned her RN in Nursing in South Bend and became a licensed vocational nurse when she came to California, receiving certification from Orange Coast College in 1958. For many years, she worked for a family practice physician.

Lynn, Blanche and Rose, South Bend, Indiana, 1947

In later years, Blanche also studied for her real estate license, and she was very good with finances and investing the modest income she and Mike made. When the family moved to Tustin, they bought a new home for what she considered a very good price. At the time, the area was still fairly rural.

Rose, Lynn, Mike Sr., Mike Jr. and Blanche, June 1959

Blanche and Lynn, Tustin, California, 1958

Blanche enjoyed cooking and spending time with family and was involved with a variety of local and women's organizations.

She died at the age of eighty-four, a little more than a year after her husband, Mike, passed.

Julie and Lynn (authors), Rose, Blanche, Mandy and Amy (Lynn's daughters; Julie's sisters), August 1970

Richard (Dick) – (March 9, 1910-September 13, 1969)

Richard (Dick) graduated from Highland High School in 1928 and moved out of the area in 1939 to South Bend, Indiana. There, he met Cecile Denman, who was born in Mishawaka, Indiana on September 24, 1914. They married on February 10, 1940, and in July 1948, adopted twins—a son and daughter—Jonathan and Janice (the latter Lynn's cousin Jan).

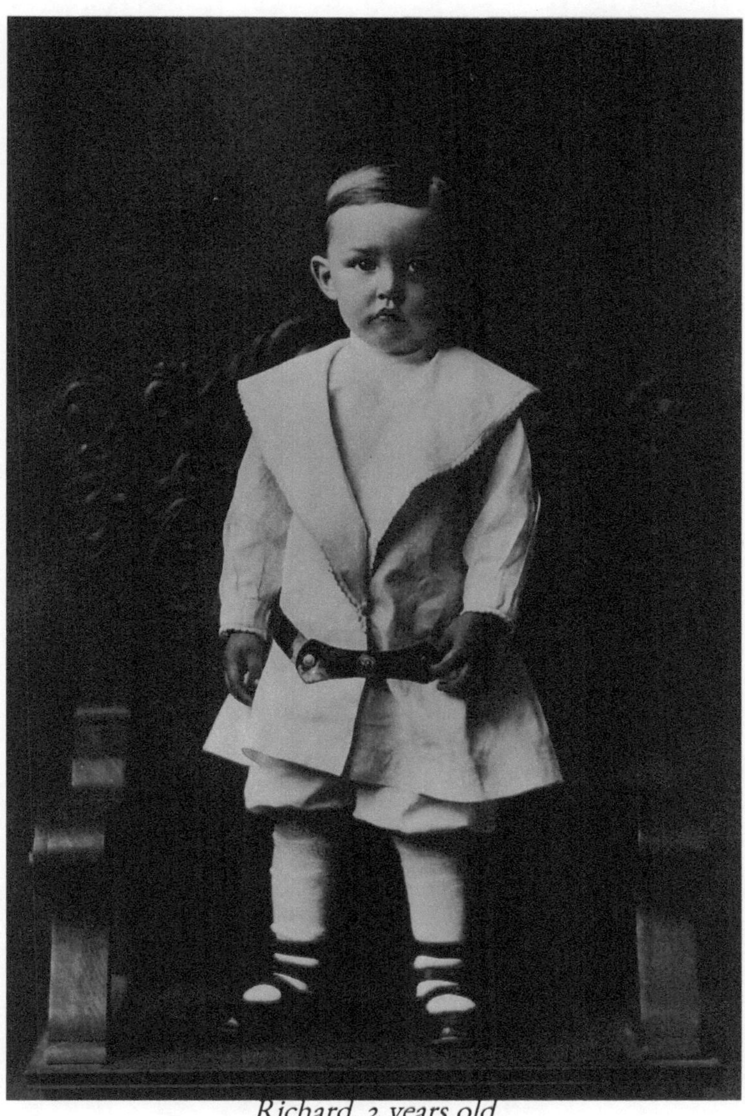

Richard, 2 years old

Richard (right) on his pony

Richard, 1917

Dick was a loving father, who spent a great deal of time outdoors with Jan and Jon, including playing baseball with them and the neighborhood children. The family lived outside of town on a lakeside property with two beaches within walking distance. They had a large garden loaded with vegetables and a strawberry patch, and their home was a gathering place for family cookouts, as well as boating and swimming. Dick also enjoyed taking the family on summer vacation road trips to various areas throughout the United States, including west to California.

Richard (Dick) with children, Jon and Jan, Christmas-time, December 24, 1958

Until 1963, Dick worked for Studebaker, until the company moved to Canada. Initially unable to find a job in his field after Studebaker, he temporarily worked as a prison guard. That job, which likely brought up memories of his father's incarceration and hanging, was very difficult for him. He followed that with a position at Selmar Band Instrument Co. in Elhart, Indiana. He was a member of the Terre Coupee Lodge 204 F and A.M. of New Carlisle and the Loyal Order of Moose, 599 Elkhart, Indiana.

Dick had a fatal heart attack at the age of fifty-nine. Cecile passed away some years later on July 5, 1981.

Arline (November 4, 1903-January 5, 1998)

After Eldo Sr's conviction for life imprisonment and her father's hanging, Arline divorced her husband and left the area, eventually settling down for many years in Shreveport, Louisiana.

She married Alvin (Al) Fred Luehm on December 5, 1937. He tuned pianos and taught his stepson, Eldo Jr., the craft.

Richard and Arline

Arline, 1940, Caseyville, Illinois

Arline and Al Luehm

Blanche and Arline, 1948

Arline was dedicated to being a mother to Eldo and had no other children. The two remained very close throughout her lifetime, including enjoying world travels together.

A go-getter, Arline worked for many years for Avon, the income of which allowed her to buy a house. She also won a pink Cadillac as one of the company's top saleswomen.

Arline, 1972

Arline remained active for many years, including with her church and local women's groups. She died at the age of ninety-four.

Eldo Jr. (Little Eldo) (April 27, 1924-June 18, 2004)

Eldo Jr. with friend, Lillian, June 1945

Eldo remained close with his mother, Arline, throughout her lifetime. He served in World War II in the Army Air Corps. Some years later, on October 8, 1972, he married Jean DeLaney. They had a son and daughter.

For many years, Eldo lived in Collinsville, Illinois, where he was a member of the Holy Cross Lutheran Church. He worked for Dow Chemical as a metallurgical engineer and at Wicks Organ as a cabinet maker. An accomplished woodworker, he also enjoyed bicycling in his free time. He died at the age of eighty.

Minnie (March 31, 1895-June 12, 1959)

In 1926, Minnie married her third husband, Charles Lang, a farmer. They raised her two children from John Nungesser. She died at the age of sixty-three and was buried in Highland.

Photos and Heirlooms

Rose and Emil Early in their Marriage

This is the only photo Rose kept of her and Emil.

Rudolph Fricker (father to Emil)

Children at Fricker School, including Richard. The school was started by Rudolph Fricker, who was well-respected in Highland.

Samuel Ludwig Jenny, Sr. (Rose's father), December 5, 1920. Samuel was well-respected in Highland.

Sam L. Jenny, Jr., younger brother of Rose and Inductee of the Trapshooting Hall of Fame. He was one of the world's best trapshooters for 20 years.

Family Heirlooms

Rose's Rocking Chair

Rose's handmade silk handkerchief from 1900

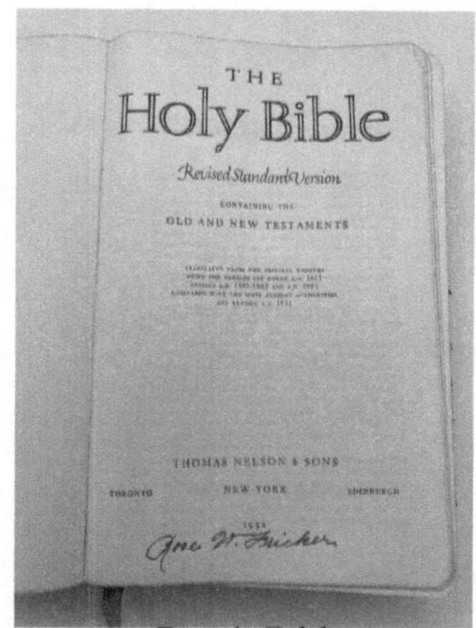

Rose's Bible

Cowbell from Fricker Dairy Farm

Richard's Toy Car

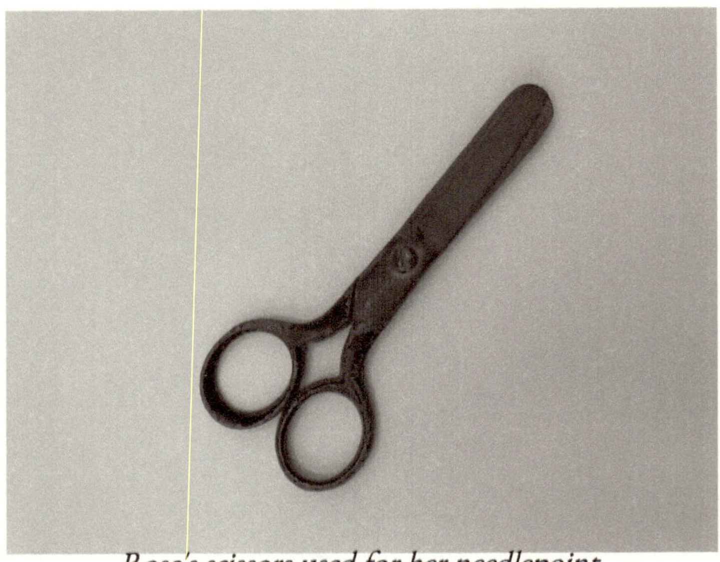

Rose's scissors used for her needlepoint.

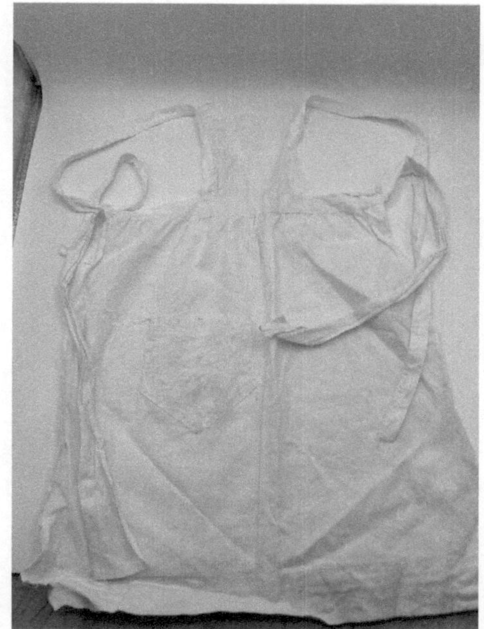

Blanche's apron on the farm

Richard's christening shirt

Blanche's christening gown made by Rose

Richard's Shorts Set

From Rose's Kitchen and Cafe

Sugar bag from Rose's cafe

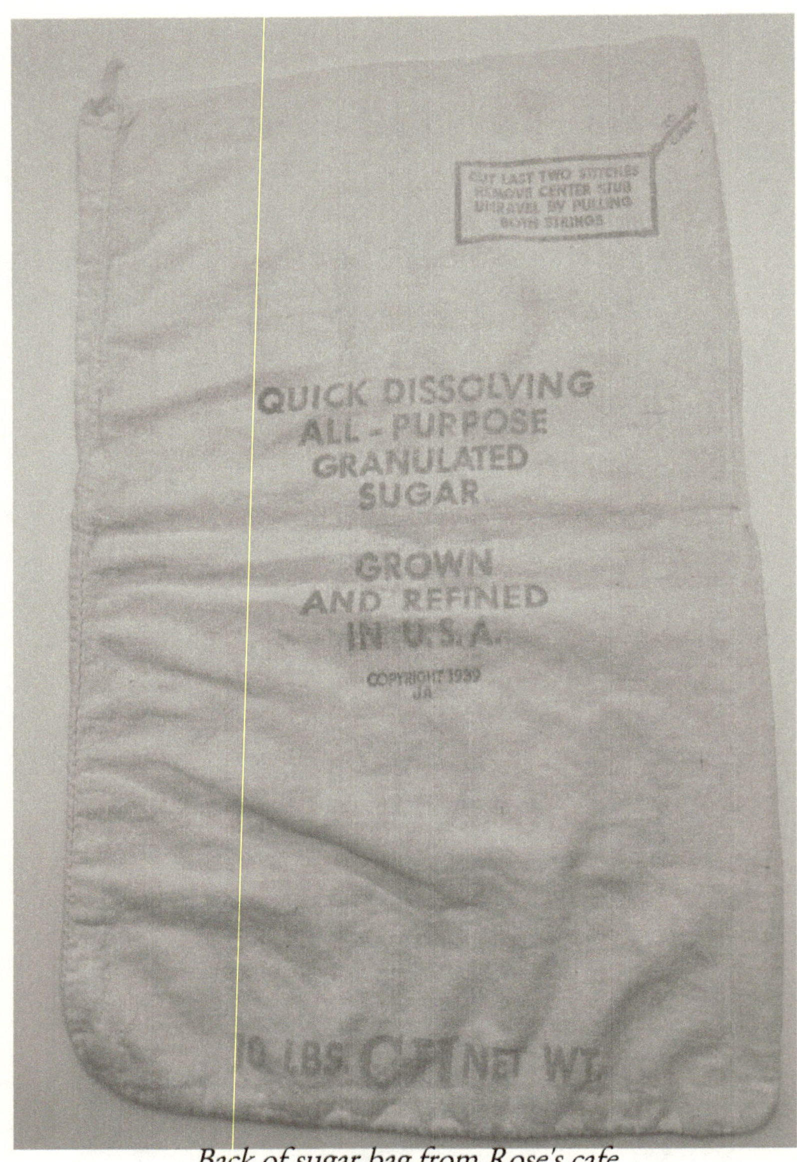

Back of sugar bag from Rose's cafe

Top of one of the spoons containing the Fricker family emblem that Rose hid in her petticoat drawer before the lawyers cleared the house of all valuables.

Fork and cup from Rose's kitchen and spoon containing family emblem. Fork is still used in Julie's kitchen.

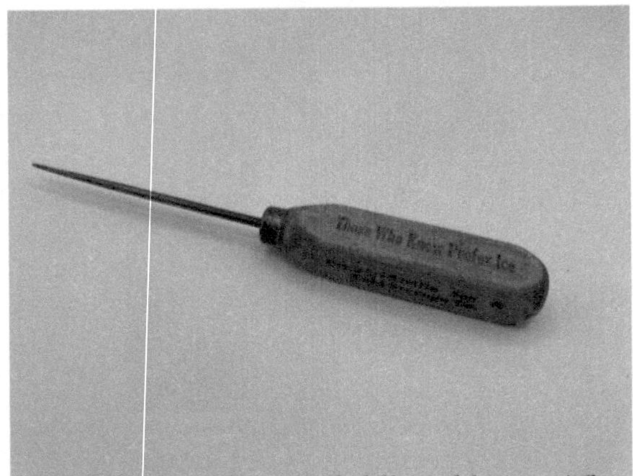

Ice Pick from Rose's childhood home. The side in view says, "Those Who Know Prefer Ice." Another side says, "Save With Ice." The remaining two sides have the company name and address in Highland.

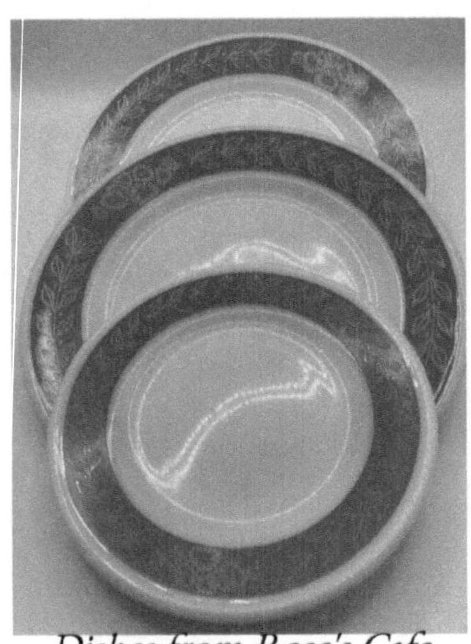

Dishes from Rose's Cafe

Rose's Recipes

Rose's Recipes used in her Cafe

A lifelong baker and cook, Rose loved to be in the kitchen. She found great joy in sharing her food with friends and family and customers at the cafe.

Rose compiled her recipes in composition books that she labeled as cookbooks with her name. She likely did this so her cafe employees could replicate her recipes and for future generations, as Rose was known for creating her own recipes and cooking from memory.

You will see that some of these recipes are well-suited for short-order cooking, which makes them a great choice when you are in a hurry to get a meal on the table. This is especially the case with the entrees and side dishes.

Here is a small selection of popular recipes Rose recorded for posterity and served up often in her cafe.

Quick Hamburger Loaf

1 pound hamburger
1/2 teaspoon salt
1/2 cup chopped onion
1/4 cup breadcrumbs, soaked in milk
1 egg

Mix all ingredients and form into an oblong shape. Place in a greased pan and bake at 350 degrees F. until cooked through and browned. Make a gravy after the meatloaf is done in the pan drippings by adding water and thickening with flour.

Cabbage Delight

4 cups shredded cabbage
1 green mango, diced
1/2 cup chopped nuts
Mayonnaise

Mix all ingredients and add mayonnaise to desired consistency.

Fast Fried Chicken

Chicken pieces (drumsticks, wings, thighs, breasts)
Milk and Flour

Boil chicken pieces in water until done. Mix flour with a small amount of milk to create a heavy batter. Coat chicken pieces in batter. Drop pieces into a heavy skillet half full with hot lard and cook until coating is brown and crispy. Serve at once. (Reserve leftover chicken water for soup.)

Hot Biscuits

2 cups flour
4 tablespoons shortening
4 teaspoons baking powder
1/2 teaspoon salt
3/4 cup milk

Mix ingredients. Roll dough to a desired thickness, cut out circular biscuits, and bake in a 425 degrees F. oven for 10 minutes until golden brown.

Angel Food Cake

This recipe, and Angel Food Cake in general, was a favorite of Lynn's.

Whites of 8 or 9 eggs, beaten to a froth. Add a pinch of salt when beating.
1 1/4 cup sugar
1 cup flour
1/2 teaspoon cream of tarter
1/2 teaspoon vanilla

Mix all ingredients except egg whites. Then fold egg whites into mixture until well combined. Do not stir; only fold.

Bake in an ungreased pan for 35 to 40 minutes at 325 degrees F. Remove from oven when the cake is done and springs back to the touch. Invert pan immediately.

Lemon Sponge Pie

Rose noted that this pie was "swell."

1 cup sugar

2 eggs

2 tablespoons melted butter

4 or 5 tablespoons lemon juice

Grated rind of 1/2 lemon

6 1/2 level tablespoons flour

1 1/2 cups milk

Pinch of salt

Mix 1/2 cup sugar, butter, egg yolks, lemon juice, and rind together. Beat until smooth. Add the rest of the sugar and the flour, beating again until smooth. Add milk and salt and stir well. Beat whites of eggs and fold carefully and evenly into the mix. Pour mixture into unbaked pie shell. Bake at 350 degrees F. until pie browns on top, then decrease heat to 300 degrees F. and bake until the filling is firm and set, about 40 to 50 minutes.

Almond Cream Pie/Crunch Topping

3/4 cup sugar
3 tablespoons cornstarch
1/2 teaspoon salt
2 large eggs, beaten
1 3/4 cups milk
2 tablespoons butter
1/4 teaspoon almond extract
1/2 teaspoon vanilla

Combine sugar, salt, cornstarch, then add eggs and milk and stir until smooth. Cook mix 5 minutes or until thick, stirring constantly. Remove from stove and stir in butter and almond and vanilla extract. Beat 1 minute. Cool, pour into baked pie shell and chill.

Crunch Topping

Crush 1 cup corn flakes cereal with rolling pin. Mix with 1 1/2 tablespoons sugar and 1 tablespoon melted butter. Sprinkle on pie before serving.

Mother Jenny's Baseler Leckerli (Swiss Spice Cookies)

This recipe was from Rose's mother and brought from Switzerland when she and Rose's father emigrated to the United States.

1 quart honey
10 citron
1 large lemon
1 pound sugar
1 pound nuts
1 glass brandy
1 tablespoon allspice
1 tablespoon nutmeg
1 tablespoon cloves
2 tablespoons cinnamon

Heat the honey, add sugar and let it boil. Cool, then add 1/2 of a nickel of baking ammonia or hartshorn. [Note: referring to a nickel is an old-school way of saying to add a small amount—about the size of a nickel—of an ingredient to a recipe.]

Add the rest of the ingredients to the cooked mix, then mix in a small amount of flour until the mixture is the consistency of bread dough. Knead like bread dough and then set aside for several hours or until the next day. Roll dough out and bake in a 350 degree F. oven until the dough is cooked through. Cut into oblong pieces and frost.

Quick, Easy Frosting

1/3 cup softened butter

1/4 teaspoon salt

1/3 cup milk

2 teaspoons vanilla

1 package of powdered sugar

Cream all ingredients well. Makes enough frosting for an 8-inch layer cake or about three dozen cookies.

Rose's Poetry

Rose enjoyed writing poetry throughout her lifetime. For many years, her poems were published in her hometown newspaper, *The Highland News Leader.* She filled notebooks with her poetry. Here is a small sampling of her work.

Summertime on the Farm

It's summertime
Down at country farm
An early dawn, roosters crow
The farmer knows the alarm

Beautiful the farm
Plenty of work to be done
As full as can be
During rains and sun

Hay lofts empty
And to be filled with hay
The golden wheat a dream
Thankful and grateful this day

Garden vegetables plenty
The pleasure to bring
With many flowers and berries
Every year at spring

Good old summertime
On the farm
For the young and old
Happily to know and sweetly told

A Small Girl

I remember the days
When I was a little girl
Back on the farm
Hair in braids, ends in curl

How well I know
Lighthearted and free
My thoughts full of joy
As full as it could be

Lived in a two-story rambling house
Near a windmill, red painted barn
Chickens, ducks, geese and turkeys
Strutting around the farm

A ball for outdoor fun

Made from woolen yarn
A game called hand it over
Over roofs to throw, higher than the barn

Numbers small and large rag dolls
To love and cuddle all day
Domino diddly winks and checkers
At winter evenings to play

Often went fishing among creeks
Fish seemed never to bite
Discouraged and disappointed
Only mosquitoes I would fight

After heavy rains or showers
What a pleasure and fun
To wade in shallow waters
Warm from rain and sun

Barefoot and bareheaded
Dressed scantily I would go
Skip on mud and pebbles
And stumble and hurt my toe

Going Back Home

I will be going back tomorrow
And see the place I was born
Doors then without a key

The farm with growing wheat and corn

I'll try to see my friends and neighbors
Where we children would play
And had together the fun
Walking in dusty lanes many days

It's years and years
The large two-story house
Now to cherish more my home
And faithfully love

The beauty more
Where I did roam
The large two-story home
Rooms large, clean and neat

Feather beds at winter nights
Kept one warm and sweet
The steps leading upstairs, sleet on roots
Soon dreaming without a care

Often at winter precious were apple trees
Where we children would swing
To shake apples ripe on limbs
Until the dinner bell would ring

Memories

(Rose wrote this poem when she was 92 years old.)

Pleasant memories
Lie deep within my heart
Today and its past
No matter where I live
At work or play
Small joys and sorrows last

I feel the warmth
The love from my family
The beauty near
A pleasure and comfort
And with my neighbors and friends
Whom I love dear

It takes courage and patience
That God has given me
A treasure in every way
And grateful to remember
So dear to know
And at my Golden Day

About the Authors

Julie Rose Bawden-Davis

The great granddaughter of Emil and Rose Fricker, Julie Rose Bawden-Davis is a bestselling journalist, novelist, blogger, and YouTuber. A prolific author, Julie writes in several genres. She enjoys creating page-turning, suspenseful novels, garden books that turn any brown thumb green, and spiritual books meant to enlighten and inspire.

Julie began penning stories at the age of 5, when she wrote sweet, little romance books for her grandmother. From there, she graduated to sneaking to a neighbor's house to watch "Dark Shadows" (because her parents thought it was too scary for her) and in her teens, rushing home after school to become immersed in the world of "General Hospital." These early influences inspired her to write suspenseful books full of intrigue.

Widely published, Julie has written 45 books and more than 4,000 articles for a wide variety of national and international publications. She lives in Southern California, where she enjoys sunny, blue skies most days and year-round gardening. Julie gains inspiration from being surrounded by plants when she writes. Like her Grandma Blanche and Great Grandmother Rose, Julie also enjoys cooking and baking.

Lynn Rose Ann Kelley

Lynn Rose Ann Kelley, granddaughter of Emil and Rose Fricker, spent her formative years in South Bend, Indiana. She moved to Southern California when she was ten years old, where she met her first husband, Monte Bawden, while in high school. They had four daughters—Julie, Amy, Mandy, and Katie. When she married her second husband, Bill Kelley in 1985, she also became a stepmother to his daughter, Alison. Bill passed away in January 2020, and Lynn followed in December of the same year.

Like her mother, Blanche, Lynn had a long, productive career as a nurse. She earned her LVN and BSN, working in hospitals and in home healthcare, the latter focused on the care of AIDS patients. Later in her career, she earned a Doctor of Psychology (PsyD) and went on to combine her skills as a nurse and counselor. She also became a Clinical Specialist in Treatment of Victims and Perpetrators of Domestic and Random Violence, and earned certification in yoga, combining the therapeutic and physical benefits of yoga with her practice Yogatalk. Though she had many accomplishments, like her Grandmother Rose, Lynn considered her greatest achievements being a wife, mother, and grandmother. She expressed this sentiment often throughout her life.

Lynn and Julie, 2018

A Note for You

Thanks for reading! Let's stay in touch. Check out my blog on my website at https://www.juliebawdendavis.com/fiction. You can also email me at Julie@JulieBawdenDavis.com, find me on Facebook, and follow me on Amazon.

Even better, join my weekly VIP Reading Gems newsletter via my website. When signing up, you get a free copy of *Discovered Beginnings*, the prequel novella to my Discovered Truth Series, and *Suspended: The Prequel*, which starts off my Past Life Prism Series. There are also lots of exclusive giveaways and contests!

If you like this book, please leave a review or just stars on Amazon, Apple Books, KOBO, Barnes & Noble, GoodReads, Google Play, BookBub, and/or any other book platform you find me on. Your opinion matters and is incredibly powerful.

Thanks again and talk soon!

Julie

Books by Julie Bawden-Davis

Secrets That Remain: The Emil Fricker Story

The Discovered Truth Series (Romantic Suspense)

Discovered Beginnings: (FREE at https://www.juliebawdendavis.com/fiction)

Discovered Secrets

Discovered Memories

Discovered Indiscretions

Discovered Liaisons

Discovered Betrayal

Discovered Denial

Discovered Distractions

Discovered Deception

Discovered Lies

Discovered Vengeance

Discovered Redemption

Discovered Obsession

Discovered Transgressions

Discovered Suspicion

Discovered Escape
Discovered Promises
Discovered Cover-Up
Discovered Intentions

The Past Life Prism Series (Romantic Time Travel Suspense)
Suspended: The Prequel (FREE at https://www.juliebawdendavis.com/fiction)
Suspended: The Beginning
Suspended Enforcement
Suspended Entrapment
Suspended Exodus
Suspended Entanglement
Suspended Control
The Past Life Prism Series Box Set: Books 1-4

www.ingramcontent.com/pod-product-compliance
Lightning Source LLC
Chambersburg PA
CBHW030524310726
48979CB00010B/1794/J
* 9 7 8 1 9 5 5 2 6 5 5 2 2 *